1^{st}_{p}

$S_{1,i,\dot{...}}$

$7^{su}_{\underline{\quad}}$

$\sim$

GOOD NEIGHBORS

GOOD NEIGHBORS

GORMAN BECHARD

CARROLL & GRAF PUBLISHERS, INC.
NEW YORK

Copyright © 1998 by Gorman Bechard

First Carroll & Graf edition 1998

Carroll & Graf Publishers, Inc.
19 W. 21st Street
New York, NY 10010-6805

Library of Congress Cataloging-in-Publication data is available
ISBN: 0-7867-0512-4

Manufactured in the United States of America

*for obvious reasons, this book is dedicated
to Casey and Mr. Kilgore Trout . . .*

*. . . and to Sunshine Jones,
who started it all*

Acknowledgments to my beautiful wife, Kristine, my constant source of inspiration and reason.

To Major Richard Covello, (retired) Connecticut State Police, for advice on police procedures and etiquette. (If mistakes were made, they're mine in the name of literary license.)

To Gary Bechard, for teaching me the ins and outs, ups and downs, of running a bar.

To Alison Tolisano and Fred Russo, for their invaluable information and suggestions.

To the Donahues, the Russos, and the Tolisanos, the quintessential *great* neighbors one and all.

To Kathy Milani (for the photo), Steve Manzi (he tried to come up with a joke), and Bob Dixon (his turn to get credit just for the hell of it), for their unwavering friendship, still, after all these years.

To Bill, Ovie, Marion, Debbie, and Stanlee, for always being there.

To Matthew Bialer of the William Morris Agency and Milissa Brockish of the Monteiro-Rose Agency, the greatest agents in the world.

To Kent Carroll, for believing in this book.

And lastly, to Archers of Loaf, Lori Carson, Wilco, Sleater-Kinney, Paula Cole, and too many others to mention, musicians whose sounds helped keep me sane during those endless days of writing and re-writing.

He who learns must suffer. And even in our sleep pain that cannot forget falls drop by drop upon the heart, and in our own despair, against our will, comes wisdom to us by the awful grace of God.

—Aeschylus

prologue

The last day of Reggie DeLillo's life started off with a bad cup of coffee, then went downhill from there.

He was sitting at the kitchen table, sipping, cringing at the bitterness, wondering why the temperature outside was higher than the temperature in his mug, when he heard the rapping at his front door.

His wife, Anabelle, seemed not to hear. Pretended not to hear. Maybe she'd gone deaf overnight. Reggie didn't know. He didn't give a good Goddamn at this point, watching her as she hovered over the toaster preparing breakfast. Eggos and half a pink grapefruit, delivered in cotton panties and a tank top. It was all she seemed to wear around the house anymore, whether cooking—if you could call it that, whether cleaning, whether lounging out on the deck. Maybe it was to remind Reggie why a fifty-six-year-old had married a woman half his age in the first place. See this body, Reggie? See these legs? Yeah, he'd been thinking lately, he needed more reminders of his mistakes.

Grumbling, his heart heavy and still, Reggie shuffled past his wife of three years, down the hallway, and to the front door. He answered before the visitor on the other side had the opportunity to knock again.

It was a policeman. The same policeman. A young man, clean shaven, but not because he had any choice in the matter. He was tall and muscular, with short brown hair. A little too short in Reggie's opinion. The style made the cop's face seem wide, his eyes narrow, his lips much too thick. Or perhaps those impressions had nothing to do with his hair.

His badge read: Castagnetti. His first name was Peter. He was one of Harmony, Connecticut's finest.

"Mr. DeLillo?" Officer Castagnetti said. He was polite. His tone respectful and tentative.

"Yeah," Reggie said. He knew what was coming. He was just surprised that this visit, this courtesy call, had taken so long. How many threats does a man have to make before those being threatened turn to the law, or violence, or both? How many threats, how much anger, before grief's fingers would unlock their hold on his throat?

Reggie nodded politely at the officer. Just doing his job, he figured. He didn't know how Reggie hurt inside. He didn't understand the rage. How Reggie's world had been uprooted by what a child found funny. A prank. You know how kids are? Boys-will-be-boys.

The officer didn't understand what it was like to have a friend, a close friend, die in your arms. The helplessness in those deep brown eyes, so eternally sad and trusting. Trusting till the end of time. The last image forever etched in Reggie's mind. A cough, a groan. And the endless wail that began somewhere south of your soul, and twisted up, battering your heart, your mind, and coming finally out your throat. A voice you never knew, frightening and frightened.

Officer Castagnetti just didn't know. He probably didn't need to. And in the end, after the young man's discourse on how important it is to be civil toward one's neighbors, after his explanation that they've decided against pressing charges, Reggie smiled sadly, and promised to behave.

But closing the door, standing in the foyer for a long moment, Reggie's smile faded. And the weariness and terror stepped from behind the curtains in back of which they hid. He knew that behaving was not an option.

He had threatened, no *promised*, his neighbors, the Robertsons, Sally and Neil, that he'd do to their fifteen-year-old, David, what the little SOB had done to his Molasses. Then they could cradle their boy in their arms, and watch him die.

In Reggie's mind they were as responsible, if only for bringing such a vile creature into the world. It was as if Neil had himself sprinkled the powdered rat poison onto the ground beef that Sally was rolling into an irresistible ball. Irresistible at least to an eight-year-old chocolate Lab.

It was as if they too must suffer. And suffer. And suffer. And die.

In a drunken rage, with his v-necked white t-shirt smeared with blood, tears, and brown hairs, with the dirt from his dog's freshly dug backyard grave still caked beneath his fingernails, Reggie DeLillo had sworn vengeance.

Then he went home. He curled himself up on the throw rug at the foot of his favorite chair. Curled himself into a ball, as Molasses would have. Curled up at his own imaginary feet, and went to sleep, dreaming of Milk Bones and chasing cats through the pearly gates.

Bypassing the Eggos and that half a pink grapefruit, bypassing his wife, Reggie moved out onto his deck.

It was unbearably hot and humid. One of those early June mornings when New England attempted to fool its inhabitants into thinking they resided in South Florida. When the air itself hummed in discomfort. And the leaves on the trees begged for mercy.

Reggie leaned against the railing of the deck. All cedar, he had built it a few years after his early retirement, finished it the year after that. Slowly, painstakingly. Remembering how the pain in his lower back and legs, as he cajoled each board into place, only made it seem that much more his. His and Molasses's.

It was a place where they could ogle the squirrels, and do combat with the mosquitos and wood ticks. Where even the morning newspaper seemed like work. And where Pabst Blue Ribbon tasted like just about the greatest refreshment in the world.

With the deck, he had put up a matching cedar fence. Picket-like, just enough to keep his dog in, and others out. Or so he thought.

Tears came to Reggie's eyes as he glanced over at the mound of freshly patted-down soil. Under the tree where Molasses would lay, roll on his back, scratching himself in ecstasy against the bark or grass. Where he'd watch whenever there was raking or mowing to do.

He could feel the breath catch in his chest, his world put on pause, as the screen door that led from the family room and onto the deck, slid open.

"Are you okay?" Anabelle asked.

Without turning around, Reggie held up a hand, a slight backwards wave. It was all he could manage.

But that wasn't enough for Anabelle. And soon her hands were on him, rubbing the muscles in his shoulders.

"Let me take your mind off it," she whispered into his ear. "I could always take your mind off anything, remember? Come inside with me, baby. I'll make everything better."

Reggie shook his head. He pulled away, cringing, raising his shoulders, hunching them inwards, his back still to her. Not able to face her now, or anymore, not wanting to.

Anabelle's hands dropped to her side. How had everything gone so wrong? How had it— She started to step away, to go back inside, when she stopped herself.

"We can get another dog," she said, wishing she hadn't as soon as the words left her mouth.

Reggie fell to one knee, and buried his face, his sobs, his sorrow, in his hands. He did his best to hold it back, hold it in. He did his best. But it wasn't good enough. There were no other dogs. There was no replacement for Molasses. How can one ever replace—

Molasses made Reggie feel that despite the shortcomings, the regrets, the mistakes, the dreams that never quite panned out, he wasn't a complete failure as a human being after all.

There was no replacement for that.

It was later that afternoon when Anabelle informed Reggie that she was going out. Grocery shopping, he thought he heard her say. At least she had some shorts on over the panties.

He waited and listened for the car door to slam shut, the engine on his dark green Ford Taurus to turn over, and for the familiar squeak in the suspension as his wife drove the passenger side tires over the curb, just as she always did.

Reggie heard all that, and more. Another car engine. This one idling a little too high. And a car door slamming shut. An energetic yell of, "See ya."

He could feel the bile rise as if on autopilot. The goosebumps went goose-stepping, the cold chill flicking at his spinal cord. Flicking. Flicking. He gripped at the rail, pressing the tips of his fingers into the wood, to the point where one or the other had to give. One or the other—

And something snapped. Eventually, he wasn't sure when, or how long the tension had lasted. It could have been seconds. It seemed like days. But it was neither fingers nor rail. It was the sanity support line I.V.-ed to Reggie's mind.

Officer Peter Castagnetti would later write in his report that he entered the Robertsons' home at three-twenty-eight PM to have a talk with David. He found the assailant, a Mr. Reginald Michael DeLillo, seated in the living room. DeLillo was covered in blood, and held an automatic pistol in his right hand. His gaze was directed downwards, toward the floor, where there, at DeLillo's feet, lay David Robertson. It appeared to the officer, that the child was dead, due to a single gunshot wound to the chest.

"Please put the gun down, sir," Officer Castagnetti asked, standing in position, his weapon aimed, his arms rigid, ready to attack or be attacked. Ready to quite possibly die.

It took forever for Reggie to look up and notice the police officer standing there. But when he did, he smiled, and whispered to no one, "Not a whisker in sight."

"Please, sir," Castagnetti implored. "I don't want to have to shoot you."

"Of course not," Reggie said, calmly, loud enough for the officer to hear. But instead of lowering the pistol, he raised it, not far, and not for long.

One shot rang out. One perfectly aimed bullet to the center of Reggie's chest, shattering what was left of his already broken heart. Officer Castagnetti only beat Reggie to the punch. Beat him by a second. Beat him from pressing the pistol to his own temple and pulling the trigger. But either way, as far as Reggie was concerned, he had the battle won. And either way, he died with only one thought in mind: Wait up, Molasses. I'm coming with you.

GOOD NEIGHBORS

monday

one

It was about half-past four when the phone rang. Juke Miller shot it a leery glance and hoped that whomever it was on the other end of the line would have second thoughts before he actually took the time to answer. It couldn't be important. Or at least *that* important. The important calls at Juke's Place came between noon and two PM, Mondays and Thursdays. They were from distributors, wholesalers, suppliers. Anything else was just a wrong number, a query about the establishment's hours of operation, or a wife begging Juke to toss her errant husband's ass off the barstool upon which he'd settled, and head him in the direction of home. And since there were no husbands, errant or otherwise, in the bar. There were no customers at all. And since the hours of operation were clearly posted on the door, and would anyone really be wondering on a Monday afternoon? That left: sorry wrong number.

But after the seventh ring, he gave in, and snatched the red plastic receiver off the wall-mounted base. The phone, a rotary dial relic from the early sixties, was hung near the waitress station at the far end of the bar, within reach of one of the two cash registers, and over the drop-gate which allowed employees to get behind the bar in the first place.

"Juke's," he said, his voice slung low. It was smooth, with a smoky edge, and worn, sort of like his patience.

There was a sucked-in breath on the other end of the line, and a pause. One just long enough for Juke's eyes to scan the rectangular space—old habits that'd never died—from the door which led to the office in back, down the oak bar which ran the length of the right side wall—thirty-five feet, its top a solid piece of wood, a playing field with draft beer taps marking the fifty-yard line—past the seven booths along the wall opposite the bar and the ten tables that filled the space between. The booths, tables and chairs were all carved by ghosts of patrons past. A name, an initial, a phone number, a heart. The real estate agent had told Juke that the previous owner felt the carvings would give the place a homey, comfortable feel. When Juke didn't respond, when his blue eyes remained steely, his strong jaw set, the price dropped another ten grand. Such a bargain. He snatched it up on the spot.

Juke kept the carved-on booths and tables. He kept the rotary dial phone. Likewise the New York Yankees' memorabilia on the walls, the banners, the bat, the autographed pictures. That one from '51, of Joltin' Joe, his long arms around the shoulders of Yogi and the rookie Mantle, signed by all three no less. He left the dust on the ceiling fans alone. And the barstool with the missing leg and the sign that read: "Sit at your own risk," he kept that too. And over in the farthest corner, between the two restroom doors, there was a fortune-telling machine. A mechanical genie's head with a moving jaw and a busted speaker, that for a penny would slip you a card promising wealth, good fortune, romance, or something more. Juke wouldn't have dreamed of ever tossing it away.

About the only addition or change he made was to the name. Though *Patsy's* had been a Tompkins Glen staple since the thirties, it just didn't work for him. At six-five, two hundred ten pounds, he didn't look like a Patsy. Teetering the fine line between early and mid-forties, he didn't feel like a Patsy. And he certainly didn't want to tend bar in a joint called Patsy, and possibly become known or thought of as Patsy.

So the name became: *Juke's Place*. And in it, he reserved the rights, all the rights. He had paid for them lock, stock and barrel.

"It's Reggie."

Juke felt the hairs on the back of his hands stand on end. It wasn't the message, but the messenger. And there was no mistaking the voice. An abrasive snap of sounds, a little too high-pitched. Like a puppy's yelp. Anabelle DeLillo, wife of his best friend and neighbor. A woman who had never called the bar trying to locate her errant husband, begging Juke to send him on his way home. Not once.

"You sure you're doing the right thing?" Juke had asked, when Reggie said he planned on marrying the woman. Not much was known about Anabelle. Originally from Arizona, her last home had been in Branford, Connecticut, and anything over the Q Bridge might as well have been in, well, Arizona. There were rumors that Reggie had met his bride-to-be when calling an Adult Services classified ad in the back of the *New Haven Advocate*, as he was known to do from time to time. "On the road to complete satisfaction," her ad supposedly read, "Let Sweet Virginia be your driver. She never runs out of gas." The charge: two-fifty an hour, for whatever your pleasure.

"Yeah," the whispers went, "Reggie's marrying a professional escort," as opposed to an escort of the amateur variety. But then, they were just rumors, no one at that time had actually had the pleasure.

According to Reggie, he met Anabelle at a department store. At the Super Kmart. They got to talking in the hardware aisle, and one thing led to another, which led to a drink, which led to, well, a wedding.

Juke had no reason to doubt his friend. But he had plenty of reason to question him. Anabelle was a good-looking woman. There was no mistaking her feminine charms. But she appeared a little too keen on marriage. And Reggie was destined to be husband number three, the first two ending in divorce. She was one for two in the alimony department.

Juke asked Reggie again right before the ceremony, "You sure?" And again looking him straight in the eye as he handed the groom the rings.

But Reggie was sure. Juke was as well. He had never believed in trophies: not Academy Awards, not a bear's head mounted on a redneck's wall, not expensive cars, not even the Pulitzer Prize. And Juke certainly did not believe in Anabelle. Which was how she appeared on Reggie's arm: the young-enough-to-be-your-daughter trophy wife.

Not much had changed in the three years since the second Mrs. DeLillo had moved in next door. Except that slowly, surely, it appeared as if Reggie came to see Juke's side of things.

"How could you let me do it?" Reggie would ask on those long nights at Juke's Place, when the Monday Night Football crowd had since exited gracefully to cries and yawns of "I'll catch the second half at home," and the few patrons that remained were a lot more interested in what filled their glasses, than in field goals and fourth-down conversions.

But Juke had already spoke his piece. And Reggie had made his decision. Not a life or death decision, but a smile or suffer. And Juke figured Reggie was batting about .300 as far as Anabelle was concerned. He had expected the Mendoza line, or worse. While Reggie had fantasized about seasons of dingers, nothing but dingers. That ball is outta here.

Juke ran a hand over his mouth, his chin, feeling the three-day growth of whiskers. He never shaved on Sundays and Mondays. There was no reason to. He wondered why Anabelle would be calling. Why she'd be turning to him.

"Is he okay?" he said finally, hating to have to even acknowledge her presence on the other end of the telephone line. But it was for Reggie. He knew the guy was broken up about the dog, but felt fairly sure that he'd hold it together. Reggie was—

"He's been shot, Juke," Anabelle said, the words catching in her throat, tears mixing them all up.

There was another pause, and Juke could feel the walls beginning to crumble. The denial, disbelief, anger, and acceptance all rolled into one tight little package. This wasn't happening again. This wasn't— Jesus fucking Christ, he would not allow for this to happen again.

He heard a sniffle, then an apprehensive sigh. "He's dead," she said. "Reggie's dead."

Juke placed the receiver back onto its hook. He took a few deep breaths, then as calmly as possible wiped his hands on one of the bar rags, then again unconsciously against the sides of his jeans. He stepped from behind the bar. He might have flipped over the "Closed" sign had he, or the previous owner, ever made such a purchase. But both were of the belief that if the door's locked, the lights out, and there's no one inside, most customers will eventually figure it out for themselves.

Locking up, Juke walked around back to the parking lot large enough for eight cars, and got into the red Saab 900 that he'd had for going on fourteen years. He couldn't bring himself to sell it, despite the pings and knocks. Or maybe he just couldn't separate himself from the friendly sounds.

Normally he'd have walked to work. Stepped out of his house onto River Bank Road, his sort-of messy dark brown hair combed as best he could, too thick, too wavy, Juke never could figure out what to do with it. Wearing the usual: some worn cotton shirt over those jeans. He'd then walk east the two-tenths of a mile to Wright Avenue, a street which connected everything in Harmony: its sixty-three thousand inhabitants, its various sections, Wrightville, Centerville, Olivet Hills, Sleeping Giant, and of course, Tompkins Glen. Then he'd turn south, travel six blocks, past the Tompkins Glen Pharmacy, past The Best Video Store in the Whole Wide World, past the Colonial Bank and Trust, to his third of an old Tudor-style home that housed an antique shop, a hair salon, and Juke's Place.

But today, something told him to drive. Intuition. A gut check. Those old habits he wanted to beat to death with a stick.

two

The news came just like that. A snap of a finger, a snap of a finger, a snap—

There was an alibi, the ballistics didn't match. How could the fucking ballistics not match? And the Internal Affairs Department was launching an investigation. Perhaps Detective Miller was a little too trigger happy. Perhaps Detective Miller he had become a loose cannon. Perhaps he was no longer able to protect and serve.

Protect. He hadn't. He couldn't. He had failed when it mattered most. No perhaps about that.

But the gun. The sonofabitch had reached for his gun. Pulling it from the waistband of his pants. Covered by an untucked shirt. Covered. A .45. The caliber was right. The MO was right. Everything right pointed to Johnny Marciano, a rap sheet six feet long, and that penchant for—Christ! Marciano went for his gun. How could Detective Juke Miller not shoot first? How could Detective Juke Miller not blow the SOB into the bowels of hell where he belonged?

The persistent blare snapped him back. Snapped. A horn. The light had turned green. How long had the light been green? How long had he been idling in the Saab, his blinker suggesting left. Where was that soft, smiling echo of a voice saying, "Green, honey?" That soft voice—

It was the risk. Juke couldn't take the risk. The risk of letting Marciano live? The risk of letting him walk away, due to a technicality, due to a slick lawyer, due to a fucking jury buying his charm?

Juke waved a hand at the driver behind him, and turned off Wright onto River Bank. He rubbed at his eyes, and cursed all of creation. But it was the Saab's fault. The Saab always twisted everything up inside.

River Bank Road was consistent. If nothing else. Fifty to sixty foot-wide lots, all a little under a half acre, and adorned with Colonials. Nothing but Colonials: Garrison, center hall, Dutch, and the ever-popular Alice Washburn design. It was like one of those shops you notice when driving down Manhattan's side streets: *Just Lamps, Just Shades, Just Bulbs*. River Bank Road was Just Colonials.

Juke's house, number one-four-seven—Reggie lived at one-four-three, the Robertsons at one-three-nine—was a white Garrison, wainscoted, with slate gray shutters, and a big bay window out front. It had six original rooms and a sunporch tacked on off the kitchen.

Juke bought the house for a steal in 1981, right after he got married. Thirty-one thousand, seven hundred dollars. The Robertsons had lived in their house for less than a year. They paid a little over one-sixty-five, getting it on the cheap. And though theirs was center-halled, the square footage was virtually identical.

There was a stop sign about halfway between the corner of Wright and Juke's house. He could see the yellow plastic crime scene tape from there, encircling the Robertson house like a fence of misconduct. It held in the evidence, and kept out those curious and grateful that a white picket was all they'd hopefully ever know.

He counted seven police cars of both the marked and unmarked variety, one ambulance, and the Medical Examiner's van which was backed up on the lawn, its back doors open. There were two satellite news-gathering trucks, one from a New Haven-based network affiliate, the other Hartford-based. Plus a couple of reporters, guys who had been working the greater New Haven beat for longer than anyone would care to remember. A lot of manpower. A lot of coverage. But then people were rarely shot in Tompkins Glen.

Juke pulled into his driveway, got out of his car, crossed over his front lawn, and stopped in front of Reggie's house. It was a light blue Dutch, its lawn meticulously groomed, the marigolds and hedges that surrounded the fieldstone foundation giving it the feeling of just having stepped off the pages of *House & Garden* magazine.

Anabelle was sitting on one of the stairs leading up to their grand front porch. Its wide floorboards painted white to match the house's trim. The swinging loveseat hung at the far end, near a stack of firewood. It was probably the perfect place to wind down, a glass of whiskey in one hand, a good book in the other, back when the house was built in the late twenties, before decks and privacy, before television and indifference, came into vogue.

She wore shorts and a tank top, her shoulder-length blonde hair pulled back into a tight ponytail. Anabelle looked less like a grieving widow, and more like a woman who'd just finished working out. The sweat-covered upper lip. The flushed cheeks. Were those tears? Or had she just run a four-minute mile?

"What happened?"

Juke wasn't asking Reggie's wife. He was speaking to the detective who stood hunched over before her in a rumpled blue polyester suit that looked as if it hadn't seen the inside of a dry cleaners in years, and instead had gone through the weekly spin dry cycle in a Maytag. Filling the suit above and beyond its capacities was a rumpled man, a lot overweight, with a bad haircut to over-compensate for his rapidly balding head, and though Juke could never break it to him, never knew how, the worst breath he had ever encountered. In fact, Detective Tom Piccerillo's breath was stale donuts and Taster's Choice synthesized, and was, when Juke thought about it, most likely the real cause for Anabelle DeLillo's tears.

Piccerillo straightened up, and crinkled his mouth into what might pass as a smile. He bobbed his head a few times, snapping shut the notebook which held lines of mostly indecipherable scribblings.

"Was wondering when you'd show up," he said, adding the word "partner," not as an afterthought, or as sarcasm, but because it still sounded right to him.

"Soon as I got the call," Juke said.

Piccerillo tilted his head toward Anabelle.

Juke nodded, and looked, finally, in her direction.

"He was crazy, Juke," she said. "That dog dying was the last straw."

"You're saying your husband was unstable prior to the dog's death?" Piccerillo asked in his most cautious, most comforting tone. He had the notebook open again, his ballpoint poised to strike.

"He was crazy about the dog, period," Juke said, not about to let her toss around such stupidity.

"He loved that dog more than me," she said, her voice stinging with resentment, her glare aimed not at the detective, but at Juke.

"Can't say that I blame him," Juke said, returning her glare, searching her soul for an answer to the first question that came to mind: *Did you have anything to do with this, Anabelle?*

She looked away from Juke, standing suddenly, brushing at the seat of her shorts. "Anything else, detective?" she asked Piccerillo.

"Not at the moment," he said.

"I'll be inside," Anabelle said. "If you need me."

Juke watched her walked away. Her head held high. The soft sniffles. The murmurs of pain. *You're a good actress,* he thought.

11

"Can we talk?"

"About?"

Piccerillo snapped shut the notebook. "You knew Reggie better than anyone, Juke."

"Yeah," Juke said, nodding, adding in a cheerless whisper, "Better than anyone."

"Come again," Piccerillo said.

Juke turned then to face his ex-partner. "Only if I'm allowed inside."

"I, um." He stammered for the right words. "I don't know if that's such a—"

But Juke wasn't about to wait for permission. He stepped away from Piccerillo, already crossing the Robertsons' driveway, on his way to their front door.

Piccerillo shrugged, then hurried off in Juke's direction.

"If it were up to me," he said, catching up.

"You've got top rank as far as I can see."

"All the assholes have yet to show."

"So until then?" Juke said.

Piccerillo pinched his nostrils together and sucked in the snot. Juke always thought of it as one of his more endearing traits.

"Yeah, sure," Piccerillo said, tentatively. "Until then."

They were in the living room. It was the first time Juke had stepped foot in the house since the Robertsons had moved in. Somehow he wasn't surprised to see the old oak floor now covered by wall-to-walls. He wasn't surprised by the collection of matching French Provencial-style furniture that filled the living room. The gold crushed velvet cushions. The end tables and coffee table laminated, and detailed in gold paint. About the only thing that surprised him about the way the new owners had decorated their colonial, was how the house no longer felt as if it belonged in Tompkins Glen. As if, through cheap furniture and bad taste, it had become a Raised Ranch, or a motor home.

"Castagnetti stopped by to talk to the kid," Piccerillo said, his voice hushed. "He was going to suggest he try and make amends with Reggie. Do some yard work, clean out his garage, something."

"Can't see Reggie agreeing to that."

"That's pretty obvious now."

A Scientific Investigation Division (SID) tech was photographing the bodies of Reggie and the boy from every possible angle. The tech was young, with a beer gut, and some heavy-duty sideburns. Probably weaned on horror movies and MTV and somehow not all of this seemed real, or even all that gruesome. He just went about taking close-ups that would forever sit in a manila envelope, in a file marked "Robertson/DeLillo" or vice-versa. Making their way from a squad room file cabinet stuffed with only the most recent, to a final resting place in a cardboard box on a steel shelf somewhere in the basement of the department headquarters.

Other techs crawled on their all-fours searching for clues, dusting for prints. They weren't allowing a carpet fiber to go untwisted, just in case the obviousness of it all became less so. There was always storage space available for clues. File cabinets and cardboard boxes lining up, ready to be filled with the debris of shattered lives.

SID was based out of New Haven, as was most of their work. The division was shared by the neighboring towns: East Haven, North Haven, Harmony, Woodbridge, Orange, and West Haven. The pooled resources bought a lot of man hours and equipment. They were always ready to jump at a moment's notice. Even the Connecticut State Police Major Crimes Unit exploited their expertise from time to time.

Juke watched them as they worked, hardly recognizing a single face. Seven years and the names did change. The old faces had mostly faded away. Or had they just grown tired of death? To be replaced by these kids, an endless cycle of anaesthesia.

"Castagnetti was trying to keep the peace," Piccerillo said. "Instead he walks in, finds the kid dead, and there's Reggie in the Laz-E-Boy, holding a 9mm in his hands. When Castagnetti asked Reggie to drop the weapon, he raised it instead."

Juke nodded. And Piccerillo didn't have to say another word. He knew the routine. Up close and personal. Had lived with it day and night for over seven years. He would live with it for the rest of his life. Officer Peter Castagnetti acted appropriately, under the circumstances. *Under the circumstances*, that was the kicker, the hard to swallow. But it's what IAD would conclude, after ripping the rookie's life to shreds and back again. God bless fucking Internal Affairs.

"Where are the parents?" Juke asked, changing the subject.

"Mrs. Robertson's at work," Piccerillo said. "She's a teller at the First Harmony Savings and Loan over in Centerville. We sent a car to pick her up."

"She know yet?"

"Guess that's my responsibility," Piccerillo said.

No cop ever wanted the duty of next-of-kin notification. But this was especially brutal. How do you tell a woman her fifteen-year-old's been shot to death by a neighbor in her living room? There was no etiquette, no training at the academy that could ever prepare.

"She should be here soon. Russo's picking her up."

Fred Russo was one of the real old-timers on the Harmony force. One of the nice guys that could still give cops a good name. He brought to mind Norman Rockwell and mom's apple pie, a time when even the bad guys really weren't all that bad.

"Good choice," Juke said.

"Told him to take his time."

"What about the husband?"

Piccerillo let out a long breath. Juke could tell he wanted to be somewhere else, anywhere else.

"He's at work down in Jersey. Left a note by the phone in the kitchen. A meeting or some shit like that. Wrote that he wouldn't be home till late. His work number was on speed dial. There was a list of those numbers, Neil's work, Sally's work, David's school, taped to the wall over the phone. Y'know, his was *pound-one*." He checked his notebook. "Peroni Auto Parts. Based out of Watertown, New Jersey. Guess he's the tri-state sales rep. I gave it a ring. But, ah, no luck, he'd already left for the day."

"Something to come home to."

"Fuck," Piccerillo said. "If I knew this was waiting for me at home—" He just shook his head, his words trailing off as the medical examiner, a small man with big glasses, wheeled the boy past on a gurney. A bloodstained sheet draped over the thin corpse.

"Keep it covered up," Piccerillo said. "We don't need sight of that on the six o'clock news."

As the ME nodded his understanding, Juke went over to the chair where Reggie still sat. Bulky and covered in brown vinyl, the chair was one of two non-provincial pieces of furniture in the room. And it was aimed at the other, a rear-projection television. Its remote control within reach on a nearby end table.

Juke dropped to one knee in front of his friend, and stared into the face. Reggie's normally ruddy complexion, redder because of the time of the year, the time he spent lying like a dog with his dog in the pre-summer sun, was already pasty and gray. His hair, so white and thin, was messier than usual. The right side of his mouth was curled up onto a partial grin, a smirk of satisfaction that Juke knew all too well.

He clamped one of his large hands over Reggie's, and could almost feel what little heat, what traces of life that remained, trickle into him. As if some part of Reggie's being lingered behind—the clean-up crew: Lock up, set the alarm, and find another earthly home.

Juke closed his eyes and said a silent prayer. Not to God, or Christ, or some sainted holy spirit, but to the one soul that might help Reggie adjust. That might invite him and Molasses to some heavenly cookout. Who would toss a tennis ball to Molasses, and hand Reggie a cold one. And they could talk over old times, her laugh, her smile warming the galaxies. And together they'd wonder aloud when Juke was joining them.

"Not soon enough," he whispered, squeezing his dead friend's hand.

three

Piccerillo held out an evidence bag. In it, a Walther P-88 automatic. A 9mm, with a fourteen-round magazine. The checkered black finish was specked with blood, both Reggie's and the kid's. The droplets of purple pressed against the inside of the plastic bag, smearing, running, as if the weapon were freshly cut from a side of beef.

"Ever see it before?"

"Shouldn't you be asking the widow that?" Juke asked.

"I did," Piccerillo said. "According to her, Reggie didn't own a gun. He didn't like guns. He never talked about guns. Guns were just not part of Reggie's bigger picture."

"What about Anabelle's?"

"She never saw this particular gun before." Piccerillo snorted loudly. "I'm beginning to think the fucking thing doesn't even exist."

Juke shook his head. The gun didn't fit. Where would Reggie have gotten a pistol on such short notice? As much as it pained him, he had to agree with Anabelle on this one point: never in the

seventeen years that they'd been neighbors had Reggie ever mentioned guns, in general, in particular, period. Just the opposite in
fact—how safe Reggie felt in this relatively crime-free neighborhood, how secure. And a Walther of all brands. Christ! If Reggie
had managed to keep the pistol a secret for all those years, and
that wasn't likely, it wouldn't have been German-made. Not a
chance. Not with Reggie "Fly the stars and stripes high on the
Fourth of July" DeLillo. He'd have bought an American-made gun,
a Colt or a Smith & Wesson. No doubt about that. And not a
9mm automatic. Reggie was a .45 six-shooter sort of guy. Or
maybe a .38.

"What are you thinking?" Piccerillo asked.

"I was just about to ask you the same Goddamn question,"
came a voice from behind. Though Juke hadn't heard the voice in
a long while, it still made him a little nauseous, a little angry. It
made him want to hit something, preferably its source.

"Chief," Piccerillo said, suddenly looking down at the floor, or
away, anywhere but at Juke or in the Chief's face.

"Bradbury," Juke said, not about to call the ex-IAD sonofabitch
by any title worth repeating in mixed company.

"Am I mistaken, or did you retire from the force seven years
ago?" Harmony Chief of Police Marion Bradbury, *Old Maid Marion* to a lot of his troops, stared at Juke as he spoke. He wore an
expensive suit, blue, with a white shirt, and a striped tie. With his
squinty eyes, thin lips, and military buzz-cut, he looked like someone born and bred in Internal Affairs. The double-dose of cheap
after-shave was the kicker.

"I, um, asked him in, Chief," Piccerillo explained, a little sheep-
ishly, clearing his throat.

"I didn't give him much of a choice," Juke said. "Reggie was
my friend."

Piccerillo cleared his throat again. "I, um, thought—"

"You thought?" Bradbury said. It was a statement of disbelief.

"Yes, sir," Piccerillo said, "That he, ah, might be able to shed
a little light—"

"And have you?" Bradbury asked, cutting the detective off.

"Depends on your perspective, I guess," Juke said. "I was about to say that as far as I knew Reggie DeLillo didn't own a weapon."

"And my perspective would say you were wrong," Bradbury said. "Not only did he own a weapon, he used it on a fifteen-year-old boy. He probably would have used it on Officer Castagnetti as well, had Castagnetti not shot first. Seven years off the job can dull your instincts, Miller."

So what's your excuse, Juke thought, though the words came out sounding like, "And that's all she wrote, Bradbury?"

"It's as open and shut as they come."

"Just the way you like them."

"Makes my job easy, and we can move on to the next item on the menu."

"I'd think this town's first murder in—"

"Three years," Bradbury supplied. "On my watch."

"—would warrant a little special attention."

"Not when we catch the perp with a smoking gun and a body at his feet."

"Didn't know the gun was smoking."

"Coming through," the ME called out.

The three moved aside, and were silent for a moment, as the medical examiner wheeled a second gurney out to his van. Juke watched as Reggie took the bumpy ride to the morgue and whatever humiliations the small man with the big glasses had in store for his beaten old corpse.

A beeper attached to Bradbury's belt began to sing its cheerful song. The Chief snatched it up, grimaced slightly, then told Piccerillo he'd see him back at HQ. He took a step toward the door, but had to turn around. Juke knew the SOB couldn't let it go.

"I'll assume you remember how to conduct yourself at a crime scene?"

"It's all coming back to me," Juke said.

"Then, maybe you should reapply to the academy," Bradbury said, snorting a satisfied little laugh. "I can always use a good traffic cop over at Harmony Plaza."

They watched him as he walked away.

"The wife's still got him by the short and curlies," Piccerillo explained, pinching at his nostrils again. "All she's got to do is beep."

"Let's take a look upstairs."

Juke had put in almost fourteen years on the job before calling it quits, before hanging them up, and taking his position on the wrong side of an oak bar, a different sort of shield, waiting till judgment day rolled around. But if there was one thing he learned, especially in those last eight years as detective, was that nothing was ever as it seemed. Rarely was anything open and shut. And when in doubt, focus, open your fucking eyes and see. He had learned more about most suspects, most victims, than they knew about themselves, by simply observing. The way they kept their clothes, their cars. How they decorated the personal spaces where they planned, dreamed, fucked, ate, and slept.

David Robertson's bedroom was on the second floor, in the rear of the house. It had two windows. One looked out at the Mad River, a stream of unconscious litter and little else, which ran behind all their homes, which cut Harmony in half, until it trickled north toward Cheshire and beyond. The other window looked onto Reggie's deck, and his garage, which was set back to the far edge of his property line, and Juke's one-car garage beyond that. He'd get around to painting it, one of these days.

Juke wondered how many hours the kid had spent watching Reggie and Molasses. Scheming, speculating. How much rat poison? To how much ground beef? Was he jealous of the companionship? Did he want to know what it was like to kill? Or perhaps he wanted to see the battered old guy suffer and cry. Maybe he just hated dogs.

The walls were papered. A beige on ivory stripe. Judging from the frayed seams, the wallpaper had been up for two decades, if not three. The floor was carpeted. A medium beige, to match the walls. But the carpet was new, a covering for those old hardwood planks.

There was a single bed, made, covered by a dulled brown blanket over white sheets. The headboard was of a cheap wood, probably pine, and painted pale blue. A pair of expensive sneakers peeked out from under the foot of the bed. There was an upturned milk crate which doubled as a night table. On it, a lamp, a combination clock/radio/telephone, and a mostly empty glass of water. Inside the crate, a stack of paperbacks and schoolbooks.

All of the kid's clothes were either hung in the closet, or folded neatly in a matching blue bureau, on top of which were more books: textbooks, notebooks, and a copy of *The Catcher in the Rye.*

Juke picked up the books, and fanned their pages. Most of the textbooks were used, but clean. The notebooks contained outlines and summaries from his English and Math classes. The Salinger was worn, a few pages and chapters circled. But no notes in the margins. Nothing to suggest David Robertson wanted to eliminate the phonies of the world, starting with his next-door neighbor's dog.

"Christ!" Piccerillo said, looking through the one drawer of a small, also blue, desk. "The perfect room of the perfect son of the perfect parents."

"All too damn perfect," Juke said. "Too damn tidy."

"Tidy?"

"Spick-and-span."

"Huh," said Piccerillo. "Maybe the kid had a maid."

Where were the heavy metal posters, Juke wondered, the crinkled issues of *Penthouse*, the piles of dirty underwear and jeans? Where was the Nintendo, the skateboard, the basketball/ baseball/ any sort of ball? Where were the prepubescent snickering fantasies of fast girls and fast cars and life as a guitar player in a rock and roll band? Where were the signs that a teenager, a fifteen-year-old boy, actually had once stepped foot in the ten-by-fourteen foot space?

"Maybe it's open and shut like Old Maid Marion says," Piccerillo suggested.

"Yeah," Juke said. "Maybe."

But he really wasn't paying his ex-partner any attention. Instead, he found himself drawn to a framed black and white photograph mounted on the wall over David's bed. It showed a girl, thirteen, maybe fourteen years old. With long, curly blonde hair. She was sitting on the edge of a boulder, which overlooked a river. Her feet dipped ankle deep in the crystal current. Her white t-shirt and shorts were wet, and clung to her still-developing body. There was a look in her eyes of wisdom. Wisdom achieved through pain, through rushed childhood experiences, a reluctant end to innocence. There was a look as if she had been crying, crying her whole life, that the river in which she dipped her feet was a river of tears, her few years of sorrow sweeping by, cooling her toes, and that she only stopped crying now in time for someone to take a picture.

The image made Juke want to reach out a helping hand to the girl. Tell her to turn back, to savor every moment. That there was no reason to cry, at least not yet. Tell her to never grow old. Warn her that nothing lay ahead but heartbreak and pain. Worse than she could ever imagine. But the look in her eyes told Juke she was well aware. Told him he was too late.

He would have expected to find such a photograph in an art museum. Its tone and unconventional quality reminded Juke of images he'd seen at an exhibit at the Museum of Modern Art about a decade earlier. Or in one of the galleries off Chapel Street in New Haven that catered to the Yalies and their parents. Or perhaps in a coffee shop, a showing of some local photographic talent.

But on the bedroom wall of a fifteen-year-old who had murdered his best friend's dog. Juke had a problem with the open and shut of that one.

four

There was something about the way old plaster walls played with sound. If a noise hit a wall just right, it would bounce off, amplify. Become a superball blare, all echo and speed and anger. Nothing could stop it, as it ricocheted for an infinity, keeping the rooms alive.

Sally Robertson's screams would never leave that River Bank Road house. There was grief so real, that it made Juke step back for a moment, step back from the official proceedings. Made him want to melt into those plaster walls, if only they'd have him. This wasn't a crime scene, it was a scene of anguish, of how could such a thing happen to me? The yellow police tape should carry just that warning. Then no one would ever venture near. All the curiosity seekers would scamper away frightened that some of the misery might follow them home. Juke had news for them: it already has. It's here, there, everywhere. And forget about getting used to it. He had tried.

"I'm used to B&E's and grand theft auto," Piccerillo said, as he sucked in a breath. "Not this." He walked down the stairway that cut the house in two a few steps ahead of Juke, and headed over to the stricken woman. The detective introduced himself, then began, "This is never easy."

"Easy?" Sally Robertson said, her voice teetering on the edge of hysteria. "Easy? All that blood? All you people. You come get me out of work. Don't tell me anything. What's going on here? Did something happen to Neil? Is that it? Is my husband okay? Please—"

"I'm afraid," and Piccerillo paused. He took another deep breath. "It's your son, Mrs. Robertson."

"David?" Sally Robertson said, and she began to shake. "What's, what's—no. My boy? No. Where is he? I have to see him."

"I'm sorry, Mrs. Robertson."

"No. No, it can't be—no."

"Your son is dead," Piccerillo said, telling her what she must have already surmised. Not that the noun mattered much: son, daughter, mother, father, husband—wife. It all carried the same impact. A confirmation of dread. Why else would you be called down to an emergency room at four in the morning? Why else would you return home to crime scene tape and TV news crews? Why else would your partner meet you at the mouth of an alley in which an unidentified woman was raped and murdered, and tearfully beg you not to go any further? *"No, Juke. Please. Don't go down there."*

Juke stood behind Sally Robertson. She sat at the table in the dining room, in the other half of the house, away from the living room where her son was murdered. Piccerillo sat to one side of her, not looking at her, but away. Officer Russo sat to the other side, gently holding the woman's hand.

She wore bank teller clothes. A light blue ensemble that helped her exude purpose as she cashed checks, accepted deposits, and collected payments on mortgages and car loans. All day long, Juke thought, Sally Robertson accepted payments on people's dreams. Twelve hundred, fifteen dollars and seven cents for a safe haven.

23

Two hundred, forty-six dollars and seventy-three cents for that bright red Honda. Thank you for banking at First Harmony. Have a nice day.

Juke watched her shoulders. Hunched in and small, they were rising and falling with her muted sobs. The screaming, the stream of *no's*, had become sobbing. Just sobbing. And eventually the sobbing would become tears. The tears would become sniffles. And they would dry up.

Turning toward the living room, seeing it again, Juke now noticed the similarities to David's room. Personality was missing. The clutter that passed for history. Where were the mementos? The small-framed photos that should have been crowding the mantel? Where was the Robertson family shrine?

The walls, recently painted ivory, were barren except for another black and white photograph. Hung a little crooked on the wall over the sofa, it was framed much like the one of the girl in David's room.

Moving toward it, past the crimson stains, past the chair in which his friend had died, Juke noticed it was of Sally and Neil Robertson. She was waving. He was forcing a smile. The Magic Castle slightly out of focus in the background. She looked pretty in the picture. Very blonde, frosted and teased. Very tall. Her smile curly and big, much like her hair. She wore a cut off top, revealing a very flat stomach for a woman in her late thirties, and flowered leggings. Neil wore a polo shirt, and Docker shorts. He hadn't shaved in perhaps a day or two, obviously living on the edge. They were just another happy Disney family, in the happy Disney world.

"It's a small world after all," a voice said.

Juke turned. It was a cop he didn't recognize. He was standing near the entrance to the kitchen, his thick arms folded. "What's that?" Juke asked.

"Disney World," the cop explained, pointing at the photograph.

"Right," Juke said, nodding. Not that the location was important. It was the body language that made him wonder. Neil's body language, to be specific. A small man, a few inches shorter than his wife. With a rapidly receding hairline. And here in the photograph, a tightly clenched jaw. Clenched fists. A focused glare. Juke tried in vain to read the look in Neil's eyes. Was there an ongoing tiff between him and Sally? Or did he just hate Mickey Mouse? He looked as if he wanted to slap the camera from the photographer's hands. From David's hands? Was the youngest Robertson the photographer? And if so, what had he done on that Disney day to warrant his father's wrath? If so, had he also taken the photo of the girl hanging on his bedroom wall?

"Went there once with the wife and kids," the cop said, continuing the conversation beyond any point of interest to Juke.

"Never got a chance to," he said, walking past the cop, not looking at him, not looking back.

The Robertson kitchen had been remodeled in the seventies. It was a testament to orange Formica and particle board, golden linoleum and fake brass. Not attractive now, but still functional. It was the one room Juke surely would have remodeled.

He moved through it, taking note that the front of the sunburst-colored refrigerator was like a blank canvas. No coupons, no announcements, no reminders. Not even a lone magnet, in case. Opening the back door, Juke stepped into the small three-season sunporch, and from there, into the Robertsons' fenced-in yard.

Fenced-in seemed to be another Tompkins Glen prerequisite. Living the cliché that good fences made the best neighbors. Keeping the dogs and kids in, right where you can see them. Keeping the neighbor's dogs and kids at bay, for a little peace of mind and quiet. As Reggie would have testified, the fenced-in theory didn't always work.

Juke looked about for what differentiated this backyard from the others. What made it special, or worse? There were a few bushes in need of pruning. A two-car garage, a rarity in the neighborhood. And the lawn. Mostly green and recently mowed. Juke was pretty sure he saw the kid out mowing on Saturday.

It was stark in its side-by-side comparison to Reggie's backyard. His deck, spectacular in its design. The meticulously groomed shrubs and flowers that surrounded the fenced-in perimeter, that surrounded the deck. The ivy that grew up the eastern wall of his one-car garage. The beds of cedar chips, the Kentucky Blue Grass, all naturally fertilized so as not to be a danger to his dog. And that sixty-foot tall evergreen which provided the shade he and Molasses so adored on those detestably hot summer days. It was an ongoing project. One that started the day he brought Molasses home. It seemed Reggie's green thumb could flourish, as long as he had the dog to crack wise with. Though sometimes, as a casual observer, Juke believed that it was Molasses who was really calling the shots. Pointing with his snout where to plant the seeds, or what branches to trim. And Reggie lapping it up. Patting the dog on the head. "Good idea, boy."

Much like the Robertsons', Juke's lawn seemed rather paltry by comparison to Reggie's. He had a small maple tree, a couple of bushes, patches of grass that actually outnumbered the patches of dirt. And his own cedar fence that kept it all in. Not that it mattered much. Juke didn't have a green thumb. He didn't want one. And he didn't have anything left worth keeping in.

The doors to the Robertsons' garage were locked. Juke peered into the darkened interior, courtesy of a side window. Pressing his face to the glass, he could make out the shape of Neil's old Corvette, covered as it was with a specially designed tarp. He had once told Juke its model year. It was a Sunday, and Neil was taking his Sunday vehicle out, alone, for a Sunday drive. Juke was just returning home, probably from shopping. Neil pulled up to a stop at the end of Juke's driveway, waved "Hey, neighbor," and beamed as he told Juke everything he never wanted to know about the history of the Corvette. Specifically, Neil's Corvette. It was a cherry red convertible, with those white indented panels running along its side. Everything original. Juke wished now that he could remember the year, mid-sixties, he thought. But all that came to mind was the license plate, *TORRID*, and Neil's unabashed pride. It confused the hell out of Juke. He wanted to tell his neighbor, "Get a life, it's only a fucking car."

On the other side of the garage, Juke could make out the lawn mower, the spreader, the weed whacker, all the tools of a lawn-man's trade. But he was living proof that just because you owned them it didn't mean you knew how to use them.

There was a bike, some boxes, firewood stacked against the far wall. Didn't Neil know that the wood needed to be kept a few inches *away* from the wall? Termites. Another Tompkins Glen imperative. Though not by choice.

There were tires, an extra cast iron radiator—Juke had two of them in his garage—and one of those kiddie wading pools.

Reggie also had a kiddie wading pool stored up in the rafters of his garage. He had purchased it for Molasses, filled it on the hotter days, and watched as the dog just moved in perpetual circles in the tiny tub. Around and around and around, just splashing really. Making a mess. Getting everything wet. Wagging his tail. And Reggie, laughing almost till he burst.

The Robertsons' pool had cartoon designs all over its interior, some blue little man that Juke did not recognize. The pool Reggie bought for Molasses was pink, and covered with Barbie dolls. Reggie got it at a tag sale for fifty cents. Molasses didn't seem to mind, or be emasculated by its design.

As Juke turned away from the window, he heard a snap, distinctive and sharp. It cut above the din of movement coming from the front of the house. A twig, or more likely a branch breaking in half. He spun toward the Mad River, and the Water Company property beyond the fence. He thought he saw a flash of color. Yellow. Or gold. No, blonde. Then movement. Forward. Rushing. Silently rushing.

He ran toward the fence, his eyes scanning, but there was nothing. Not a sound. Not a hastened breath, other than his own. Juke stood there still for many moments, waiting. Eyeing every branch, every leaf, every stone. Was there anything out of place? The river beyond the banks. Still. A dead current.

Perhaps Juke's imagination had just been playing with him. Creating an imaginary killer, hiding out in the woods behind the scene of the crime. Apprehend me I'm yours. To clear the name of his friend. Or perhaps a small animal, one of the many chubby

Tompkins Glen felines, had climbed onto the wrong branch. Or perhaps a branch simply snapped of its own accord.

Juke was about to turn away, when a bird, a slightly withered blue jay, its feathers still an exquisite contrast to the greens and faded oranges of greens from seasons past, began to sing. To fly. It perched on a nearby limb, looking down curiously at him. Turning its head first right, then left. Holding on Reggie's house. Looking at it, as if for one last time. Then flying away.

He watched the blue jay fly, soaring up and up and into the heavens. He imagined it was Reggie. Just checking in, checking out the details, making sure that Juke was on the case.

five

There wasn't much in Juke's house that was less than seven years old. Very little had been changed in those years. The sheets, sure. He had to replace the motor on the dishwasher, but even that took him almost a year to get around to. Like at his bar, he saw no reason to change what was functional. He saw no reason to remove the memories, the fingerprints of souls that had left their mark for a moment or a lifetime. Juke had had enough change to last forever. And if he couldn't go back, there seemed no reason to go forward.

The kitchen was filled with country touches. Nothing orange, nothing gold. Just soft oak cabinets, wide plank floorboards, and a row of plants lining the sill of the double-wide window, which looked out onto his backyard. Atop the cabinets there was a collection of old tins and small wicker baskets. In a corner, an antique hutch, which made even the phone and answering machine seem homey. And his white-fronted refrigerator was covered with magnets, and notes, and coupons. Some for products that were not even manufactured anymore: breakfast cereals that weren't such a good idea after all, clear colas, and salad dressings from a small company long chewed up, swallowed down, and spit out, by one of the conglomerates.

He was sitting at the kitchen table. A square cherry wood design, whose top was covered by scratches from the bottoms of less-than-perfectly finished coffee mugs. In particular there was a Boston Red Sox mug that had done the most damage. He wasn't the fan, she was. But still it remained in the rotation, and the scratches grew at an imperceptible pace. Juke drank coffee from it now, Ethiopian, black, no sugar. And he probably added a scratch or two.

Taking a long sip, he replayed what information he had. The facts as he knew them. On Sunday, the Robertsons' only child, David, had poisoned Reggie's dog Molasses. Reggie made threats. Officer Castagnetti investigated. The kid admitted to killing the dog, said he was sorry. His parents were sorry. Everyone was sorry. But Reggie was not to be placated. He made additional threats. *"He threatened to burn down their house,"* Piccerillo had told him. And though the Robertsons were not about to press charges, Castagnetti nonetheless paid Reggie a visit. At the time, Reggie promised to behave. And Castagnetti went on his way, returning hours later to have a heart-to-heart with David. But he never got the chance.

The kid was dead. Reggie was dead. That much Juke could not change. But the opinion that Reggie had killed the kid, and then was about to shoot a cop. That didn't sit.

Juke drained the mug, and shook his head. Then pouring himself another cup of joe, he walked out of the kitchen, through the dining room which he had not used in those seven or so years, and into the living room.

This was Juke's favorite room in the house. It was also the most painful to be in. The history of their short time together was here, for anyone to see. Photos, so many photos in so many frames, frames of every shape and size, covering every flat surface. The built-in shelves lined with books and compact discs. A dark green sofa, the centerpiece of the room, facing the fireplace. A Stickley chair off to one side of that fireplace, an old rocker to the other. The rocker was covered by an afghan her grandmother had knitted her. She used to cover her legs on those cold winter nights as they'd sit together on the couch, her head resting on Juke's lap. The fire would always be whispering, crackling. Some music on the stereo. She always had music on. He hadn't had music on since.

Juke took a seat in the Stickley chair, and gazed at the comings and goings out his front window, watching the curious as they gathered on the lawns and sidewalks across the street. Faces and murmurs. *"A boy had died,"* those wide eyes said. *"A crazy man had killed a kid."* They pointed and covered their mouths with the palms of their hands. Reggie was the crazy man. Reggie was guilty. No trial, he'd never get one. No chance that he'd ever clear his name, not in *their* minds.

Juke could feel his own heart rate rise. The breath catching in his chest. He was angry at their accusations. Angry about their murmurs. About the pointing and the gasps. No matter how it looked. They didn't know the man. Reggie DeLillo was a good man, a good friend. He'd been there for Juke when the lights had gone out, and it seemed as if the only respite would be at the end of a six-shooter, or at the bottom of a bottle. Sitting for hours on end, perhaps days. Just silence. Waiting for when Juke was ready to talk, if he'd ever be ready. Waiting for the words to form, the confusion to dissipate, the anger—Juke shook his head, the anger would never go away.

The ambulance was long gone now, as was the Medical Examiner's van. Even the SID techs were through crawling around. Only three police cars remained: Piccerillo's unmarked Park Avenue, and two cruisers. The satellite news-gathering trucks had also called it a night, along with most of the reporters. Only one held vigil, an old news hound named Cross. Wilbur Cross. A rumpled raincoat sort of guy with a complexion as silky as a nickel cigar, and a voice just as rough. Juke was pretty sure the man invented reporting. He seemed ancient back when Juke was a rookie. He didn't seem any younger now.

Wilbur Cross was standing on Reggie's lawn. He had his hands shoved deep into the outside pockets of a tweed sports jacket, a small notebook peeked from its breast pocket. The *New Haven Register* didn't get to cover many murders in Harmony. Usually the killings were limited to drug deals gone bad in Newhallville or The Hill. Or a stray bullet hitting the wrong kid in Fair Haven. But a fifteen-year-old getting shot down in his living room. A rookie cop killing the perp in an alleged act of self-defense. Well, that was front page, above the fold, fodder for Cross for days and weeks to come. This was the mother lode. He might as well just move into Reggie's guest bedroom. It'd be a hell of a lot more convenient for everyone—

The phone rang.

"Yeah," Juke said, snatching up the receiver on the second ring. There weren't many who'd be calling him at home. There weren't many who had the number. That was one other thing he managed to change. It eliminated a lot of sympathy. A lot of pity. It stopped the reminders, outside of his normal day-to-day. The answering machine messages from friends who just did not know what to say.

"Town's parched," came the half-mumbled reply. It was Quintin Jones, who, on the busier nights, manned the other half of that thirty-five foot oak bar. He spoke fast, usually leaving a word or two out from most sentences. Still, they made sense. Most of the time. "Got the keys in hand."

"Then open up," Juke said.

As Quintin so eloquently stated, Tompkins Glen would need a drink tonight. It would need a little quenching, a little numbing.

"And you better call Zoë," Juke added. She was the waitress at Juke's Place. And could fill in behind the bar in a pinch. Zoë could probably run the bar in a pinch. And when he thought about it, Juke realized, she probably did.

"Ahead of you," Quintin said, then asked, "Specials?"

"Usual, for now."

"Comin' in?"

"Probably."

"Later, then."

Juke let the receiver bounce in his hands for a few moments, then turned back to look out the window. The crowd across the street had started to thin. Even Cross had finally called it a night, probably off to the city desk to pound out a suitable two thousand words.

The doorbell rang.

Juke replaced the receiver, finished off the last gulp of coffee, then placed the Red Sox mug atop the nearest scratched end table surface, and headed to answer the door.

"Juke Miller," Wilbur Cross said, a warm smile, an extended hand. "Haven't seen you in a dog's age."

"Scotch?" It was what Juke remembered Cross drinking, back in the days when he'd been a regular Friday night customer at the bar. A double shot of Johnnie Walker Red, a splash of water, no ice. A few too many of them. But Juke always took Cross's keys. Always called a cab. He figured that was why Cross stopped coming around. The cab fare taking too big a bite from the weekly paycheck.

"Juke. The only thing worse than drying out, were those steps. Those twelve Goddamn steps. They'd drive you to drink, if only you didn't realize somewhere in the back of what's left of your mind that you'd only end up back at step one. Fuck, no. I'm dry. Been dry for years." He smiled, and suddenly Wilbur Cross didn't seem as old. "Couldn't afford the cab fare anymore."

"Coffee, then?" Juke said, wondering why someone hadn't told him that old Cross was dry. Was he that far removed from the loop? That old customers, or worse, old friends, had moved on without question? Had got on with their lives while he stood mostly still? Yeah, of course he was. He'd seen to it. "Was just gonna make another pot."

"Perfect."

Cross followed him into the kitchen, and took a seat at one side of the square table. "Shame about Reggie," the reporter said.

"You knew him?"

"Seen him around. Used to walk his dog up at Greystone Park on the weekends. Me and the missus just sort of walk each other."

That brought a small smile to Juke's face. The idea of Cross and his wife power-walking the circumference of Greystone Park.

Half in Harmony, half in New Haven, just off Wright Avenue, the park was like a commune for gardeners, dog-lovers, couples and kids seeking refuge from Yale or concrete or whatever it was people still sought refuge from. The park was fenced in by an eight-foot fieldstone wall that would have seemed more appropriate surrounding a castle in England. Perhaps it protected the greenhouses. Perhaps it assured the couples. Perhaps it just felt right at the time it was built.

"He sure didn't seem like the sort who'd off a kid," Cross said.

"Guess looks are deceiving," Juke said.

"Guess? The cops seem pretty certain. It's wrapped up. Old Maid Marion told me so himself." He pulled out his notebook, and flipped a few pages. "And I'm quoting, 'It's an open and shut case of revenge. David Robertson paid the ultimate price for playing a foolish prank.' End quote." He smiled. "Might use it as a lead."

"Doesn't seem that open and shut to me," Juke said, "But then, as Old Maid Marion himself pointed out to me earlier, seven years off the job have dulled my instincts."

Cross laughed. "He said that?"

"I ever lie to you, Cross?"

"Tons of times. But c'mon now, Juke," he said, shutting the notebook. "You can still call me Perez."

That name brought Juke back to the days when he was carrying a shield. Perez was the name Cross would leave at the station house when attempting to get whatever info he could from Detective Juke Miller. A relationship with the press was frowned upon in the department, not just Harmony's, every police department. As far as Chiefs and Commissioners were concerned, the fourth estate should be the last to know, if at all. But Juke felt that sometimes the local paper could help. A well-placed tidbit of information, whether true or false, had cracked cases wide open. Cross had always been there to assist in the cracking. As long as Juke tossed him back the occasional cookie.

"I don't need to call you Perez anymore. Besides," Juke said, "haven't you assigned that code to some other cop?"

"Actually, yes. Just a few weeks ago. A very pretty lady." He cocked an eyebrow. His tone became man-to-man. "I think you'd like her."

"I don't date cops."

Cross nodded. "Yeah. Okay. Not in this lifetime, right?"

It was the last thing Juke would ever want, would ever need. A reversal of roles, to be constantly reminded of crimes solved, suspects apprehended. The right suspects for the right crimes. To forever hear shop talk, cop talk. He got out for a reason.

"Not in any," Juke said capping that part of the conversation with a curt, "I don't date."

"Period, right?"

"Something like that."

"But would you?" Cross asked, not letting him off so easy.

"Would you believe me if I told you I had?"

"I'd'a heard about it, Juke."

"Yeah," Juke said softly, holding his glance for a long moment, before finally looking away. He really was that much out of the loop.

Juke poured out two cups, steaming and black. He didn't need to ask. All old drunks and ex-cops drank it black.

"Thanks," Cross said, taking a sip. "Good."

"So what are you here for, Cross? What do you want?"

"A Pulitzer."

Juke shook his head. "What the fuck is it with trophies? Reggie had Anabelle. Neil Robertson has his Corvette. And you want a Pulitzer?"

"Got nothing to do with the trophy," Cross said.

"What then?"

He rubbed the fingertips of one hand together in a sign that made Juke laugh. "I want the cash prize that goes with it."

"Forgive me for underestimating you," Juke said, himself taking a sip. "Short of that?"

"How 'bout a gut feeling from a good cop."

"Ex-cop."

"You'll always be a cop, Juke."

"Sure." Juke took another sip. "My gut tells me it's a little *too* open and shut. My gut tells me that wasn't Reggie's gun. My heart tells me he didn't shoot the kid."

"The facts—"

Juke held up his hand. "You asked for a gut feeling. If you want facts—"

"Old Maid Marion."

"He's full of them."

"Among other things."

"Yeah. Do me a favor, Cross," Juke said. "Leave a little doubt. In case Reggie didn't do it. The guy deserves that much."

Cross nodded, then gulped down the rest of the coffee. "He sure loved that dog."

six

It was pushing nine by the time Juke made a move toward work. He ate, showered, and changed into something clean. He even shaved. Something he normally wouldn't have bothered with on a Monday night. Maybe it was out of respect for Reggie. Maybe it just postponed facing the crowd down at his bar for a couple of minutes. People who'd be looking to Juke for answers. He wasn't sure, shaving just seemed like the thing to do.

Stepping out of his house, Juke caught sight of Piccerillo sitting on the Robertsons' front steps.

The detective was staring blankly at the walkway at his feet. His palms upturned, resting atop his knees. He looked up, and nodded his hello as Juke stepped over.

"You look like hell," Juke said.

"I feel worse," Piccerillo said. "Y'know, normally me and Cathy are away this time of the year. First two weeks of June, we rent that house up on the Cape. I go fishing. Lie back, drink a lot of beers, grill up some big steaks, or lobsters. Or whatever the fuck we're in the mood for. But not this year. No. This year I get the fucking brilliant idea to go away at Christmas time. Y'know, we got no kids. So, Christmas don't matter much. We spend the last two weeks of the year down on the islands. New Year's on Aruba. That sounded real good to me. Already got the plane tickets and all. Cathy, she could have gone either way. Whatever makes you happy dear. That's what she said." He shook his head thoroughly disgusted. "Fuck."

"You and your bright ideas," Juke said, wondering for a second how Cathy Piccerillo was. It'd been so long since the four of them—

"Yeah," Piccerillo said, laughing at himself.

"How she holding up?" Juke said softly, motioning with his chin toward the house.

"About what you'd expect," Piccerillo said. "Her doctor tried to give her a sedative, but she wouldn't take it." He rubbed at his eyes with the fingertips of both hands. "I just want her husband to get home so I can leave this scene. There's gonna be reams of paperwork on this one—"

"Detective." The voice was quiet, tentative. Another rookie cop Juke didn't recognize. He was standing on the lawn about five yards away, and looked lost in his uniform. A kid playing dress-up. He pointed at some approaching headlights.

Piccerillo stood, and wiped his hands against the side of his jacket. "Part two," he said. "Wish I had listened to my dad and gone to medical school."

"Instead of next-of-kin, you'd be notifying the victims," Juke said. "Telling them they have three months, or a year."

"Yeah, you're right," he said, straightening his tie, combing back what few hairs he had with his fingers. "Not much difference, I guess."

"Want me to go?" Juke asked.

"That was a joke, right?" Piccerillo said. "If I could, I'd let you do this."

"Old Maid Marion would appreciate that."

"Yeah," Piccerillo said.

The headlights cut their conversation short. Both men turned to face the blue Dodge as it pulled to a quick stop before them in the driveway.

Watching the man through the windshield, Juke doubted that Neil Robertson would need to be notified of anything at all. There was a wide-eyed look of terror frozen to his face. Like a deer caught in the headlights of its own mortality, he knew there was something terribly wrong, and it would all be over, just like that—

"Is this a joke?" Neil Robertson asked, almost hopefully, stepping from the car, running a hand through his rapidly graying hair, nervously pulling at his moustache. He motioned at the crime scene tape, at the two cruisers parked in front of his house, then at the half-dozen or so neighbors standing across the street watching him, watching his house. The people across the street motioned back, whispering to one another, as if it were a secret that Neil was now home. Hands once again covering their mouths in shock, or sympathy, or maybe just because they'd seen people act that way on TV.

"Mr. Robertson," Piccerillo began.

"My wife," Neil said, spinning back to face them, his voice rising, his breathing short. He called out her name, "Sally. Oh, my, God. Oh, fucking God, no. Sally."

She came rushing from the house, a streak of tears and mascara, eyes puffed and confused, gleaming homeless and hesitant. She ran into her husband's arms. All sobs, muttering fractured words, a broken explanation.

"It's David, isn't it?" Neil asked, looking over Sally's shoulder at Piccerillo and Juke.

"David's dead," Sally cried. "Our boy is dead."

His gasp cut through the humid night. The final breath of Neil Robertson's old life. The fractured pants of oxygen which would take its place. Nothing would ever be the same again.

Piccerillo shot a quick sideways glance in Juke's direction, then placed a comforting hand on Neil's shoulder. "Mr. Robertson," he said. "If you could come inside. I'd like to ask you a few questions." Then added, softly, "It's routine."

It appeared to Juke as if it took his every ounce of strength for Neil to respond.

"Maybe to you," he said.

Juke stepped back, watching as Piccerillo hopelessly followed Sally and Neil Robertson into their home. He walked over to the Saab, got in, and sat quietly for a moment. He'd witnessed two notifications over the course of a handful of hours. And here he'd thought never again. Not after the last time. When he was on the wrong side of the information.

Five minutes later he pulled the Saab into the parking lot large enough for eight cars. But despite the warning, "Park here at risk of life, limb, and windshield," Juke's space was occupied by a brown minivan with a bumper sticker on its rear window which read: "My child is a Tompkins Glen Guerrilla of Goodness."

He headed back down Wright a block, but every space was taken. He opted finally for The Best Video Store in the Whole Wide World parking lot across the street and down a block, thinking as he walked to his bar that a convention must be in town, or Jesus Christ himself had made an appearance over at Saint Joseph's Roman Catholic Church. Though Juke knew better. These were the vehicles of patrons. A neighbor had died. Two, if you counted the kid. The circumstances sensational. What better night than to head down to the neighborhood pub to talk, to mourn, but mostly to listen?

Crossing Wright, Juke approached the Tudor. It was one of the older buildings in town, dating back to the 1830s, probably once a home for some well-to-do family. Its brick facade had worn glossy and smooth over the decades. Its slate roof in need of constant repair. And the leaded glass windows. Juke maintained they looked great, but damn what a pain in the ass to clean.

The bar shared the first floor with the *Antique Boutique*, a little overpriced, a lot snooty. Juke's Place took up the left side of the building, the antiques were on the right. The hair salon, *Snips*, was on the second floor, just over the bar. Over the antique shop were two apartments, both recently vacated by graduating Yalies.

Juke pulled open the door and stepped into the noise. Zoë, mixing equal parts gin, sweet vermouth and green chartreuse, with a dash of orange bitters, and straining the iced concoction into a cocktail glass, greeted him as he walked up to the bar. "Welcome to the monkey house," she said, garnishing the drink with a twist of lemon peel and an olive.

"Good evening to you, too," he said.

Juke's Place was New Year's Eve packed, minus the fancy suits and pretty dresses. Minus the revelry. There was definitely a somber feeling in the air. A few of the patrons had been crying. Most of the conversations were private, speculative. Juke was pretty sure he heard more references about the dog than anything else. One woman, whom he recognized from her frequent walks with her pair of greyhounds, said loudly, "I'd have shot the little sonofabitch too."

"If the election were held today," Zoë said. "Reggie would win over the kid by a margin of at least two to one."

"But the election isn't going to be held today," Juke said.

"Moot point, then."

"It's all a moot point, right?"

"Right," Zoë said, then, "So, you working, or just paying us a social call?"

"I'm working," Juke said. Not like he had a choice.

"Then I'll snap my fingers and magically morph back into a waitress before your very eyes," Zoë said, doing just that, as she traded places with Juke, stepping from behind the bar, tray in hand.

Half the guys in the joint turned, a few tactfully, some staring in open-mouth awe, watching Zoë as she zigzagged up to the first table in need of refills. She always seemed to have that effect on men, gathering their eyes, their looks, their desires. She had that effect on some women as well, but their stares were usually more discreet. Zoë was a striking young woman—her application said she was twenty-two when Juke hired her about four years back, though he'd have guessed nineteen or twenty—whose looks shocked you into looking, then defied you to look away. Whether it was the short-cropped platinum blonde hair, or the short-cropped skirts. Or the platinum navel ring that always seemed to peek out from her short-cropped shirts. Or her blue eyes, that smile, a laugh with such promise that it could give the Pope a hard-on, just like that. All of the above. None of the above. Juke was never quite sure. And it didn't matter. She did her job well, was on time, and at night's end always balanced out.

Juke turned to Quintin James, just as the bartender dropped a familiar vodka bottle into the glass recycling bin.

"Abs'lut's outta sight, outta mind," Quintin said.

"All out?"

"Not a drop."

"Who knew?" Juke replied, a shrug, palms up toward the heavens. "Offer Finlandia at house prices to anyone asking for Absolut."

"Done."

"And do a special on Pabst," Juke said.

"Reggie's fave?"

"Yeah."

"Buck a pop?"

"Make it fifty cents. Reggie'd like that."

Juke watched Quintin as he nodded, then backed off to work the front end of the bar. He was about as lanky as they came, almost as tall as Juke, but probably eighty pounds lighter, with a shaved head and a black goatee. He had lived across the street from Juke back in the early eighties. His parents had been pretty good friends with Juke, Reggie, and their wives. But when teenaged Quintin got into gangs, drugs, and worse. When he got busted for grand theft auto, and police found crack cocaine in his back pocket, along with a loaded automatic in the glove compartment. His parents left town. Ran away in the middle of the night. As if the embarrassment would kill them, or worse, make them face their shortcomings. Juke heard they moved to New Mexico, or at least that's what Reggie had said. Then years later, after Juke had long since lost track of time, Quintin was released from prison. Out on early parole from a ten-year sentence. He asked the cop who had put him away for another chance. Juke couldn't think of any reason not to give it to him.

"Aren't you worried about him stealing?" Reggie had asked at the time. "I mean—" He shrugged. "C'mon."

Juke took a deep breath, then began his reply. "One. There's giving away drinks for tips. Here's a free one on the house. You leave a couple of bucks, when normally fifty cents would do."

"I don't leave anyone a couple of bucks."

"Two," Juke continued, "Guy comes in for a fast drink. Slaps his cash on the bar. And he's off. The money stays there for a long while, then finally ends up in the tip jar. Another way, buy a six dollar bottle of vodka, replace the inventory at night's end. That's a hundred bucks' worth of drinks, at least. And no missing booze. But he's got to keep track in his head. Don't want the drawer too far under, or worse, too far over."

"Worse?"

"Yeah. And if he's counting. Forget about it. He's gone. Anything. Pennies off to one side. Or peanuts. Or little checks on a bar napkin." Juke reached for a matchbook, flipped its lid, and began bending back individual matches, one at a time. "One match for every drink. That's the most obvious."

"Not obvious to me."

"Then there's working with a partner. You buy a beer. Slap down your five. I give you change for a twenty."

"I like that."

"Stealing from customers. You're half in the bag. Slap down a twenty. I give you change for a five. Or there's counting out tips. Get rid of their singles. Put in ten, take out a twenty, don't ring up the next ten dollar round."

"Wouldn't the customer notice?" Reggie asked.

"In most bars, the cash registers are stuck in a corner, or against the back wall where you can't see the total."

"Not here."

"Not here," Juke said, continuing, "Then you can flat-out over-charge, or forget to put in a new register tape, or—"

"Okay, okay," Reggie said. "I get the picture. Jesus H. Christ, you read a book on this, or something?"

"Yeah, *Stealing for Dummies*," Juke had said at the time. "There's a whole chapter on how to take a barkeep for a ride."

"Shame, isn't it?" Dominic Santorelli said. He was as regular as any of Juke's customers. An old-timer who lived over on Wood-bine Street, with his wife of forty-seven years. He drank rum and Cokes, heavy on the rum. And ice. Lots of ice. Santorelli liked his drinks cold. His jokes, anyway they came.

"Yeah," Juke said, taking position at the back end of the bar. His territory. The regulars knew it. Reggie had known it. On all those nights when Anabelle didn't call and beg for Juke to send him home.

"I mean the part about Reggie, and the boy."

"It's all a shame, Dom. Every last detail."

"Scratches on the veneer of the human race."

"Scars," Juke corrected him. "Scratches heal."

Santorelli nodded a few times, then took a sip of his drink. When Zoë returned to the waitress station, he spoke up again, as if he were waiting for the larger audience, "Got one for you."

"Not tonight, Dom," Juke said.

"Really."

"It's appropriate."

Juke and Zoë shared a look, as they always did, on more oc-casions than they'd like to admit. Chalk it up to customer service. Then they turned toward Santorelli.

"Okay," he said, happier than he should have been. "A woman goes up to a priest. She's crying. She's hysterical. She says, 'Father, my dog just died. Will you bury it for me?' The priest says, 'Madam, it has never been, nor will it ever be, the practice of the Catholic Church to hold funeral services for a dog.' 'Aw, I'm sorry to hear that,' the woman says. 'I was prepared to pay five thousand dollars for it.' 'Oh, hold on a minute,' the priest says. 'You didn't tell me the dog was Catholic.' "

Juke and Zoë watched Santorelli for a beat, both nodding slightly, not so much as cracking a smile. It was an unwritten, unspoken rule they shared to never laugh at the old-timer's jokes. Even the best customer service had its limits.

"C'mon," Santorelli said, frowning a little. "That was a good one."

But before Juke could respond, another customer sidled up to the bar.

"What you hear, love?" Malvina Washington squawked, loud enough for everyone to hear. In her early sixties, she smoked unfiltered Camels, drank Budweiser, and was deaf in at least one ear. She leaned in, placing her empty beer bottle at Santorelli's elbow. "Hmm?" she went, tapping her fingers in rapid succession against the oak.

"Just a lot of bad jokes," Juke said, only loud enough for Santorelli to hear.

"What's that?" Malvina said.

"Nothing more than anyone else," Juke said, a lot louder this time.

"You're a cop. You always know more'n everybody else."

"There are people who'd disagree with you about that."

"Let 'em."

Juke handed her a fresh beer, then waved off the crumpled five spot she handed back.

"You're just bribing me to stop asking questions," she said.

"You got me figured out, Malvina."

The old woman smiled, then snorted out a laugh. She lit up a cigarette, took a deep drag, then grabbing her beer, turned, and headed back to her booth.

"Guess it worked," Santorelli said.

"You're all crazy!"

Mary Simson was standing over by the mechanical genie. There were tears in the woman's eyes. A divorcee, with four teenaged children, Mary worked three jobs just to make ends meet, just to make her Tompkins Glen mortgage.

"Take it easy," someone yelled.

"She's right!"

"A child is dead!" Mary screamed. "An innocent fifteen-year-old boy—"

"Innocent!"

"Reggie was our friend."

"—And you people are talking about the dog like it was—like it was—I don't know what? Have you no shame?"

Rachel Altimari, the greyhound woman, spoke up. "How can you defend that little bastard after you know what he did to Reggie's dog? How dare you call him innocent?"

"How can you defend Reggie?" Mary asked. "He killed that boy."

"That dog was like a son to Reggie."

"It was his kid."

"It was a dog," Mary said, sitting back down. Crying freely now. "It was just a dog."

"The kid should have been punished," Sam Ehrhard said. He lived across the street from Juke, about three houses down. "But this," he shook his head. "This is just bad."

"Sam's right," Santorelli said, spinning around on his barstool. "Reggie went too far. I mean, Christ! Two people are dead. And for what?"

"A dog is dead," Rachel said. "And for what?"

"You disgust me," Mary said, picking up her purse, and storming past Rachel, past the others, out the door.

"What comes around, goes around," Rachel said.

"Uh-uh," Malvina said, wagging a finger. "What comes around, runs away."

seven

Zoë called to Juke over the din of the crowd. She was standing at the waitress station, a tray full of empties in front of her, bouncing the red telephone receiver in one hand.

"No wives calling tonight," Juke said. "They're all here."

"You'll want to take this in the office," she said.

Juke didn't question her. He lifted the drop-gate, and squeezed past her, as she stepped behind the bar to take his place.

"Who's calling?" Dominic Santorelli asked.

Juke shot him a decidedly nasty look, then stepped toward the office.

Santorelli shrugged a little guiltily, then turned back, catching Zoë's stare.

"It was the phone company," she said, in a conspiratorial whisper. "They wanted to know if Juke would switch long distance carriers. And that was a decision I knew he'd want to make in private."

* * *

"Found something out I thought you might like to know." It was Piccerillo, he was at headquarters.

Juke could hear the tension in Piccerillo's voice. He could sense the perspiration on his hands and face. Something was up. He glanced at his watch. It was pushing midnight. At least his ex-partner had finally escaped the Robertsons.

"From Neil Robertson?" Juke asked.

"No," Piccerillo said. "Neil Robertson hardly said a word. He just stared out the window at Reggie's house the whole time."

"Only Reggie's not there to hate," Juke said.

"Yeah. Sometimes closure ain't all it's cracked up to be," Piccerillo said, then, "Before I left, I asked if he knew why David poisoned the dog. He started to say something, but it was all jumbled up. And, um, well—that's when he broke down. He was leaning against the wall, and just slid down to the floor. Face buried in his hands. His wife put her arms around him, and they just cried—Christ. I hate to leave people that way, y'know?"

"I know," Juke said.

"Anyway—"

"Shoot."

"That's the problem," Piccerillo said. "Reggie couldn't. The gun was empty."

It took a beat for the words, their meaning to sink in. "Had it been fired?" Juke asked.

"We're running tests now. But the thing is—" Suddenly Piccerillo's words dropped off, and Juke could hear mumbled conversations. The word "Chief" being prominently pronounced. Piccerillo was talking to Old Maid Marion, and he wanted Juke to know it.

Juke leaned back in the desk chair. He had to turn sideways, otherwise risk banging his head against the shelves lining the wall, and knocking over the bar napkins, the plastic swizzle sticks, the straws, and other non-alcoholic supplies that were stored above his head. The office was small, just a desk, a couple of file cabinets, a safe, and some shelving. There was a calendar on the wall from one of the liquor distributors. And a bulletin board posted with schedules, important phone numbers, and some must-be-posted information from the Connecticut Department of Labor. A door led to the liquor storage room, another to the walk-in cooler.

Closing his eyes, Juke wondered what the hell had Reggie been thinking? What was going through his friend's mind at the end? Christ! Did he even know the gun was empty? That'd be just like Reggie to never check for bullets. Or was it all planned out? A police suicide? Threaten an officer with an empty gun, knowing that the cop would be forced to shoot. That's what they'd claim, the official line. But, no, that didn't play right either. None of this did. None of it sat right in Juke's gut. Sure, Reggie was despondent, but he would have found another way out, or perhaps in time, he'd have gotten over it. He was a survivor—

Juke had been with Reggie when the first Mrs. DeLillo passed away. The slow agony of it all, the year of chemotherapy, and nothing that seemed to help. Not a Goddamn thing.

He was there when the pains in his neighbor's back and knees became too much to bear, and Reggie was forced to retire from his foreman position at the Genovese & Sons Construction Company, a job that he loved, a decade and a half too soon. The job was as much a part of his personality as Pabst Blue Ribbon, and Reggie had never been able to give that up. Of course, he was never made to.

But this—this was revenge. This was anger. And Reggie knew how to make anger pass. How to let it slide. How to get on with it all, somehow.

"Ya there?"

Juke pinched the bridge of his nose until it hurt. Then he snapped his eyes open. "Yeah," he said.

"Old Maid Marion just doubled me up," Piccerillo said. "Gave me a new partner."

Though he wanted to ask who? Juke asked, "Why?" instead. There had to be more now. More than what Piccerillo had just told him. That Reggie's gun was empty didn't prove much of anything. One bullet was all anyone needed to put down the kid. Even Marion Bradbury didn't need extra manpower to prove that.

"The gun Reggie was holding was a 9mm."

"Right," Juke said. "I saw it."

"The slug they just pulled from the kid was a .38."

eight

Juke figured that Wilbur Cross would still be at his desk at the
Register. Reworking the lead, fine tuning it just right. Still taking
a crack at winning that Pulitzer.

He answered on the first ring.

"Perez?" Juke said.

"Perez has left the building. He's living on an island with Elvis,
Marilyn, and JFK."

"Then, I guess, you'll have to do."

"Tell me something that'll break my heart."

Juke told him.

Cross let out a long, low whistle.

Juke heard the "uh-oh's" in the background. Cross's co-workers
must have known the signal. They must have gone scurrying, the
presses must have stopped printing, and somewhere an editor was
developing a migraine.

"So what are you thinking?" Cross asked the ex-cop.

One scenario in particular had been playing in Juke's mind.
He talked it through with the reporter. "Reggie walked in on a

murder. He found the kid that way, probably even tried mouth to mouth."

"Would explain the blood. But not the gun."

"It belonged to the kid—"

"He was fifteen. C'mon."

"C'mon, nothing, Cross. You've seen the statistics."

"Yeah, alright, alright. I, um," there was a rustling of papers, "Did a piece on it a few weeks back. Yeah, here. Last year, over six thousand pistol-packing kids expelled from schools in twenty-nine states, and all the numbers aren't even in."

"And those were just the kids they caught," Juke said. "Christ! You know as well as I do, half the high school students in New Haven are carrying. Why not Harmony High?"

"You're suggesting this is gang-related?" Cross asked.

"Another kid pulled the trigger. Yeah, Cross, that's what I'm thinking. David Robertson stole a girl, a pair of sneakers. He looked at someone the wrong way. He cut ahead of someone in the lunch line. Who the fuck knows? We're living in a world where you can get shot at for cutting another driver off. And this kid poisoned a dog. I doubt it was the first time he's pissed someone off."

"Killing a dog ain't got nothing to do with gangs."

"Initiation. Proved he was worthy. Or maybe he was just show-ing off. Playing God's little game of life or death. He killed the dog because he could. That violent impulse we all know a little too well."

"Speak for yourself."

"Maybe he liked carrying a piece. Little big man. Acting tough. Go with me here."

"You're stretching—"

"Okay, maybe he got the gun to protect himself from Reggie."

"Could it have been his dad's?"

"The wife would have given it up. Walther's have a very specific look. It's not just any gun. Besides, Neil Robertson's not exactly the gun-toting type," Juke said. "He's more your classic Corvette, Chinos, and White Zinfandel."

There was a long beat of silence at the other end of the line. Juke could tell Cross was thinking, and jotting down notes, eyeing his just finished lead, and wondering what the hell he'd write now.

"There's another possibility," Cross said finally.

"Give it to me."

"A trigger-happy cop."

Though he said nothing, Juke was nodding. That scenario had also played out in his head. Castagnetti goes to see the kid, sees he's carrying, and when the rookie tells David to drop the weapon, the kid goes for it instead, and gets himself shot. Castagnetti wouldn't have known the gun wasn't loaded.

Then the rookie hears a noise. Reggie. He panics, hides, then thinks things through. Reggie had all the motive in the world. So when Castagnetti reenters the room, when he finds Reggie covered in blood, the kid's gun in Reggie's hands, every last piece of the puzzle falls into place. A rookie cop probably wouldn't have noticed the kid was packing a 9mm. Or thought about his service revolver being loaded with .38s.

"Sorry, Juke," Cross said finally, his tone suddenly cautious, as if that last suggestion was like pouring salt on an old friend's wound. "I, ah, didn't mean anything by—"

Juke cut him off. It had never even crossed his mind. "Ballistics will tell all," he said. "We'll know in the morning."

Juke let Zoë and Quintin handle the cleanup. It'd take a good hour and a half, but he'd tack on a little bonus to their paychecks at the end of the week to show them gratitude. Take care of those who take care of you.

He was unlocking the Saab when he heard the voice behind him. The words were slurred, and a little too loud, but then Brett Genovese's words were always slurred. He was always a little too loud.

"Juke," Genovese said. "Can I talk to you for a second, Juke?"

Juke could feel the muscles in his back immediately tense up. Brett and his kid brother, Christopher, had inherited the Genovese & Sons Construction Company from their father. The younger brother ran the company. Brett ran himself into the ground. Turning, Juke spotted Brett leaning against the back of his red Ferrari. He was drunk, though not on Juke's booze. Not tonight. On this night a lynch mob, the friends of Reggie DeLillo, might have been waiting to string him up.

"Not tonight, Genovese," Juke said.

"She—" Brett said, stopped, then, "Anabelle."

Juke shook his head. "What about her?"

"She broke it off with me."

Juke could feel the anger beginning to surge. He wanted a piece of Brett Genovese. He wanted to pop him one. Yeah, just because he could. His violent impulse. The punch that Reggie could never throw. Would never throw. Reggie didn't believe in violence. He believed in words, in sarcasm, in that rude slam the door in your face. Juke balled his hands into fists, thinking, none of this made any fucking sense.

"She—"

Juke unclenched one of his hands, then slammed the other into the palm. Not drunk. He wanted Genovese on an even playing field, but knew he'd never get the chance.

"Cry on someone else's shoulders," Juke said turning, opening the driver's side door.

"You don't understand," Brett said, taking a step forward, stumbling.

"What don't I understand?" Juke said, a little too loudly. "You were fucking Reggie's wife, and now you're not fucking her. Seems pretty clear to me."

"No, it—"

"Why would I care?"

"She's, um." Brett shook his head, as if trying to clear it. "Aw, shit. She's been seeing a cop."

Juke let the words sink in. Why would Anabelle trade in a millionaire for a cop's salary? But then, what Anabelle was interested in had little to do with bank accounts.

"For how long?"

"At least a month," Brett said. "She hasn't had anything to do with me since at least that long."

"What's his name?" Juke asked.

"Don't know. But I—"

"That why you haven't been coming around?" Juke asked. He turned back to face Brett. "Not as much fun when you don't have anything to throw in Reggie's face."

Brett straightened himself up. His three thousand dollar Italian suit hanging off his physique like a three thousand dollar Italian suit. He wasn't as tall as Juke, just a lot wider. With a round, still-boyish face—boyish for a man in his late forties—and long hair tied back into a short, tight, ponytail. He'd been a linebacker in college, till the partying put a quick end to that extracurricular activity. He looked at Juke, wounded for his troubles. Then he took a step forward, then another, walking around to the other side of the sports car.

"Yeah, Juke," Genovese said, fumbling with his keys, bending, trying to unlock the door. "Just like you said."

But Juke was by his side, taking the keys away, hooking a hand under one of his arms and leading him over to the Saab, ready to drive him home.

"How many times, Genovese?" Juke asked, not expecting an answer, not getting one.

There was a small section of Tompkins Glen, on the other side of Wright from where Juke lived, where the houses were mansions. Stately six, seven or eight thousand square foot estates, with gleaming white columns out front, tennis courts and in-ground pools out back, and slate roofs on top. It was where New Haven's wealthy called home. Close enough, without the high property taxes.

Brett Genovese's home was as opulent as any. A twelve-room, brick Colonial, probably worth high six figures, sitting on a two-acre parcel of flat, pristine land, surrounded by a fieldstone wall. Fenced-in, but not really.

Juke turned the Saab into the circular driveway, and pulled to a stop alongside a black Range Rover.

Genovese went to open the door, but stopped himself from completely pulling back on the handle. "I liked Reggie, y'know," he said. "He was a stand-up kind of guy."

"You have some way of showing it," Juke said. "Anabelle was—"

Genovese cut Juke off. His voice raised with emotion. "Me being with Anabelle didn't have anything to do with Reggie. It didn't have anything to do with Reggie at all. I'd have been with her no matter who she was married to. She isn't a one-man girl."

"Obviously."

"Most times I wished she wasn't married to him."

"Why's that, Genovese?"

"I don't know. I guess that way Reggie probably would have enjoyed the stories more. He was a drinking buddy—"

"He enjoyed them plenty, Genovese."

"Yeah," Genovese said. "I bet he did."

He pulled on the handle, and swung the car's door open, then looked down, staring at his hands for a long time. He turned them over, and back again, as if they weren't familiar. As if they weren't his hands. His brow scrunching, confusion clouding his features.

"Genovese," Juke said.

"Yeah, I, ah—" he said finally. "My dad tried to keep him around, y'know?" His voice was surprisingly contemplative and sober. "Offered him a desk job. It was all Reggie could do with that bad back of his."

Reggie had put in twenty-seven years with Genovese & Sons. "He could do plenty," Juke said.

"Dad couldn't take that chance. Reggie got hurt on the job, he would have owned the company."

"Reggie wasn't the type to sue."

"Tell that to my father." He rubbed at his eyes as if they hurt. "I was there. Reggie looked at us like we were nuts. He didn't want any part of it. If he couldn't be out with the crew, swinging the hammer, lifting boards into place, then he just wasn't going to do it. He could have inspected for us—"

"He didn't like the idea of having to inspect other people's work," Juke said.

"That's what he told us. And I can't say that I blame him." He shook his head ever so slightly. "I just wanted you to know."

"I know," Juke said.

"Yeah," Genovese said, reaching out, pulling himself from the car, and trying to stand on wobbly legs. One step forward, then another. Getting his balance.

Juke watched as Brett Genovese disappeared into his mansion. Closing the double-wide front door behind him. All that space. All that emptiness.

nine

Like the Robertsons, Juke had an old sunporch tacked on to the back of his house. A long while back he had thought about building a deck, but without shade, it would have been unbearable on those summer scorchers. And without the screening, the mosquitos that bred ravenously in the Mad River would have eaten him alive at night. So the sunporch stayed.

It was where he sat now. On an Adirondack chair, its wide arms and back long weathered from mahogany red to a laid-back gray. His feet rested atop a small side table. No lights were on. He'd seen enough for one day.

It had cooled off considerably since the mid-afternoon highs that reached into the low nineties. It had quieted down even more. There was a breeze moving through the backyards of River Bank Road. By the trees and bushes, around the garages, and back porches. It swooshed the leaves, and the flaps of umbrellas that some residents had propped upright in the center of their patio tables, making the only sound on an otherwise soundless night.

Juke was playing with the couple of pieces from what he knew would be a thousand-piece puzzle. Turning them over in his mind, fingering the edges. He had one link. He was sure Reggie had gone to talk to the kid. Scare him even, Walther or not.

Could the 9mm have belonged to Reggie? Perhaps. An unloaded handgun in these days of Uzi's and grenade launchers. That was Reggie, all right. But the other links were missing, so far. Or were they? What about Anabelle and the cop? What about—there was a rule about tips from drunks. Half of them were dead on the mark, the other half pure bullshit. If only Juke could figure out which half was which.

"All the secrets in the universe would be revealed," he said, in half-jest, to the shadows.

He held a beer in his hand. A bottled amber made locally. He had been trying for years to sell it at Juke's, but the brewers felt it would affect sales at their own micro-brew pub in downtown New Haven, and would only supply six-packs to a few select liquor stores. Such was life, Juke thought. And though he disagreed with their business sense, he couldn't argue with the taste of their beer.

He remembered once offering Reggie a bottle of the amber. It had been one of those airless summer days. Anabelle was out, God knows where. Though he probably cared less than Reggie. And the two neighbors found themselves in their respective backyards. Reggie sitting with his dog. Juke sitting with his memories. When the feeling hit, Juke headed inside for a fresh-me-up, but came out with two instead.

"Thought you might like a beer," he had said, popping the top, handing Reggie the dark brown bottle.

"You know better than anyone I only drink Pabst Blue Ribbon."

"Try it."

One sip was all it took. Reggie laughed. And so did Juke. It was worth a try. Reggie then offered the beer to Molasses, but even the Lab was biased. He too would only drink Pabst. Like father, like son.

"Juke."

The voice caught him off guard. He looked over at the screen door which hung just slightly crooked in its frame, but still kept most of the mosquitos out. She was standing there, wisps of sweat-stained hair falling into her face. She wore a white v-necked t-shirt like a mini-dress, and Juke was pretty sure she had nothing else on underneath. She opened the door and stepped into the sunporch, moving over to him in a way that clawed at his heart.

"Aren't you going to offer me a beer?"

He shook his head and turned away. Juke couldn't look at her, for fear of the rage it would spark. He hated her so much right then. More than ever. More than he could imagine, or would even try to.

"We can be together now," she said. "We need to be together now."

When Juke spoke, his voice was flat, even. Controlled, considering the situation. "Why don't you give Genovese a call?"

"You hate me, don't you?"

"I hate what you represent," he said. "It's nothing personal."

"You're so good—"

"He's not even cold, for Christ's sake!"

"So above everyone else—"

"Not even cold."

"No, Juke. That's your domain."

"Fuck you, Anabelle."

"That's why I'm here."

She wouldn't give up. Not even now, on this night of the dead. How many times in the past three years had she come on to him? How many times had she stopped into his bar on a listless afternoon, when Reggie was asleep in the backyard with the dog, and Juke's Place regulars were still a few hours away? He wanted to tell Reggie, but had always stopped himself short. How many times had he told her to leave? To go home to her husband? That he wasn't interested, not now, not ever. How many times would he need to tell her to leave him the fuck alone?

"Get out of here."

"You don't know what you're missing."

"Of course I do."

"What do you mean?"

He turned away, and thought about what he was about to say. He could picture the look on Reggie's face. He'd get a kick out of this scene. Despite everything.

"Why do you think Reggie married you, Anabelle?"

"Because—"

"I'll tell you. So he'd have something to brag about to the guys down at the bar."

"You're full of shit."

"He could spend hours mimicking your moans," he said, his voice clipped with hostility. "The look on your face when you gave head. The things you could do with your tongue. And then, well, when some of the other regulars began to know what he was talking about firsthand, when Brett Genovese spilled the beans, it all sort of got old for Reggie. Got old real fast."

"How pathetic."

"We're all guilty of that."

"You especially, for listening."

Juke looked at her now. Glared at the woman who thought she was taking his friend for a ride, when really it was a mutual fucking. Both parties getting what they wanted, probably what they deserved.

"I might be pathetic, but not because of that. 'Cause no matter how much I turned away, no matter how many times I tried to change the subject, your deeds were there, slapping me, slapping everyone, in the face." He shook his head angrily, and spit out the words, "There's nothing I don't know about you. There's nothing more I need to know."

"You sonofabitch."

"You were his fuck, Anabelle. Molasses was his friend."

She stared at him, clenching back the tears, biting at her top lip, muttering the phrase over and over. But her calling Juke a *sonofabitch* meant nothing. There wasn't anything Anabelle DeLillo could say to Juke that would carry any weight, any meaning.

He watched her as she backed away, off the sunporch, to disappear into the darkness of the night. He could hear her mumbling as she moved, as the door to her own house slid open, then slammed shut. Then the screams. The rage coming to her surface, exploding. It was the reaction Anabelle DeLillo should have been having on this night, but for other reasons.

Juke sat there listening to her pain. Could rejection, could humiliation really feel that bad? He doubted it. And instead hoped that some of those tears were for Reggie. He hoped anyone else listening, waking to her cries in the middle of this night, would believe that. That Reggie was being mourned by his wife.

He stood up then, walked into his kitchen, to the fridge, then returned a moment later to his Adirondack chair. He had a fresh beer. This one a Pabst. He always kept a few bottles on hand for when it was his turn to supply the backyard brews. Twisting off the top, he took a long sip. It tasted light, foreign, a little watered-down, but still so cold. And as he drank it, Juke began to cry. He could feel the salty droplets streaming down his face. He could taste them mingling with the beer. He couldn't stop the tears. There was no reason to. So, sobbing and sniffling, he drank it all down, then raised the empty bottle high.

"This one's for you, old friend," he said, toasting the heavens.

ten

A backyard barbecue. Reggie provided the yard, the shade, the new deck. Juke provided the barbecue and the beer, lots of cold beer. Pabst for Reggie. And Becks for Juke, the micro-brew stuff had yet to completely catch on.

Molasses was there. A puppy, six or seven months old. Not fully grown. But tall, and scraggly, and still trying to fill out all the wrinkly chocolate-colored fur. He had a red collar on, a soft cotton weave that was embroidered with the phrase "good dog" written over and over again. Reggie had paid twenty bucks for that collar. There was nothing too good for Molasses.

And she was there, as well. Leaning against the railing of Reggie's deck, watching Juke as he tended to the grill. Or as he flipped a tennis ball across the yard to the dog, who could catch it like a seasoned outfielder. Reggie maintained there were at least a couple of pro teams that could use a player with Molasses's ability and enthusiasm. "The Yankees for one," he said. "The Red Sox for another."

Juke could feel her eyes on him. Such a deep brown, and so

wide. He could picture her as she lifted a beer bottle to her lips. A slight dimple on the left side of her face, as just the hint of a smile played around the bottle's neck. The wisps of dark brown hair escaping from the single ponytail that held most of it back out of her face. So tall, lean and beautiful, she wore old jeans on this day, and a soft black t-shirt. No shoes. No jewelry, except for the gold wedding band and her engagement ring.

He didn't dare turn and look. Lest he fall to his knees trembling. She had that effect on him. Always had. Since the day he'd first walked into B-side Records, in downtown New Haven, and saw her behind the counter. He had special ordered an old Billie Holiday album. Someone had called and said it was in.

"I like your name, Juke Miller," were the first words she ever said to him, reading his name from the special order list. There was a warm smile on her face as she looked up at him, handing him the vinyl LP.

"You can have it," was his reply, immediately in love with her voice, her smile.

She didn't know at the time how serious he was. But Juke knew he'd marry her right then and there. He could have asked her on the spot. Skipped all the rituals, and simply said, "I do," in front of the cash register. But it would happen, fourteen months down the road. The tall, handsome cop and the beautiful girl from the record shop.

When he finally turned, the feeling hit. How he could ever imagine living one moment of life without her. To wake without her, sleep without her, to sit at the kitchen table reading the Sunday papers over a strong cup of joe and some fresh croissants without her. The notion collapsed his lungs. Broke his heart from inside out. It killed him just to leave her every morning. And the only reason he made it through each day, past the pain and suffering, past the domestic squabbles and attempted shoplifting, was because he knew she'd be there waiting for him when he got home. And he'd take her into his arms. Hold her for a moment, squeeze her to him as if for the first time, as if for the last time. No, there'd never be a last time. And they'd kiss. And often, they'd put aside dinner to whenever, they'd put aside everything, and go to bed, to lay staring at the ceiling, holding hands, talking. There was always the most ridiculous news story of the day, each was required to uncover at least one. They'd plan dream vacations, discuss what colors they should paint which rooms, what movies they'd watch that weekend, or about day trips to parks where they'd bring a picnic basket and a bottle of good red wine. Then, when the conversation faded, one would inevitably turn to the other and there'd be back rubs, which would lead to soft endless kisses, long tireless caresses, which would end with them making love.

"What are you thinking?" she asked, stepping over to him, taking the spatula from his hand, and expertly flipping one of the burgers.

"Oh," he lied, "How maybe we should get a dog one of these days."

"I'd like that," she said. "Give Molasses someone to play with." She'd squat down and give the pooch a scratch behind the ears. Molasses would roll over onto his back, scrawny legs out all over the place. And she'd rub his belly. "You'd like someone to play with, wouldn't you, Molasses."

Juke would look over at Reggie, and wonder how he survived the death of his wife. There were no children to lend support, no real family. Was it booze and friends? Could building a deck, could a dog, ever take the place? Or did they all just pass the time? He had asked Reggie once, and the guy just sort of shrugged, and got a far away look in his eyes. "The time passes whether you've got something to do with it, or not," he answered, drinking up, paying his tab, heading home.

When the food was gone, and the supply of beer had run dry, she and Juke crossed the fenced boundaries back into their own yard, and watched the day fade from the sunporch, holding hands, having new variations of those old conversations. And when it was dark, when most everyone else on River Bank Road had retired for the night, they made love in that old Adirondack chair, laughing riotously at the sheer discomfort of it all. Getting more turned on with each bump and bruise, yet trying to keep the sounds down so as not to wake the neighbors. So Molasses would not start to howl.

But no such luck. And when Reggie dragged himself from bed to see about the frantic barking, they did their best to hide and watch in the shadows of the sunporch, giggling like teenagers who thought they'd gotten away with something. Though they were pretty sure Reggie knew what was going on. His smile said as much, as did the comment to Molasses, "C'mon boy. Let's give our neighbors some privacy."

Juke turned now, so lost in sleep, so alive in his dreams, and reached an arm over the empty pillow that remained on the right side of the bed, her side of the bed. There was a smile on his face. All of those who mattered were with him.

tuesday

eleven

Juke lay awake in bed. The ceiling fan caught a glint of the early morning sun and filled the bedroom with a slow-motion, hand-cranked, strobe-light flicker. A freeze-frame glow of nothing much at all. He turned on his left side, and faced her pillow. If he removed the case and pressed the old down to his face, he could still catch her scent. Lemony, and fresh. Like the smell baby powder only wished it could have.

The room was just as she had last left it. Stressed pine night tables bookending the bed. A vanity which he had built, sanded and stained from a kit. It wasn't perfect, but she thought it was. An old pie chest with heart-shaped cutouts in the door and an Ethan Allen nine-drawer pine dresser, covered with keepsake boxes, knickknacks, perfume bottles, photographs, and a small stuffed teddy bear wearing a black Zorro mask. And three framed wedding photos mounted on the wall over the dresser, the happy faces, the proud, loving glows.

Juke stared now, not at anything in particular, but at the space, into the space, trying to recall everything he knew about the Robertsons.

David and his parents had moved into Maria Onofrio's center-halled Colonial last August. Ten months back. The house had been on the market only a few weeks. But after the old woman passed on, at the age of ninety-four, her children stripped it of its antiques and memories, then underpriced it by about fifteen percent for a quick sale.

The Robertsons came from Watertown, New Jersey. He now knew that Neil worked as an auto parts sales rep, and Sally as a bank teller. And the kid. He had been two weeks away from the end of ninth grade, a freshman in high school.

What was it about *two* houses away that made it seem like another galaxy, another lifetime? As if the Robertsons weren't his neighbors, just Reggie's, and—Goddammit! Juke couldn't remember the names of the people who'd lived for at least four years in the pale yellow house beyond the Robertsons'. They also had a Saab in their driveway, and he thought the husband might have been a writer of some sort, and the wife ran a coffee shop in New Haven, but beyond that—another galaxy.

Had he ever spoken to the Robertsons? No conversations that he could remember, except the one about Neil's usually garaged Corvette. And that struck him odd now, after seeing the furnishings in their home. That car had to be worth thirty grand, if not more. And thirty grand could replace that French Provincial. Thirty grand could remodel that kitchen. Thirty grand could—

And, yes, once, earlier this spring, in the Tompkins Glen Pharmacy. The over-the-counter pain medication section. Juke was picking up some aspirin, when Neil wobbled in. Looking a lot worse for wear. Bags under his swollen, bloodshot eyes, clothes wrinkled. He was hungover. Juke could have spotted the symptoms anywhere.

It took a double take for Neil to recognize his neighbor. But when he did, "Oh, man. If anyone'll know, it's you."

"What's that?" Juke asked.

"Best cure for a hangover." Neil picked up a package of Tylenol. "Went a little overboard with a bottle of wine last night."

Juke knew one bottle of wine could never cause so much damage, but he let it slide. "That's the last thing you want," he said.

"Why's that?"

"Acetaminophen and alcohol don't mix."

Neil glanced at the label, then returned the Tylenol to the shelf. "What then?"

"Nothing here," Juke said. "Go home. Drink a lot of water, and work up a good sweat."

Neil had misgivings. "That works?"

"It's the only thing that works."

Juke recalled seeing them in the bar once. Just Sally and Neil, a busy Saturday night, maybe a month or so after they'd moved in. He sent them a couple of drinks on the house, with a message delivered via Zoë: "Welcome to the neighborhood." But Juke's Place was crowded and loud. And the Robertsons stayed for only an hour or so, sipping their free drinks, never ordering a second round. Perhaps they were on their way to a movie or dinner or— Juke hadn't a clue. He didn't know their habits. He never had a reason to. They said thank you on the way out, Sally mentioning how friendly everyone seemed to be.

Friendly—other than the obligatory and very neighborly wave as he or they drove or walked past the other's house, Juke really hadn't seen more of Sally. He'd catch the kid mowing the lawn on occasion, or shoveling. Yeah, he remembered seeing David a lot this past winter. Seventeen snowstorms, and yet all Juke ever got was a wave, a "How ya doin'?" Of course, he had offered no more, usually less, in return.

David was a tall, lanky kid, with chiseled features and clear blue eyes. His complexion was clean, his hair long, straight, and dirty blond. He avoided that baggy pants/hip-hop look, which Juke could never even begin to comprehend, and instead seemed to go for blue jeans and t-shirts. He was probably popular with the girls at school, and Juke remembered Anabelle once conceding, as she barbecued Reggie's steak, that David would be a real heartbreaker when he got a little older. Juke believed her. Anabelle seemed to be an expert on such things.

As for Reggie, he never said much about the Robertsons, one way or another. No gossip, no fuzzy recollections of Sally and Neil screaming at each other in the middle of the night. Nothing, except for a small encounter he shared with Juke over a couple of late afternoon cold-ones back in April.

"Unfriendly motherfucker," Reggie said.

"Who's that?" Juke asked.

"Neil Robertson."

"You have a run-in?"

"Wouldn't call it a run-in, exactly."

"What then?"

"I was watering the front lawn last night, like I do every night this time of the year, and some splashed a little on the guy's driveway. Maybe six inches along the edge. Y'know, those sprinklers aren't an exact science."

"Yeah, so?"

"Yeah, so, nothin'! Listen to this. Neil Robertson rings my doorbell at six o'clock this morning, and asks if I could refrain from wetting his driveway. Refrain. That was the word he used: refrain."

Juke laughed. "What'd you tell him?"

"Not a fucking thing. But I didn't *refrain* myself from slamming the door in his face."

The doorbell rang as Juke was stepping into a pair of Topsider deck shoes. They were old and worn and comfortable. He wore them without socks on those days when the temperature in Connecticut reached the preposterous point, as some blabbering weatherman on the radio had forecasted while Juke was taking a shower. The shoes had once been black suede, topped with a deep brown leather trim and just as deep brown laces. But the colors had all faded and turned the same after so many summers of wear.

He shut off the lamp on his night table, and headed downstairs. He could make out the top of Tom Piccerillo's head through the half-circle cutouts of glass that topped his front door. He opened up without any further inspection.

"On our way to visit Castagnetti," Piccerillo said in lieu of a good-morning. "Care to join us?"

"Old Maid Marion know about this?" Juke asked.

"Not exactly," Piccerillo said. "But, um, we'd like you there. No one knew Reggie better than you."

Juke looked from his ex-partner and into the eyes of the other part of Piccerillo's *we*. They were blue, flecked with gold as the morning sun seemed to catch them just right. The centerpiece of an oval face, plain, but pretty nonetheless. The woman, Juke guessed her to be in her very early thirties, had shoulder-length, rather dark hair, curly, and an olive complexion, making her appear Mediterranean. She was of medium height, perhaps five-six, and medium build, and wearing serious clothes: a white blouse, a light blue blazer/pant combo.

Piccerillo caught him looking. "This is my new partner," he said. "Greta Zaretsky." Then he nodded back at Juke, "Juke Miller."

Zaretsky extended her hand, and Juke shook it.

"Nice to meet you," he said, feeling an uncertain jealous twinge at meeting his ex-partner's new partner. It had been so long. And about the time he called it quits, the Harmony department went through a metamorphosis, deciding to let their detectives ride solo on most trips. There wasn't enough manpower, enough money, or enough crime. This, after all, wasn't New Haven, or worse, Bridgeport or Waterbury.

"Actually, we've met," Zaretsky said. "Seven years ago I was a rookie on the New Haven force. My beat was downtown."

Greta Zaretsky didn't have to say any more. The look in Juke's eyes gave away the sudden recognition. The memory of a young female officer pulling him away from the scene, trying to calm him down, to soothe the denial, the anger, the grief. Clutching him finally to her chest as he cried, as he wailed, as he screamed to almighty God to end it now, take him too. As he pushed her away finally and ran. Sometimes Juke felt like he'd been running ever since.

"I never knew your name," he said.

"Now you do."

Both Juke and Zaretsky reached for the handle to the passenger door of Piccerillo's unmarked and oversized Buick at the same moment. It was just a gut reaction for Juke, a reflex set in motion from ancient repetition. Then as quickly, they both backed off, and with an open palm she motioned toward the chrome handle. Looking away, he tugged up on the chrome. The door swung open, then Juke stood aside, holding it for the detective.

"Old habits die hard," Juke explained.

"Maybe there's a part of you which thinks you should still be a cop," Zaretsky said.

"It's wrong."

Juke pulled himself into the back seat, wishing he could retract some of his legs, making do instead by sliding over behind Piccerillo, while keeping his feet behind Zaretsky.

As Piccerillo started his car, and pulled out of Juke's driveway, Juke glanced over at the Robertsons' Colonial. It was painted brown, and had yellow trim and shutters. And a yellow front door—which swung open now. Neil just stepping out onto their stoop. Sally standing in the open doorway watching her husband as he walked to his car. He wasn't looking back at his wife, but to Juke appeared to be concentrating. Focusing on every little detail, to prevent anything else from going wrong. His eyes were swollen and bloodshot, the bags heavy. Not from drinking. Not from too many glasses of wine. But from crying. His footsteps were tight, as if each took his every ounce of energy. As if each might be his last. Perhaps he wished for just that.

Sally glanced up at the Buick as it moved past their house,

catching Juke's eye in the back seat. He held on to the familiar look in her face, a death mask of a response, just to the left of anguish, so far beyond confusion and disbelief. He'd seen it before, known it before. A little too well. From mirrors, and his reflections in windows and windshields and chrome.

"You tell the Robertsons yet?" Juke asked. "About Reggie not being the shooter?"

"We're waiting on ballistics," Piccerillo said, as he turned left onto Wright, and headed toward Centerville. "And I want to see what Castagnetti has to say."

Made sense, Juke thought. Maybe they could bring more to the table that way. More than just, someone else murdered your boy, and we haven't a clue as to—

"You're thinking he might have shot the kid in a panic?" Zaretsky asked.

"I don't know what I'm thinking right now," Piccerillo said. "Other than I could use a few more hours sleep."

She turned to face Juke. "He always complain like this?"

"Only one way to keep him happy," Juke said.

"How's that?"

"Donuts."

"Thanks a lot, *partner*," Piccerillo said. This time the sarcasm was there.

"Keep the donuts coming, and he's too busy to complain about anything," Juke said, a good-natured grin creeping about at the corners of his mouth.

"At least a donut has substance. Not like that low-fat granola shit you used to eat."

"I love granola, Tom," Juke said, starting to laugh.

"And I love donuts." The guffaws from the back seat were contagious.

"How long were you two together?" Zaretsky asked.

"Too long."

"Not long enough."

* * *

Castagnetti lived in a complex behind the Super Stop & Shop. And though the buildings were all less than a decade old, the Garden View Apartments seemed run down and tired. The units resembling some of Juke's regulars who'd been drinking hard all their lives.

As the Buick pulled around a depressed quarter acre patch of overgrown hedges and dried-out plants—the garden of which Castagnetti had a view—Zaretsky pointed out the side window and said, "Unit three-three-one. Up on the left."

Piccerillo pulled into an empty space with the number "three-two-nine" painted in faded yellow paint on the faded black asphalt. As the three exited the vehicle, a young African-American woman, with a child in each arm, screamed from behind a screen door.

"That's my space you parkin' in, Mister. I call the tow truck you don't move it."

Piccerillo flashed his badge. "Police business, ma'am," he said. "We'll be commandeering your spot for the next hour or so."

The woman glared at Piccerillo. There was such a hatred in her eyes, a misunderstanding and anger, as if he were responsible for every indignity ever inflicted upon her race by his. Juke wondered if she gave that same look to Castagnetti as he passed by. He wondered as well, how it might make the young officer feel.

"She looks at everyone that way," came a steady force of a voice from behind the screen door, next to which the numbers "three-three-one" had been painted in black. "Peter used to think it was just him. Because he was a cop. But then one day we noticed she gave it away to everyone."

"Gave it away?" Juke asked.

Robin Castagnetti nodded. She had a troubled sound to her voice, a hardened look in her face which Juke could have recognized from a hundred yards. Premature wrinkles stressed the sides of her mouth and her eyes. Flecks of gray marked her otherwise brown hair. And she couldn't have been more than twenty-five. A cop's wife.

"Her pain," she said. "She gives it to everyone—"

Juke looked back at the woman. She was still behind the screen door, scowling, clutching the two children to her chest. He wanted to go over and ask her if it was easier that way. Easier than just storing it up, keeping it all locked away inside.

"—Whether they want it or not."

twelve

Peter Castagnetti looked as if he'd been on a weeklong bender, but Juke would have bet the kid hadn't touched a drop. The strain, the sweating it out, was all from pulling back on a trigger. Whether he had rightfully shot Reggie, or whether he had in a panic killed both Reggie and David Robertson. The first time you pulled the trigger had a wobbly edge. The first time was vertigo.

They were in the living room of Castagnetti's townhouse, a typical two floor, two bedroom. And though it looked as if the couple had only lived there a short while, there were still a lot of homey, personal touches. Framed photographs and paperback novels lined the built-in bookshelves. Magazines covered the coffee table. And a dozen popular feature film videos were stacked atop the TV.

Juke and Zaretsky sat on a soft-print sofa, Piccerillo on the matching loveseat, and Peter Castagnetti on an antique wingback chair the couple must have picked up at a yard sale. His wife stood behind him, her right hand resting on his left shoulder. A portrait in courage.

Castagnetti unconsciously bit at his fingernails, working on a hangnail on the ring finger of his left hand. The plain gold wedding band caught some shimmers of sunlight which streamed through the front window of the condo.

"They think I shot the kid, don't they?" he blurted out. Obviously something he'd been mulling all night. The only thing on his mind.

Piccerillo shrugged. "Did you?"

"I can't believe you'd—" Robin said, shaking her head, then looking away. There was a flash of anger in her eyes. So vivid. Juke knew what the woman was thinking: my husband risks his life every day, and yet gets treated like a criminal.

"No," Castagnetti said, glancing at his wife, then back. "I did not."

"I believe you, Peter," Piccerillo said. "Honestly, I do. And hopefully ballistics will clear this all up. I'm waiting on word right now. But in the meantime, maybe we can go over the incident one more time. Maybe something jogged loose in your memory. A little detail. Anything. Just start at the beginning."

"On—"

"Take your time."

"—Sunday afternoon," Castagnetti took a long breath, "I answered a call at Reggie DeLillo's home at one-four-three River Bank Road. Mrs. DeLillo answered the door. She, um—" he scratched at the side of his face. "She was the one who called it in. Anabelle. Mrs. DeLillo. She walked me through the house, and onto the back porch. That's when I spotted Mr. DeLillo crouched down on his knees out on the lawn. He was—he was leaning over a large brown-colored—" A shrug.

Juke thought about where he'd been Sunday afternoon. At the local Price Club, the monthly visit, picking up supplies: paper products, vat-sized cans of green olives, five gallon jugs of orange, cranberry, pineapple, and grapefruit juice. And cleaning supplies. Always a lot of cleaning supplies. By the time he'd arrived back home after dropping most of the stuff off at the bar, Castagnetti had come and gone. And Reggie was digging, silently, angrily. Already a little drunk. And the dog—Juke couldn't believe Molasses was dead.

He remembered a July afternoon, about two years before Anabelle came on the scene. Not that long after the first Mrs. DeLillo had died. Reggie had rented a twenty-six-foot motor boat for a week in July. It was like a small yacht, and he and Molasses were going to sail to Martha's Vineyard, Block Island, Nantucket, back and then some. Juke spent a day with them—a Sunday, the usual day off—cruising over to the eastern tip of Long Island. "You gotta see this," Reggie had said to him, somewhere out in the middle of the Sound. He was proud about something, Juke could tell it from his voice, from the smile on his neighbor's face.

Turning toward Molasses, Reggie clapped his hands once, and said, "Pabst." The dog ran over to a cooler, pushed the lid up with his snout, and retrieved a can of Pabst Blue Ribbon from the ice. Then, putting the can down on the deck, Molasses nudged the lid shut, and brought the beer over to Reggie, whose only regret was that he couldn't teach the dog to pop the tops.

Juke hadn't asked if Reggie needed help. He pulled a shovel from his own garage, and went to work, helping dig a respectably-sized hole. Then Juke stepped back as his neighbor pulled from his house one of those extra-large Rubbermaid containers made for storing winter clothes, made for packing away and protecting what you won't need until next year, what you might not ever need again. Reggie had lined it with the green-striped dog bed which Molasses always slept on.

Carefully, Reggie picked up the dead animal, placing him in the makeshift casket. Placing him as if he were only asleep. Then covering him with a blanket which he had also taken from the house.

Giving Molasses one last scratch behind the ear, Reggie lowered the lid, clipped the plastic locks in place, then turned to face Juke. Again, without saying a word, Juke bent over and lifted one side of the casket, while Reggie got the other. They lowered it into the ground, under the shade of the dog's favorite tree.

Juke then stepped back. He watched Reggie for a long moment, wishing there was something he could say. But he knew better. There were no appropriate words. Now it was time for Reggie to be alone. Now it was time for Reggie to mourn.

Turning, he headed toward his house, along the way catching a glimpse of Anabelle. She was standing at the kitchen window, staring at her husband. She'd been crying, her eyes swollen and red, her mascara nothing but ghastly streaks.

At the time, Juke hadn't a clue as to what had brought on Anabelle's tears. Now he wished he had asked her why?

"The dog?" Piccerillo asked.

"Yes. That was the dog," Castagnetti said. "An, um, eight-year-old chocolate Labrador Retriever, named: Molasses. Mr. DeLillo told me Molasses had been poisoned. I asked him how he knew this for certain, and he explained about pieces of raw hamburg stuck to his fence about where he found the dog. And that as Molasses lay dying in his arms, the dog had regurgitated pieces of undigested raw meat.

"I confirmed the presence of the meat on the fence. It appeared to have been pushed through the slats from the other side. The Robertsons' side of the fence. The meat was flecked with white particles, which I later confirmed to be a concentrated powdered pesticide, made by Ortho."

"You confirmed it how?" Zaretsky asked.

"I found a half-empty container in the Robertsons' garage, which the boy, David, later admitted to having used on the dog."

"What did you do next?"

"After interviewing the kid?"

"After finding the pieces of meat on the fence."

"I, um, crossed over into the Robertsons' yard, and knocked on their door. Mr. Robertson answered. I explained why I was there. I had a suspicion—"

"A suspicion?"

"Mr. DeLillo's actually."

"Did you tell Robertson that?"

"No. I said that the neighbor's dog had been poisoned."

"How did he react?"

"He stared at me for a moment. Just stared. His face all tensed up. Didn't say a word. It was like he was lost suddenly. Remembering something that he preferred not to. I finally said, 'Sir,' and he seemed to snap back. He shook his head a little, looked over in the direction of the DeLillos' house, then went inside to get his son."

"How long did you wait for the kid to come down?" Piccerillo asked.

"Did you hear any of the exchange between father and son?" Juke asked immediately after.

"A couple of minutes," Castagnetti said looking at Piccerillo, then turning to face Juke, "No."

"Was the kid upset?" Zaretsky asked.

"He wouldn't really look at me. And can't say that I blame him. His father stood rigid behind him the whole time, one hand around the back of the kid's neck. Mr. Robertson is a small guy, shorter than his son, but I still kept thinking he was gonna choke the kid from behind." The rookie shook his head imperceptibly. "I asked David if he knew anything about the death of DeLillo's dog? He nodded, then answered yes. Did he have anything to do with it? Another yes. How did he do it? He confirmed the use of the pesticide. Why? A shrug. The dog was always growling at him."

Juke shook his head ever so slightly. Molasses didn't growl. He'd rarely ever bark. He was only threatening if you were allergic to canine saliva, or if a hysterically wagging tail could somehow do you harm. In the eight years Molasses had lived next door, Juke had never once seen him show the slightest sign of aggression toward a member of the human race. Squirrels, well. That was something else altogether.

"What?" Robin Castagnetti asked. She was glaring at Juke. Her tone accusatory. "You don't believe him?"

"Not that," Juke said. "It's the dog. He wasn't aggressive."

"Maybe he knew what was coming?" Robin said.

The persistent beeping was Piccerillo's cue that the interview was over. In one way or another. Everyone in the room knew it. No one more so than Castagnetti.

Piccerillo looked down at the readout, asked the rookie if he could use the phone, then stepped into the kitchen to do just that.

When he was out of earshot, Castagnetti turned to Juke. "I had a dog just like that when I was growing up. Chocolate and all. We called him Hershey. Like the candy bar. My sister and I picked out the name. 'Cause she looked like a big candy bar to us. Man—" he shook his head, and wiped at an errant tear, "—that dog followed me everywhere. I don't think I ever had a friend as good as—" he stopped mid-sentence. "I remember—I was eighteen, had just graduated high school. My mom had remarried again, this was husband number three. And I—and I come home from a date, and there was my sister. She was bawling her eyes out. Told me Hershey had died. That she was in the garage. In a Goddamn black plastic trash bag. My sonofabitch stepfather was just going to throw her out with the garbage—" His tears flowed more freely now. "—I can never forget opening that bag and seeing her fur, all matted. I didn't look beyond that. I couldn't. I just left for good. Stayed with a friend. Then I read in the paper about the test to see if you had what it took to be a cop. I figured I had what it took. Self-control. I had the mother lode of self-control. The fucking mother lode. 'Cause I didn't beat the shit out of my stepfather that night. I didn't wring his neck. And I wanted to. Still to this day I want to." Castagnetti sniffled, then rubbed the balls of his palms into both eyes, grinding the tears back. "Still to this day."

"Looks like we've got ourselves a murderer running around Harmony," Piccerillo said, breaking the sudden and uneasy silence. He was standing in the entrance way to the kitchen. How long he had listened to Castagnetti's story, even Juke didn't know.

"Shooter's using a .38. Short barreled. Something cheap. A Saturday Night Special."

"So, my husband's off the hook?" Robin asked.

"The bullet which killed the boy didn't come from his service revolver," Piccerillo said.

She stared at him for a moment, hard and a little cold, then shaking her head, turned away and whispered, "Who would shoot a fifteen-year-old?"

"You were the first to arrive at the scene," Juke said, facing the rookie. "Forget what you first thought. Reggie wasn't the shooter. He just came onto the scene a few minutes before you did. He took a seat and waited—"

"For me to kill him," Castagnetti said.

"An easy way out," Piccerillo said.

"There are no easy way outs," Juke snapped.

"C'mon, Juke," Piccerillo said. "It's like calling Dr. Death. He backed Castagnetti into a corner. And if Reggie didn't kill the kid—"

"Who would have believed him?"

"The ballistics—"

"Bullshit! He wouldn't have survived a night in lockup."

"That's bullshit!"

Juke shook his head and turned away from his ex-partner. Lockup was a piss-poor example of life gone bad back when he left the force. He doubted that it had become all rosy in the seven years since.

He again faced the rookie. "Could anyone else have been in the house?"

Castagnetti played back the scene. How he knocked on the front door, and watched as it swung open.

"The front door?" Juke asked.

Castagnetti nodded.

"But wasn't the gate separating their backyards also open?"

Another nod.

"Then Reggie came in through the kitchen," Juke said.

"Are you sure?" Zaretsky asked.

"I lived next to the guy for seventeen years. Never once did I see him come or go through the front door. He went there to scare the kid. Not sell him insurance."

Castagnetti nodded. "Okay," he said. "Sure. But—" He was straining to remember, pressing at the sides of his head. "It's all such a blur. David on the floor. Bleeding bad. I could see the bullet wound in his chest. He wasn't breathing. I was pretty sure he was dead. Pretty sure. Mr. DeLillo was on the Laz-E-Boy. Covered in blood. Just covered. The gun in his hand. He was staring down at the kid. And I said, 'Please put the gun down, sir.' "

"Did Reggie say anything?" Juke asked.

"I said 'Please, sir. I don't want to have to shoot you,' and he said, 'Of course not.' "

Juke nodded, wondering what could possibly have been going on in Reggie's mind if he thought Castagnetti's bullet was the only way for the misery to stop.

"Why me?" Castagnetti said, burying his face in his hands.

Juke had asked himself that question more times than he could ever begin to recall. But he never found an answer. There was no answer. It was all just luck of the draw. God dealing out the cards.

Today *you* win a million dollars.

Today *you* fall in love.

Today *you* begin to suffer. The worst sort of disease. One not terminal, and of which there is no cure.

thirteen

It looked like a warehouse from a block away. A four-story cin-derblock building, its walls covered by decades of graffiti, scrubbed off, painted on again. There was a parking lot big enough to hold a few hundred cars, its asphalt cracked and faded. The grounds were surrounded on all sides by an eight-foot high chain-link fence. Even the old football field and the overgrown, weed-covered baseball diamond out back. Locked in, enclosed, their games failing to breathe life into such an ugly structure.

Harmony High School was located on the town's other main thoroughfare, Deerfield Avenue. It ran parallel to Wright for most of its length, before veering right, and meeting up to form the corner in Centerville which the city fathers felt most appropriate for town hall. But the school was situated at the far, south end of Deerfield, closer to New Haven, and the Newhallville section. A lot closer to that city's problems, than it was to its abundant cul-tural offerings. So close, that the building almost looked at home in its neighborhood.

As Piccerillo pulled the Buick into a space marked, "Principal,"

Juke noticed that the flag out front was flying at half-mast. He wondered about the significance. Why not fly every flag at half-mast, every day? A requiem for every senseless death, a reminder that it's all so fragile, and can be taken away like—he heard the quick snap of a finger in his head. Yeah, like that.

They were given David's homeroom, as well as the name of his teacher, Mrs. Rinehart, who lived only two streets away from Juke in Tompkins Glen, on Walker Avenue, a dark green Dutch Colonial, if his memory served correctly. He had once investigated a break-in at the old woman's home. Nothing was missing, except for her cat, which Juke eventually located in a tree out in her backyard. About half the cops on the Harmony force would have told the woman that the police weren't paid to rescue animals. But not Juke. Instead he climbed up, carried the cat down, then calmly spoke to Mrs. Rinehart about home security. He told her she was lucky nothing was taken this time. That the cat and the burglar probably scared each other away. To which she readily agreed, stroking her tabby, calling it a "watch-cat," and asking Juke for the umpteenth time if he'd like some iced tea.

And here she was now, at least ten years older, running a homeroom for fourteen- and fifteen-year-olds who all honestly believed they'd never live to be her age. Why would they want to?

"Detective Miller," Mrs. Rinehart said, shaking Juke's hand. Her grip was still strong. Her hair shocking white and pulled into a tight bun. "How good it is to see you again."

He nodded pleasantly. It was okay if she chose to forget that Juke was no longer a cop. She was old. It was her right to remember what she wanted. It was her right to be correct all of the time, damn convention and common sense and facts. She was in her golden years, what precious time she had left should not be wasted on trivia.

Introducing Detectives Piccerillo and Zaretsky, Juke told her they were investigating the murder of David, and could they, perhaps, speak to some of his friends?

Mrs. Rinehart nodded, and pointed out the window at a number of children congregating in the school yard out back. "Today's one long recess," she explained. "We're talking to everyone in small groups. To offer counseling, you know? Even though David was only here for a year, he was a very popular boy. His grades were excellent, straight A's. He was involved in sports, he was the school's quarterback last season, you know? We went twelve-and-oh. He wrote for the school newspaper. Oh, it's so sad. Everyone loved David." The old woman began to cry softly, pulling a tattered handkerchief, which looked as old as she did, from the pocket of her dress, and dabbing at her eyes. "Oh, my," she said.

As Juke and the two detectives walked to the school yard, Piccerillo commented, "Great. We're investigating the murder of the all-American quarterback."

"There has to be at least one person who hated his guts," Zaretsky said.

"Mrs. Rinehart was only showing us one side of David," Juke said. "Hopefully, we're about to meet the other."

"Po-po in the house."

"Chill yo, roanie alert."

They approached a group of four teenaged boys. Thirteen to fifteen, Juke figured. Somewhere in that gray area. The kids all attitude. One tall, exceedingly scrawny, with a Caesar haircut and thick lips, two rather nondescript—medium/regular in every respect, the last short, heavy, the roly-poly comic of the group. All white boys playing from the hood. But their hip-hop clothes were about as authentic as a ten-dollar Rolex. It was all suburban chic. *Jnco* and Vans. Mom's trip to Nordstrom, instead of the corner surplus shop.

"What the hell are they saying?" Juke asked.

"This week's slang," Piccerillo explained. "Can't keep up with it."

"Po-po's a synonym for cop," Zaretsky said. "So's roanie."

"Good," Piccerillo said. "Then you can be the official translator." He stepped forward and flashed his badge a few inches from the tallest kid's face. "We'd like to talk to you about David Robertson."

"The ex-David Robertson," the fat kid said.

"Dog-man did him."

"I'm aware of the fact that David is deceased," Piccerillo said. "But," and he took a deep breath, "Dog-man's not the culprit."

One of the kids fanned away the smell of coffee and donuts. "You fronting us?" he asked, making a face.

Making a face of his own, Piccerillo turned to Zaretsky.

"He wants to know if you're lying," she said.

"No," the detective answered. "Someone else killed David. And we're going to find out whom." He drew out the *oom* of the last word, then in a bad Spanish accent added, "Comprende?"

The kids shot one another sideways glances, as if they suddenly were suspect. The two medium/regulars stepped back a little, shaking their heads. The fat kid shrugged and turned away. Only the tall one stood his ground—the leader. Or, at least, the leader now, if David was the model of popularity Mrs. Rinehart hinted at.

"Did he have any enemies? Ever get into fights?"

It took a minute, but finally the tall kid spoke up "It's the bitches that fight," he said, motioning over at some girls with his chin. "They always getting into it over something."

"Okay, then what about girlfriends?"

The fat kid began to laugh. "David had more cheese than Pathmark."

"Yo, he was the chicken-head king," one of the medium/regulars said. "Man, he was fucking Frank Perdue with a Jimmy Hat on."

"Jimmy Hats are condoms," Zaretsky offered. "Cheese is slang for girlfriend."

"Bet the National Organization for Women must be very proud."

"Chicken head is, well—"

"I can figure it out," Piccerillo snapped, his face flushing red. But before he could continue, Juke stepped forward.

He placed a calming hand on Piccerillo's shoulder, then said, "Why don't you two take a break."

The frustration suddenly evaporated from Piccerillo's face. It was as if he had been thrown a lifeline, a drain for his pending ulcer, an old-fashioned breather.

"Good idea," he said, then turning to Zaretsky, "There's a coffee shop up the block. Best damn corn muffins you'll ever taste."

"But, we shouldn't leave—"

"Don't worry about it," he said, leading her away. "Juke's got a way with children. And I don't know about you, but all this talk of food has made me hungry."

The four kids shared a chuckle and wide grins as they watched the two detectives walk away.

One of the medium/regulars said, "Yo, like he needs another corn muffin."

"What he needs is Scope," the fat kid said.

They all laughed harder.

And Juke laughed right along with them, staring at Piccerillo's and Zaretsky's fading forms, waiting until they turned the corner, then waiting not a second longer.

His hand snapped up at the tallest kid's throat. Pushing him back with a loud clank against the chain-link fence. And pressing. Not that hard, but just hard enough. Using his considerable height—Juke towered over the kid by a good six inches—and strength as an advantage. The lines were drawn in the vernacular of the school yard: I'm bigger, I'm stronger, I'm in charge.

"This is police brutality, man," one of the medium/regulars said in hasty panic. "This is Rodney King all over again."

But Juke never took his eyes off the tallest. "Only problem with that," he said, "I'm not a cop."

"Then chill the status datus, man," the fat kid said.

"What's up, yo? You chrome, or just crazy?"

"We're going to cut the shit," Juke said evenly, staring down at the tallest kid, watching his face turn a little paler by the second. Feeling the perspiration collect and drip around his fingertips as they pressed into the kid's throat. "You're going to speak in grammatically correct English. Perfect, complete sentences. So much as one conjunction out of place, I'm going to wring your fucking neck, then move on to—" he shot quick glances at the others, making them all take quick, frightened steps back, "—one of your buddies, and repeat the process. Understand?"

The kid nodded.

"Are you with me?"

Another nod.

"Can you speak?"

"Yes, sir," he said. "I'm sorry, sir."

"What's your name?"

"Todd Scillia, sir."

"Nice to meet you, Todd. Now—" and Juke gave the kid his most winning smile, even letting up the slightest bit on his neck— give a little, get a little, Juke always figured, "—let's talk about David Robertson."

fourteen

They were sitting around Zaretsky's desk. Juke leaning back in a chair, his head pressed against a four-drawer file cabinet. He had just started relaying a detailed account of David Robertson's social life according to Master Todd Scillia, when the yelling began.

"I just got off the phone with some hysterical woman whose kid came home from school crying 'cause some cop roughed him up. Stupid kid crapped in his pants."

Piccerillo stood. "Must have been the fat one," he said, trying to lighten the situation.

But Old Maid Marion wasn't in the mood. The Chief was fuming, pointing a finger in dangerous proximity to Piccerillo's face. "You know anything about that?"

"Not a thing, Chief," Piccerillo said, "I, ah—"

"I did the interrogation," Juke said, standing as well. "You got a problem with it, you talk to me. But I'll tell you right now. Put that finger in my face, I'll break the fucking thing off."

Chief Bradbury looked as if he wanted to spit. "Piccerillo.

Zaretsky," he barked, "My office. Now. And you—" he seemed to resist an overwhelming urge to point.

"Your cubicle," Juke said, correcting Bradbury. There were no offices, no office doors. Never had been, for as long as he remembered. An old Chief had redecorated the division back in the late sixties, back at a time when private spaces were tantamount to police brutality, at least in the weary public's mind. There'd never been cash in the city budget to rebuild the walls, to re-redecorate.

Bradbury just shook his head. He made a growling sound, deep in his throat. "Why bother?" he said, focusing his anger on the detectives instead.

Juke cracked a little smile, then turned and looked around. It had been, well, years. But not much had changed in the detective division. It was still an ugly room in an ugly building. Crammed with mismatched furniture, and mismatched people who smoked too much, drank too much coffee, and ate too much crap. What a job, Juke thought, stopping at the desk that had been his home away from, seven years earlier, but was now covered with knickknacks and the life of a stranger. Even the wall behind it had been newly painted. The small scribblings of phone numbers and names when a piece of paper wasn't handy long covered over. To be replaced by a poster proclaiming the dangers of unprotected sex.

The other detectives were off, or on call, or already headed out to lunch at eleven AM. No one else was around except for an administrative assistant whom Juke didn't recognize. She was young and perky. Chewing gum, and glancing through a fashion magazine. She seemed oblivious to the yells coming from Old Maid Marion's cubicle, a corner space with file cabinet walls. And the largest desk. The Chief was afforded that much.

"He knew Reggie DeLillo better than anyone," Piccerillo said, his voice angry and frustrated.

"Reggie DeLillo is no longer a suspect. Reggie DeLillo did not kill the kid."

"Juke was a good cop. He's got good sense."

"He's a loose cannon! For Christ's sake!"

"That's bullshit, Chief. And you know it."

"I'll tell you what's bullshit, Piccerillo. Bringing in a civilian on a homicide investigation. Letting Juke Miller interrogate a group of teenagers. But maybe after all these years I should come to expect that from you." Bradbury turned on Zaretsky, "But you! What's your excuse?"

"Sorry, Chief," she said. "I don't have one. But I—"

"You're damn right you—"

She cut him off, continuing loudly, "—firmly believe we can use all the help we can get. Juke Miller lives next door to these people. They know him. They trust him. Hell, he probably knows more about what's going on in Tompkins Glen than we do."

"The testimony of drunks amounts to less than—"

She cut him off again. Even louder, this time. "And personal politics aside. He was a damn good cop. Take a look at his arrest record."

"He shot a suspect to—"

"What the hell would you have done? Think about it, Chief. Take everything into account. What the hell would you have done?"

Juke was nodding to himself as he walked past the assistant— she never even looked up from her magazine—and stepped through the door, down the steps, toward the street. Tom Piccerillo had lucked out, he thought. Not only was Greta Zaretsky easy on the eyes, but she was stand-up. And that in a partner was hard to come by.

Juke didn't wait around for Piccerillo and Zaretsky to get through with Bradbury, or vice-versa. The station, a two-story red brick building put up before the turn of the century, was located next door to town hall, only a ten minute walk to River Bank Road. So he headed home, at a brisk pace, where he could make a call, pick up his car, then head over to the bar. Juke had a business to run. He'd meet up with the detectives for a late lunch, they could go on from there—

A small man in a cheap blue suit was knocking on the DeLillos' front door as Juke passed. Noticing the dark green Taurus was not in the driveway, he called to the stranger. "I don't think there's anyone home."

The man turned and appraised Juke. He scratched at his cleanly shaved chin, then ran the same fingertips over his mostly bald, and sweat-soaked scalp.

"Do you have any idea when Mrs. DeLillo might be back?" he asked.

Juke shrugged. Anyone else would have been holed up, surrounded by family and friends coming in from all parts to lend support and sympathy in this time of sorrow and need. But this was Anabelle. He winced at the thought of exactly where she might be.

"Well," the man said, stepping off the porch. "If you see her, could you please tell her I stopped by." He handed Juke a card and began to turn away.

Juke read the name: Patrick Hobby. He recognized the familiar insurance company logo, then read the line of self-promotion that claimed Hobby was a "life insurance specialist." And smiling, Juke called to the middle-aged man who carried an oversized briefcase toward his economy-sized car.

"Y'know," Juke said. "I was thinking it was about time I invested in some life insurance."

That was all Patrick Hobby needed to hear.

Juke let out a long, low whistle.

"I know," Hobby said. "She probably won't be staying in this neighborhood for long."

They were sitting in the kitchen. Juke had just poured out two cups of joe. He cringed, watching the insurance agent load his up with four sugars, and about three ounces of milk. *How does he taste the Goddamn coffee?* Juke thought, but instead he played up the mock shock for all it was worth.

"Two million dollars!" he said.

Juke figured Reggie had some coverage. Everyone did nowadays. And his neighbor had never been one to do things on the cheap. Everything always the best—Reggie felt the best lasted longer.

He undoubtedly had the cash flow to cover it, having done well for himself buying three adjoining apartment buildings from the city of New Haven in the early seventies. They were not far from Yale, and he fixed them up over time, in his spare time. He was still with Genovese & Sons back then, so the buildings were more like a hobby. Something he'd one day be able to retire on. Then gentrification hit the neighborhood, along with the boutiques, art galleries, pizza parlors, and coffee shops. It became the in place to live, a little Bleecker Street in New Haven. And Reggie's original investment of about a hundred grand turned into a cash machine that pumped out more than twice that annually in rents.

It certainly eased the burden of the early retirement. But still—

"I know, I know. It sounds excessive. But with the rate of inflation these days, Mr. DeLillo just wanted to be sure his wife would never have to work a day in her life," and here Hobby's tone became comically solemn, "in the event of, well, something like this."

Juke lowered his voice to an almost conspiratorial tone. "But don't the circumstances—" He finished with a circular flourish of his hand.

"If Mr. DeLillo died during the perpetration of a crime, well, then, yes. The policy becomes invalid."

"Hmm," Juke went, scratching at his chin the same way he'd seen Hobby do it.

"But I spoke to a—" Hobby reached into his open briefcase, and pulled out a steno-pad to check his notes, "—Chief Bradbury—"

"Nice fellow," Juke said, almost making himself crack up.

"Then today must not be a good day. Because if I do say so, he was a little short with me. Actually, he was a lot short with me. Very rude."

"Pressures of the job. Especially," Juke motioned over in the direction of Reggie's house. "We don't get many murders in Harmony."

"Well, nonetheless," Hobby made a face, "He didn't even give me a chance to tell him what I was calling for—"

Big surprise, Juke thought.

"He just informed me—how did he put it." Hobby mimicked Old Maid Marion's mock gruffness, " 'DeLillo didn't kill the kid. He's no longer a suspect.' And *click*."

"You don't say," Juke said, suddenly behaving a little unnerved. As if the thought of a killer in this neighborhood shook him to his very bones. "I wonder who did?"

Hobby shrugged, "Only time will tell," then pressed on. "Now," he said, flashing a smile that could sell termite eggs to the foreman of a lumber yard, "about that policy."

fifteen

Juke pulled out the phone book he kept in an otherwise junk-filled kitchen drawer, and opened up to "Schools" in the yellow pages.

Saint Thomas High was considered the safe alternative to the school which educated David, Todd, and all their friends in the fine art of street slang. It, along with the grade school and middle schools, twelve years of Catholic education plus kindergarten and day care, was also the expensive alternative. Juke remembered reading a story about the rising cost of education in the *Register* not that long back, with Saint Thomas's twelve thousand dollar annual tuition setting the local standards of excess. And parents worried about *college* tuition, Juke thought, as he dialed the number.

As it rang, he scanned the front page of that morning's paper. The headline read: "Double Murder in Harmony." Wilbur Cross's reporting was hard, but cautionary: "All may not be what it seems—"

"Saint Thomas," a stern voice answered.

"Hi," Juke said, in his friendliest, most fatherly voice. "We're thinking of sending our little, um, Wilbur, to private school—"

He didn't expect Juke's Place to be open. The lights on. TV playing. Booze pouring. But then, Juke figured, that's what good employees were all about. A little initiative.

"Hey, boss," Quintin yelled from behind the bar.

"You're reading my mind again, Quintin," Juke said.

"That'd be Zoë," the bartender explained. "Said you'd be doin' a little B&D."

Juke felt as if he were back at Harmony High speaking to Todd. "What's that?"

"All tied up," Quintin said. "So, we pulled a Juke and opened this popsicle stand up."

"Appreciated," Juke said.

"And it just keeps getting better."

It was Zoë. She was returning from the office with a foot-high stack of bar napkins balanced in her arms. She jotted her chin toward the other end of the bar. A rocks glass. Half filled with ice. A bar napkin nearby. The slight indent from the drink. Placed down by Quintin. No other water rings in sight. Whoever finished the drink, lifted it quickly off the napkin, downed it, and slammed it back onto the bar. The color of the liquid that remained was of a golden amber. There was a sumptuousness to the streams that flowed, tilted to the edge of the glass. The imprint of a bottom lip, heavy, no lipstick.

A Macallan on the rocks, Juke guessed. A twenty-five-year-old single malt Scotch that sold for twenty-five dollars a shot. A bottle retailed for a hundred seventy bucks. Beyond top shelf, beyond smooth, it was the best booze in the bar. The best booze in any bar.

"How long's he been here?" he asked.

"Time it took for him to down that Scotch," Zoë said. "And he's smiling."

Juke was behind the bar when Brett Genovese returned from the men's room, reclaimed his seat, and rapped his knuckles against the oak for a refill.

Quintin pulled a bottle of Macallan from its cozy nesting place, but Juke stopped him.

"Allow me," he said, taking the bottle of Scotch, walking the length of his bar, slowly, ponderously. "You look like a new man," he told Genovese.

"I feel good, Juke. Everything's good."

"Oh, yeah?" Juke said, placing the bottle squarely atop the bar, about halfway between infinity and the empty glass. "Why's that?"

Brett did a cocky little shuffle with his shoulders and leaned in close. "Anabelle. She took me back."

"You don't say."

"Came to see me this morning. And let me tell you, Juke, it was good. Like old times."

"You don't say."

"Yeah. She's some woman. When she kisses me, I get so lost, so tied up inside. My stomach in knots. I could die. Y'know. Like, what if I never got to kiss her again?" Brett said, "I think about that a lot." He scratched at the side of his face, and pointed finally at the bottle. "You gonna pour me some of that?"

"I don't know," Juke said. "Am I?"

"I mean, ah, c'mon now, Juke. Don't look down on me 'cause I'm a drunk."

"Got nothing to do with you being a drunk. Lot of my best customers are drunks. Most of them can't help it. Most of them don't want to."

"You always took my money before."

"Listen, Brett." And Juke lowered his voice so that only the intended party could hear. He leaned in close, his forearms encircling the Macallan bottle, shielding it. "I'd have thrown you out on your ass a long time ago. But Reggie asked me not to."

"Reggie?"

"Yeah."

"He did that for me?"

"Uh-huh. Said you kept everything in perspective."

"What do you—what do you mean?"

Juke leaned back and lifted the bottle. He answered by pouring Brett Genovese a generous shot of Scotch.

But Brett didn't move, at least not at first.

"You going to drink that?" Juke asked.

Brett nodded. He reached out hesitantly, and lifted the glass to his lips, a little embarrassed, a lot thirsty. And he downed the shot. The visible wave passing over him as the booze hit its mark.

He lowered the glass, and said, "I'll take another, if you don't mind."

"Don't think so."

"But—"

"That was your last drink, Brett," Juke said.

"What are you talking—"

"I don't want to see you again. Not in my bar. Not on my street. If I had my fucking way, I'd see you run out of this town."

Juke's meaning suddenly became clear to Brett, even through the haze. "Reggie ain't around anymore, right?"

"And I certainly do not, I repeat *do not*, want to see you at Reggie's funeral."

"But what if—"

Juke cut him off, a sharpness in his tone to which there was no arguing. "I've got all the perspective I need," he said.

sixteen

"Did you hear her? Did you hear the way she stood up to Old Maid Marion?" Piccerillo was gushing. He had a schoolboy crush on his new partner. Or at least her backbone when it came to dealing with Bradbury. "Forget brass balls. Hers are made of steel."

"I heard some of it," Juke said, seriously. "Maybe I should lay low. You don't want to find yourself on desk duty."

Desk duty was purgatory, punishment. A day, a week, maybe more handling the walk-ins. Complaints from people who didn't want a police cruiser pulling to a stop at their front door. Who didn't want a cop ringing their bell. Who usually just didn't want their neighbors, or anyone else for that matter, to know. The abused, the raped, the beaten. Mortified that they'd become a victim. A statistic. A number. At the hands usually, of someone they knew, or loved. Someone they once trusted.

"Don't worry about it," Piccerillo said, waving the possibility off. "Old Maid Marion's full of himself, and," he was laughing now, "he's afraid of Zaretsky."

"How do you mean?" Zaretsky asked.

"No one cuts that asshole off."

"He was pissing me off."

"You were walking on water."

"No, you think?"

"You're my new hero," Piccerillo said, adding respectfully, "partner."

"Good," she said, smiling warmly, a little blush coming to her face. "Then maybe next time you'll give me a little warning before pulling a stunt like that."

The smile faded from Piccerillo's face, and Juke had to laugh. "Like you said, made of steel."

They were seated in a booth in Anthony's. Located just a few doors down from Juke's Place, it was an old Italian restaurant, always crowded in the predominantly Italian Tompkins Glen. Its food warranted a twenty-eight out of a possible thirty in the state's *Zagat's Guide*, and Juke thought they were getting short changed.

He ate sautéed shrimp on a bed of spinach, Zaretsky had a Caesar salad, while Piccerillo gorged himself on the homemade sausage and more garlic bread than any public servant should ever be allowed to eat. Exactly what the doctor ordered, Juke thought, but then he no longer had to ride with him.

"So," Juke said, wanting to get on with it, "where do you want me to start, the two million dollar insurance policy, or the kid's sex life?"

"You really miss this, don't you?" Zaretsky asked.

"No," Juke said. "That isn't it."

"What then?" she asked.

"I feel I owe Reggie this much," Juke said. "He was a good friend."

They went back so many years. The newlyweds moving into the old River Bank Road Colonial, the cop and the girl from the record shop. Reggie, the seasoned vet, especially when it came to matters of prehistoric houses and overgrown lawns. Always there to lend a hand, with a snow plow, a paint brush, a screwdriver. Always there. And then came the barbecues, the parties, a friendship that expanded beyond the boundaries of property lines, beyond being neighbors. Always there, period. And when, well—

"He helped me out when I needed it most."

"Then you're just really good at it," she said.

"I might have been," Juke said. "At one time. Right now I'm just running on autopilot."

"Like riding a bike?"

Juke shrugged. Perhaps it was that easy for him. To step back into the role he always felt he was born to fill. But that he had walked away from completely, when the thought of just making it through the day, just getting out of bed, seemed suffocating. Perhaps it was all instinct, gut check and old habits. A cop gene passed down from some great-grandparent that aroused a sixth sense. But most likely, and Juke believed this to be true, he had no choice in the matter. Once again murder had hit, if not home, then too damn close. Only difference, this time he could see straight. He might, just possibly, do something right. Get the right answers to the right questions.

"How'd you find out about the policy?" Piccerillo asked between bites.

Juke told them about Patrick Hobby. About the life insurance policy which was now lining his kitchen garbage bag. About his feigned shock and dismay that Anabelle DeLillo was now a millionaire.

"As long as Reggie didn't die during the commission of a crime."

"So the grieving widow didn't set him up?" Piccerillo said.

"Most likely not," Juke said.

"Unless—" Zaretsky said.

"Unless?"

"She put him into a situation where his only option was—" She shrugged.

"Killed the kid, then let Reggie walk in on it, knowing the cops wouldn't be far behind?" Piccerillo said.

"She's the one who called 9-1-1 in the first place, didn't she?"

"That's giving Anabelle an awful lot of credit."

"So's two million bucks," Zaretsky said. "You'd be surprised how that kind of money can stimulate the intellect."

"I wouldn't be," Piccerillo said, with a laugh.

"We can't check her hands for nitrate residues?" Zaretsky asked.

"What judge would let us?" Juke said.

"And if we're wrong," Piccerillo said, "the department's sued up the wazoo, two million bucks can buy a lot of legal advice, and you and me are directing traffic. Old Maid Marion don't like getting sued."

"What did the kid's friends have to say?" Zaretsky asked.

Juke told them. It was a lot of what they'd already heard from Mrs. Rinehart. The street slang was just a tough front. David's delinquent behavior seemed limited to sneaking into the occasional R-rated movie, and once he talked Marvin—"

"The fat kid?" Piccerillo said.

"You got it."

"How'd you know?" Zaretsky asked.

"Life sucks that way."

"—into stealing a copy of *Penthouse.*"

"No *Penthouse* in David's room."

"Marvin still has it. Wanted to know if he'd get arrested."

"What'd you tell him?"

"The statutes of limitations had run out."

"Regular Al Capones."

"Regular kids, period."

"Any girlfriends?" Zaretsky asked.

"Yeah," Piccerillo said. "Was he a Mr. Super Stop and Shop?"

"Pathmark," Zaretsky corrected.

"No one at the school," Juke explained. "Though they seemed pretty sure he had a girlfriend at Saint Thomas High."

"Wonder what the slang is for Catholic high school girls?" Piccerillo said.

"You really want to know?" Zaretsky asked.

"No," Piccerillo said. "I'll just use my imagination."

"Did they give you a name?" Zaretsky asked.

Juke shook his head. "Some big secret. David never wanted to hang with them on weekend nights, Fridays and Saturdays. When they would ask him what he was doing, the kid would just shrug and smile. All the teasing in the world couldn't get him to spill the beans. He wasn't talking."

"Or so Todd says?"

"Or so Todd says."

"Don't sound like any guy I ever knew," Zaretsky said.

"Maybe you know all the wrong guys."

"No maybes about that," she said. "Is it worth checking out?"

"Even if we limit it to, say, thirteen- to sixteen-year-olds, you're talking a couple hundred girls, easy," Piccerillo said. "And that's going on the assumption that, one, there is a girlfriend, and two, she goes to Saint Thomas and not one of the other nunneries. Yeah. I can see Old Maid Marion approving that overtime." He shook his head. "Not unless there's something that implicates the girl."

"Like she was a gang banger's girlfriend?"

"Or the parents fess up?"

"Just like that. Or we get her name, rank and serial number."

"What about the dog?" Zaretsky asked. "His friends know why he poisoned it?"

"None of them knew anything about it," Juke said, "until they heard it on the evening news, or their parents gave them the details."

"No bragging?"

"Not a word."

"Christ."

Juke shrugged. "Todd told me David was down in the dumps on Monday."

"That mean what it's supposed to mean?" Piccerillo asked. "Or is it more of that street shit?"

"It means what it means," Juke said.

"Maybe David was feeling remorse," Zaretsky said.

"If he wasn't then, he sure is now," Piccerillo said, then a shrug. "I don't get this. Kids like to brag. Am I right?"

"Males like to brag," Zaretsky said.

"But his best buddies don't know nuthin' about his girlfriend. Nuthin' about the dog. What gives?"

"The all-American quarterback was living a double life?" Juke suggested.

"We're talking about a kid, fifteen," Zaretsky said.

"We're talking about a dead dog, two corpses, two shattered families—"

"One shattered family," Juke corrected. "I doubt Anabelle's all that heartbroken."

"Give her some credit, Juke," Zaretsky said.

"No," he said, "absolutely not."

Juke held her glance for a long moment, but it was Piccerillo who next spoke.

"Fine," he said. "Like it makes a fucking difference. One shattered family. Still—" Shaking his head, the detective lifted the last piece of sausage to his mouth, inhaled deeply, then smiling, shoveled it in. "—something's got to stink somewhere."

seventeen

Sally Robertson sat at her dining room table holding her hands, nervously playing with her fingers. Juke noticed that her hands were trembling slightly, her nails ragged and bleeding, as if Officer Castagnetti's affliction was contagious. She spoke in a dazed whisper, as if caught in the middle of a nightmare, waiting for someone to shake her awake. Waiting for someone to hold her, to take the pain away.

"We were hoping to speak to both you and Mr. Robertson," Piccerillo began.

"My husband's on his way to New Jersey to break the news to his parents. They're quite old, and he's—" Sally said, stopping. "David was their only grandchild. Neil has one sister, but, she's, well—she's gay."

Piccerillo nodded. "I'm sorry," he said. Then he explained everything that had developed overnight.

She didn't respond at first to the news that her son had not been killed by Reggie DeLillo. That Reggie's gun, a 9mm, was empty. And that the bullet pulled from her son was a .38. She simply stared at Piccerillo for a long lost moment, then turned to Juke and asked if he or the detectives would like something to drink?

"Do you understand what I've told you?" Piccerillo asked.

"I'm not a stupid woman," she said, her voice angry, her eyes mortified.

"I never meant to imply—"

"How the hell am I supposed to react? At least tell me that, detective."

"This is never easy—"

"My boy's dead. David is dead. Does it really matter who did it? Will that bring him back?"

The two detectives were silent for a moment, then Juke began to speak. "No," he said. "It won't bring him back. But yes, to answer your first question, Mrs. Robertson, it matters more than anything."

"Why, Mr. Miller? So I can destroy a life like mine has been destroyed? That'll make it all right? That'll make everything fine, so Neil and I can move on, and forget about this?"

"Nothing makes it right. Ever."

"Then why bother? To stop them from striking again? To deprive some other family from feeling this pain? Do you honestly think I care? Do you? Right now I want everyone to know what I'm going through. What my husband is going through. We were a happy family, you hear me. We've had our difficulties, but, I loved my son. I love my husband. And now my life, our lives—I want every parent on earth to feel this pain. To feel—Jesus, God—I'm angry, Mr. Miller. You, more than anyone, should know what I'm feeling. What I'm going through right now."

"It's—"

Sally slammed her fist down onto the tabletop. "I'm not finished. Would it have made a difference to you, Mr. Miller? Any difference at all? Tell me, what would you do if you came face-to-face with the man who killed your wife?"

A certain familiar misery twisted Juke's face. He knew he could never have let a suspect in his wife's murder live, no matter the evidence. He had never admitted as much to anyone, never even hinted at it. Not to his partner. Not to his superiors. Not even to Reggie. But there was no doubt. Juke would have been judge, jury and executioner, in the time it took to pull back the trigger. Damn the consequences. Fuck Johnny Marciano. Fuck all the Johnny Marcianos. But he was where the trail ended. All evidence pointed at Marciano. And all hope of finding her killer seemed to die right alongside him. And as the days, the weeks, the months passed, so did the hope. The longer it took to solve a crime, the less likely that it would ever be solved. With every day a little hope vanished, until—

But the sonofabitch was out there, somewhere. Haunting Juke. Laughing behind his back. Out there—

"Mrs. Robertson," Zaretsky began. "I really don't see how Mr. Miller's—"

"No offense, detective," Sally said, cutting her off. "I was speaking to Mr. Miller."

She turned back to face Juke, whose eyes were now glued to the tabletop, as if in its reflective finish he saw the face of the man who destroyed not one life, but two.

"I'd choke the life out of him with my bare hands," Juke said, in an even, compressed tone, laying his hands flat on the tabletop, covering the gleam, pressing into the wood until the tips of his fingers flushed white.

"As would I," Sally said, reaching across the table, placing her no longer trembling hands atop Juke's. "Which is why I never want to know."

"I wish there was something I could say that could help. But I know there isn't."

Sally stood on her front porch, watching as Detectives Piccerillo and Zaretsky drove away. She nodded. "Your heart's in the right place," she said, facing Juke who stood in her driveway, half turned toward his house. "That's worth a lot."

He returned the nod, and was about to turn away completely, but instead asked the question that had been loitering in the back of his mind, ever since he stepped foot in David Robertson's bedroom. "Was your son into photography?"

The question seemed to catch the woman completely off guard. As if bringing her back, to a happier, prouder time. It was the first time Juke had ever seen his neighbor smile, except for in that Disney World black and white. But then everyone was supposed to be happy in Disney World.

"Yes," Sally said. "I'll bet you've noticed him wandering the neighborhood with that darn camera around his neck?"

"Actually," Juke said, knowing he'd never seen David with a camera, otherwise he would have remembered, and liked the kid on the spot for the memories evoked. "I noticed the black and white picture on his bedroom wall. And the one in the living room, of you and your husband."

"David was always taking pictures," Sally told him. "And he was pretty good at it. He's even got a little darkroom in the basement." Her smile faded. "I guess those photos are all I've got left."

Juke looked away from her for a moment. He thought of the pictures he had. The memories stored in an eight inch by ten inch space. Or four inch by six. Wallet-size. Any size would do. Did we all just take photos to capture moments we'd be incapable of recalling? Were they reminders of the limitations of the human mind? Or simply souvenirs from days we could never reclaim? They preserved youth. Love lasted forever in photographs. Loved ones lived on.

"Photos can be priceless," he said, finally.

"Yes," she agreed, then, "Would you like to see them?"

The basement of the Robertsons' house had been finished back in the early seventies by Maria Onofrio's children, as a fiftieth wedding anniversary present to their parents. They partitioned off a good sized area from where the normal basement necessities were located: the furnace, hot water heater, oil tank, the washer and dryer. The now partially warped walls were of a light-colored wood paneling that probably contained very little actual wood.

The wall-to-wall was of the indoor/outdoor variety, dark gray, to match the ashen tone of the walls. There was a dart board still mounted on one wall. But the old sofa and TV, the dry bar stocked with bottles of Sambuca and Bacardi, the pint-sized billiards table that Juke imagined once filling the space were gone, replaced by boxes. The unpacked. Replaced by things still waiting to belong.

The mechanical sound of a large dehumidifier greeted Juke as he followed Sally Robertson down the narrow staircase, and into the center of the room. But despite the best efforts of the machine, the basement still had a damp, musty smell. And the bottom half of the paneling was tinted a light shade of green, all those years of mold, all those years of Mrs. Onofrio not tending to the dehumidifier.

"We bought him the enlarger for his thirteenth birthday," Sally explained. "Maybe we spoiled him a little, but he was our only child. Neil's that way. Always buying the nicest presents. God, I have more jewelry than I could ever wear."

"Sounds like a good man," Juke said, softly, thinking that perhaps Neil lived by the old adage that those who died with the most toys won. Would have explained the Vette.

"Yes," Sally agreed. "And when we moved here, Neil helped him set up this space. There's much more room here than in our previous home."

She led Juke to a corner of the basement where sheets of a thick black material hung from the ceiling tiles. The makeshift, floor-length curtains, tacked up by large push pins, formed a space perhaps six feet wide by four feet deep. One curtain could be pushed aside, allowing access. Sally entered first, then Juke, each taking seats atop two barstools situated in front of a small table. It all felt so sadly familiar to Juke. Upon the table sat an Omega photographic enlarger. A beginner's model. Plus three eight-by-ten developing trays, an eleven-by-fourteen tray for washing prints, a developing tank, two reels, a pair of tongs, a squeegee, and the various brown bottles of chemicals: developers, fixers, and stop bath.

"His pride and joy," Sally said. "He'd spend so much time down here, just making pictures. Hours sometimes, on just one picture. He was so dedicated to getting it just right."

"Dodging and burning in," Juke said.

"Yes," Sally said. "He explained it to me once. Showed me what he was doing. It went—" She shook her head. "It was so complicated. How did you know?"

"My wife. She, ah—"

"Was into photography?"

"Yeah," Juke said softly.

Sally opened the bottom drawer of one of two two-drawer file cabinets squeezed in under the table. From it she pulled a stack of eight-by-tens, handing them to Juke, carefully, as if the pictures could break.

He looked through the stack, examining each photo. Photographs of nature, of vacations, of last winter's blizzard and the two feet of snow it dumped on River Bank Road, and of what Juke was sure was the Mad River out back. He listened to their stories. Sally seemed to recall why her son had chosen to freeze each of these moments of otherwise forgotten time. Or at least her interpretation of why.

"I was very impressed by the photograph of the girl," Juke said.

"Natalie," Sally said, looking down, shaking her head ever so slightly. "I could have never kept that photo over my bed. Not after—" She paused, and crinkled her mouth into a frown. Her voice sounding removed, ashamed perhaps. "Not after everything that happened. His father thought he was crazy. 'Take that damn thing down,' Neil would say."

"I'm sorry," Juke said, handing back the stack of eight-by-tens. "I don't follow."

"She was the reason we left Watertown. It was just too hard to be around there. What with the accusations." Sally placed the enlargements down atop the table. "They were friends. Natalie and David. God, they were inseparable."

Sally had just told Juke and the two detectives that David had no girlfriends. That she and her husband didn't think David should be dating at such a young age. "Wait until you're old enough to drive," was what she claimed to have told him.

"So, he wasn't too young for girls?" Juke asked.

"To me, he was," Sally said. "But—he has no girlfriends now—*had*—I have to get used to that. David *had* no girlfriends here in Harmony, if that's what you're asking. I don't think he ever got over Natalie. Not completely." She shook her head again, this time as if to dislodge some of the memories. "You had to see them together. One look and you just knew they'd get married one day, have a beautiful family, live happily ever after." She turned and looked into Juke's face. "As if that were possible."

He noticed the tears beginning, and wondered how many tears had been shed upon the grave awakening that life could never be a fairy tale? That there were no happily-ever-afters?

"Natalie told her parents she was going out with David that night. But he was home with me. Just the two of us. We were watching a movie, a video. I'm sure of it. He never went out that night. He was home with—" Sally covered her face with the palm of one hand. "Oh, God," she gasped. "They found her the next day. By the river—"

"The river in the photo?"

"Yes," Sally said. "It ran along the outskirts of Watertown. Kids used to play out there all the time. Natalie and David would go for long walks. Those pictures of those birds and that frog—"

Juke nodded. He remembered just seeing the shots.

"Poor little girl," Sally said. "She was—"

"That's okay, I—"

"It was terrible. Just terrible what happened to her. The police, they cleared David, but still. Still—it seemed as if everyone thought he was to blame. That he killed her. It, oh, it devastated him. Just—destroyed him inside."

"It must have made you and Neil very angry, to see David wrongly accused?"

"Angry. Well, perhaps I was angry at first. But really, it was hurt. To see what he was going through. It hurt us a lot. Neil, he—he's learned to control his anger over the years. He had a tough childhood. Very domineering parents. He was wild there for a while. I think that's why I fell for him. That bad boy image."

Juke smiled warmly. "Pardon me for saying, but Neil doesn't exactly come across as James Dean."

"Oh, but he was James Dean, at least to me. Back then. It's in the eye of the beholder, Mr. Miller, remember?"

"Of course."

She took a deep breath, stopping for a moment, as if recalling something fond and distant. "We moved out of Watertown, finally. It was easier to just run and hide. It was easier to start over."

"Was it?" Juke asked.

Sally looked down at the stack of photographs, and nodding her head once, let out a small disillusioned laugh.

As she began to replace the stack of eight-by-tens in the file drawer where she'd found them, Juke noticed a proof sheet at the back of the drawer. He motioned toward it, and asked if he could see it.

"I haven't looked at one of those things in years," he said.

"I'm not sure what I'm going to do with all this stuff," Sally said, picking up not one, but a thick stack of proof sheets, each containing thirty-six negative-sized images. The sheets were all numbered on the back, Juke figured, so David could find the corresponding negatives.

He held one sheet after another under a swing-arm desk lamp which was mounted on the tabletop. "It always amazes me how the photographer chooses one shot over another," Juke said, surveying the tiny images. "Sometimes they seem identical."

"I asked David about that once," Sally said. "Why this picture, and not this one? And he pointed out all the differences. God, there were so many. Shadows and angles, stuff like that. And I remember one picture of us at Disney World. I told him I thought his father looked very handsome. Until David pointed out how it gave the illusion that one of the towers of the Magic Castle was growing out of his father's head."

Juke smiled warmly, and feigned interest. He was trying to concentrate, searching the proof sheets, carefully scanning each tiny image for shots of Natalie, the girl from Watertown, New Jersey. But instead he found more shots of the Mad River, shots of plants, trees and small animals—all of them alive—and that Disney World vacation. From every angle. Close-ups and long shots. Some with amazing depth of field. Others with no depth of field at all, pin-point focusing. David obviously thought nothing of wasting a roll of film to get that one perfect picture.

As Juke finished with each sheet, he turned it over and placed it facedown atop the table, starting a new stack. The numbers were consecutive. None of the sheets—fifty-seven in all—were missing. But still, there were no pictures of the girl on the river bank. Not a one. Only that framed enlargement over his bed. Where were the others that went with it? The rejected shots? The different angles? Where were the negatives? And the corresponding proof sheets?

"This is his camera," Sally said, displaying to Juke an old Pentax K1000. "He bought it at a tag sale for ten dollars. Money he made from mowing the neighbors' lawns." She held the camera to her chest as if her son's spirit was alive within the aluminum box. As if one press of the shutter and it would escape forever, and then there'd be nothing left of him. Nothing left to hold on to.

"Ten dollars well spent," Juke said, acknowledging her pride.

"Yes," she said, placing the Pentax back down upon the enlarger easel. "But then he bought all these lenses. *I* bought him all these lenses, and filters, and—" she rolled her eyes as if it were an expensive secret she and David shared, "—it seemed to mean so much to him."

"I'm sure it did," Juke said, scanning the table in front of him, noticing for the first time the black rubber film canister with the familiar Kodak cap. Yellow and white half circles, with a green stripe separating them. It was set just off to the side of the easel, behind a stainless steel developing tank.

As Sally scooped up the stack of proof sheets, to replace them in the bottom of the file drawer, Juke leaned forward on the table, and picked up the stainless steel tank. "I always wanted to learn how to do this," he said, unscrewing its top, checking the reel inside.

"I watched him once," Sally said, straightening up, eyeing the developing tank. "But I just couldn't figure out what was going on."

Juke nodded his understanding, placing the tank back onto the table with his left hand, while casually pocketing his right. He followed Sally Robertson out of David's darkroom, through the musty basement, and back up the stairs. He shook her hand at the front door, and told her, "If you need anything, please—"

"I need for this to be over," Sally said, asking then if he would come to the funeral. "We don't have that many friends in the area."

"Of course," Juke said. "Sullivan's?"

Sally nodded.

It was always Sullivan's, Juke thought, remembering his one meeting with Ruth Sullivan. He figured everyone in Harmony had to sit down for a face-to-face in that woman's office at least once. Once was enough.

"What is it with that name?" Sally asked. "Every town seems to have a funeral home named Sullivan's. Is there a franchise?"

"It wouldn't surprise me," Juke said.

"Yeah," Sally said, a faraway look stealing in her eyes, the sadness dragging her back. "We're using his college fund to pay for his funeral, Mr. Miller. David wanted to go to Yale. That was his dream. Yale. One of the reasons we moved here. To be close." She covered her mouth with the palm of one hand. "Do you know how that feels? My husband's—Neil's parents, they'll probably offer to pay, but I told Neil, 'under no circumstances.' I don't want to owe them anything. Not a thing—" She looked at Juke suddenly, as if she realized she was rambling. "Sorry," she said.

"No love lost between you and your in-laws?" Juke asked.

Sally laughed in spite of everything. "That's the understatement of the century. They weren't happy about us moving away. That's what they're going to blame this on, y'know?" She mimicked an old woman's cackle, "I told you not to move. This would have never happened in Watertown. This—" She groaned. "I can feel it in my bones. Neil's bringing them here for the funeral."

"I'm sorry," Juke said.

"Not half as sorry as I am," Sally said, "As *we* are. I swear, Neil hates them more than I do. But he can't help it. You can't pick your parents." She took a deep breath, steadying herself as if the worst were yet to come, then, "Thank you, Mr. Miller," and after another pause, "for listening."

Nodding sympathetically, taking a step back, Juke turned, stepped off the stoop, and walked toward his house. Though many aspects of this case were running through his mind. Mainly how what was once viewed as open and shut by the town's Chief of Police was now anything but. What intrigued Juke most was the undeveloped images contained on the roll of Kodak Tri-X which he lifted from David's darkroom. A roll of black and white film which could tell so much. A roll of film which was burning the figurative hole in his pocket.

eighteen

Juke sat on the third step. He rolled the small black canister back and forth between the palms of both hands like clay. He was subconsciously molding it into evidence, the clues he needed, the answers to the questions that dogged this case. Not his case. Piccerillo's case. Zaretsky's case. But damn close enough. Right next door was too close.

He was consciously stalling. Avoiding the inevitable. Afraid to take those few steps from these basement stairs, onto the white-washed cement floor, and over to the far corner of his basement, *their* basement, and open a door which had only been opened a few times, perhaps more, over the past seven years.

Every once in a while he'd visit, he'd sit, and have a look around, remembering—Juke knew all about trapped souls—hers was so alive in every aspect of that room. The smells, the oils from her fingertips, the presence of her fingerprints, the keenness of her sight, a vision that at times Juke couldn't understand, usually as she raised the Nikon to her eye. What do you see that I can't? he'd want to know, looking at the same scene. Sometimes the answers were blinding.

It had been a complete and total surprise. A fifth wedding anniversary present which he had been planning since sometime between the third and fourth years. The timing had to be perfect. He needed a few days alone to rig everything just right. And as usual, back then, the gods smiled down upon him, granting his wish, fulfilling his needs. Juke had since learned that the gods always and eventually extract payment, in one form or another.

She would be at a three-day conference in New York. A new music seminar. Managers of the East Coast's better independent record shops being invited up to experience the latest sounds, the hottest bands. She'd returned late in the evening, the day before their anniversary. He arranged his schedule, switching shifts, pulling in notes of favors past, present, and future. And for those days, those seventy-two hours, he locked himself into the basement of their River Bank Road Colonial. Hammering, sawing, drilling, plumbing, wiring—till his hands were numb from the effort, his limbs aching, his hair caked with sawdust and paint. And when night fell, when her arrival home was only an hour or so away, he stood back and smiled with pride at the eight-by-twelve-foot, light-proof, well-ventilated, ceramic tile-floored darkroom, complete with two sinks, temperature controlled running water, recessed safelight, a refrigerator for film and paper, and the best damn enlarger a cop's salary could buy.

He spent the next half hour in the shower, the next half hour after that wrapping the key that unlocked the darkroom's door. Then he dressed, poured himself a glass of red wine, and waited, until he saw the headlights linger, turn into the drive, then go off altogether. And when the car door slammed shut, he felt the rush of goosebumps just as the first time he ever saw her. Just as every time he saw her. But a million times more so. And he walked to the door, greeted her there, taking her into his arms, holding for what seemed like forever then, what seems like not long enough now.

*   *   *

Taking a deep breath, then two more, Juke stood, finally, and walked over to the darkroom's door. The key which she unwrapped, her brow all wrinkled in confusion, the look on her face. That look on her face. Juke would never forget the look when she opened the door the first time. The *"how did you manage?"* the *"I can't believe this,"* the kiss, the passion, the love. They made love that night right on the cold ceramic tiles of the eight-by-twelve-foot room, ripping at each other's clothes, ripping at each other, so lost, so oblivious, what else could ever matter?

The key was still where she placed it that night, hid it, kept it. Recessed into the cross beams that supported the floor over their head, laying astride the valve that turned water on or off for the outside faucet—the faucet for watering the lawn, washing the car. Juke reached up, grabbed the key, slid it into the lock, and turned.

The door opened, he switched on the overhead light, also recessed, then stepped inside, shutting the door behind him. This would be a different sort of visit. One in which he'd need her help, her guidance. And though he had watched her do it a hundred times, here and before in her makeshift old-door-over-the-bathtub bathroom rig, he had never developed film before.

But placing the Kodak canister on the Formica countertop, Juke reached up high to her bookshelf stocked with how-to's and pulled down the basic. *A Guide to Black & White Photography, Revised Edition.* It had probably been revised two or three times since, but she once told him the fundamentals of black and white hadn't changed in decades. He opened to page one, and prayed she was right.

First he mixed the chemicals. These weren't seven years old. These he had purchased some months back, taking a ride, a stop at Harmony Photo. Greeting Mr. Milano. The same old man who had sold him the best enlarger one could buy on a cop's salary so many years back.

There were close to a hundred rolls of film, a refrigerator shelf full. All neatly stacked, but unlabeled. Undeveloped. Taken over the years, of what, when, where, whom, Juke hadn't a clue. So, he had decided he'd develop every roll, print every negative. Good, bad, out-of-focus, underexposed, overexposed, it wouldn't matter. He wanted to be able to hold her close, if nothing else than through her vision. But he never made it much past hanging the plastic bag of chemicals on the darkroom door's handle. Some ideas sound great in theory.

Next, and this was the hardest part, even the book promised it would be for first-timers, he placed the developing tank on the edge of the counter in front of him. Near it he placed the stainless steel reel, and beside that a small pair of scissors. In his right hand he held the roll of thirty-six exposure Tri-X, in his other a can opener.

He flipped off the lights. All the lights. She had always loaded film in the dark. He had on occasion stood behind her, his chest pressed against her back, his hands at her waist, the smell of her hair filling him with a desire that could never go away. But she would always wait until the film was loaded to turn and kiss him. She would always wait.

Juke pried off one of the ends of the film can with the can opener, removed the spool of film, placed the opener down, then felt around for and picked up the scissors. Trimming the end of the film into a point, a sideways "v," he placed the scissors down, took a deep breath, then picked up the reel.

He could remember that it took less than two minutes for her to turn the lights back on—or not, depending on whether or not there were other diversions to which she would first attend. It took him close to an hour. He was covered in sweat. His hands shaking. But when he dropped the reel into the tank, and secured its cover, he was sure he had done it right.

Not the first time. The first time he couldn't get the clip which stuck out from the core of the reel and was supposed to hold the film in place, to hold the damn film in place.

Not the second time. He had trouble bending the film just so to feed it into the grooves of the reel, which he was supposed to be turning in sync with his other hand.

And not the third time. When it seemed there was too much film for the reel. Way too much. He figured he skipped over a few of the grooves, and started again.

But the twentieth or so time, he'd lost count, that was the charm.

Everything after that was a piece of cake, just following instructions, like mixing a drink. Pour in the developer for seven minutes, agitate the tank every thirty seconds, pour out the developer. Pour in the stop bath for a minute, agitating throughout. Dump it out. Then the fixer for five minutes. Then a thirty second wash. Some hypo-clearing agent. A five minute wash using the film washer he bought her for the Christmas that followed that fifth anniversary. Then hang, squeegee, and wait for them to dry.

It was the most difficult Goddamn thing he'd ever done.

nineteen

Never touch wet negatives. The emulsion is soft, sticky, like a just-baked cookie. And just as tempting. Those desperate for a sneak peek, can gently hold the edges, and glance through the images, using what light, and whatever background are available. If you're lucky, the image will fool you and appear not to be a negative at all, but a black and white slide, almost three-dimensional. The tones and edges as crisp and sharp as just-cut glass.

Juke stood a light-box upright on the countertop, and flipped it on. He turned the hanging strip of film his way, letting his eyes float over the tiny images. They were what he expected, mostly. What he knew had to exist. Thirty-two out of thirty-six frames that would serve no purpose to anyone. Cruel and hopeless. They were taken with a telephoto lens, probably from David's bedroom window. They showed Molasses cradled in Reggie's arm. The man, Juke's friend, his neighbor, in such anguish, as he held on to the dog, as if trying to keep its life from floating away. The look as

Reggie pressed his tear-streaked face to the Lab's fur. As he pressed his mouth to the dog's ear, probably whispering, "It'll be okay, boy. I'm here for you, boy. I love you, boy." Promising walks and treats, or saying, "You'll be up chasing squirrels in no time."

Juke could see the back and forth movement of Reggie, as he rocked the dog. As he touched his hands to its face, closing Molasses's eyes for the final time. As he stood, screaming at the heavens, looking at the heavens for some sign of God. The fury twisting up his face. The helplessness—aren't we all helpless in the face of death? Reggie lifting the dog, carrying the dog, the body limp and all deadweight in his arms. Juke could sense Reggie wanting to die with the dog.

The final frame of this sequence was a close-up of Reggie's face. He was sitting on the ground. Judging from the shot that preceded it, Molasses was probably within reach at his feet. But it was over. There was a lifelessness to Reggie's eyes, so numb. The surrender in his hands, fingertips hovering near his face. So frightened at being alone. So—

Juke was glad Sally Robertson would never get to see this side of her only child. That she would never get to see what David was capable of.

But it was the last four frames, the beginning of another shoot at the tail end of this roll, which Juke wished he had never seen. Frightened by what they suggested, what they quite possibly proved, he pulled his hand away as if the edges of the film were slicing into his fingertips, severing the nerves. He studied the images. There was no doubt, not even at this small size, not even reversed, as to what was going on—

He turned away, unable to look any longer. And leaving only the ventilators on, he exited the darkroom, closed and locked the door behind him, then headed upstairs. He stopped in the kitchen first. The sweats had returned. As had the shakes. Maybe he had been away from this for too long. Seven years. Seven endless years. Time stops when you're dead inside.

Or were the clues having this effect? The evidence at hand. The piecing together of a life, of two deaths—Reggie would say three, as would she. What would Juke say? What would he do? What difference did the pieces make? Would it change anything? Bring back anything?

"Fuck no," he muttered, leaning forward, burying his face in his hands, then combing his fingers hard through his hair.

He thought about David Robertson. What his mother had said about him not having a girlfriend. Not now, at least. How he had yet to get over—what was her name? Natalie. And the contradictions, what David's friends had said about a girlfriend who went to Saint Thomas. The girl with no name. As if she didn't exist except as a fantasy. Todd, nor any of his friends, had ever actually seen the girl. This Catholic high school girl. But they knew for certain how David was into plaid. The uniforms. The knee socks. The penny loafers.

"Can you blame him?" Todd Scillia had cautiously asked, motioning with his chin toward the girls that populated his school. The baggy hip-hop no-sexual look, barrettes and black lipstick, untied sneakers, and men's jockey shorts. "You barely even know they're girls."

"Maybe that's the point," Juke had found himself saying.

Was that it? Or were the fourteen- and fifteen-year-old girls at Harmony High already past their innocent prime? Had they grown up a little too soon? No longer attractive to David? Were their manners not to his liking? Their education substandard? What exactly did a Catholic high school girl offer that wasn't available at the public schools?

Juke didn't know for sure. Though he had a few hunches. Hunches which might pan out if he could speak to Natalie's parents. Could she have attended a Catholic high school? Another hunch said yes.

He had wondered earlier if Todd and company were just sending him on a wild goose chase, covering up for a girl at Harmony High who wouldn't want to be connected with David. Now he was quite positive the kids had been straight up with him. About everything. That's how scared they were. Probably almost as frightened as the girl in those last four pictures.

But those negatives were the proof Juke needed. He not only knew David had a girlfriend. He was pretty sure about where she went to school. And now he had a rough idea as to what she looked like. Plaid uniform, and all.

twenty

"We've got a drunk cop here, and she says she won't leave until you tell her to."

The tone in Zoë Gilmore's voice was amused, at the very least. But then a lot of what went down at Juke's amused Zoë. The women who at night's end went home with men they'd never otherwise give the time of day. The men who at night's end went home alone. It was one of the perks of working there.

"Give me fifteen minutes," Juke said.

He glanced at his watch. The time was pushing midnight. He'd been waiting. After developing the negatives, he'd sat down to a road atlas while eating dinner. He figured he could make it to Watertown, New Jersey, in about two hours, fifteen minutes, if he didn't encounter any traffic on the George Washington Bridge. He washed the dishes, and had just one more chore on the agenda before turning in. But that would require lights-out in his Tompkins Glen neighborhood. It wasn't actually the committing of a crime that he planned, but the prevention of one.

"Don't you even want to know who it is?" Zoë added a little laugh, whether it was for his sake, or her own, Juke was not sure.

"I have a pretty good idea," he said.

Juke's was as crowded as the previous evening. Though on this night a dread hung in the smoke-filled air. David Robertson's killer was now a question mark, a blur, a ghost. He was the fucking bogeyman. And that frightened the residents of Tompkins Glen.

Most eyes turned toward Juke, as he pushed through the front door. It was as if he were coming with news, with answers. It was as if Juke could protect them from the invisible armed demons.

"You hear anything?" Rachel Altimari asked. She was seated at the table closest to the door.

He squeezed her hand as he walked past, shaking his head. "Nothing that hasn't been on the news," he said.

A number of the regulars nodded their hellos, or mouthed the word. Juke responded in kind, heading toward the far end of the bar. His end of the bar. He could see her there, hear her voice cutting through the din, a little high, nowhere near as apprehensive as the sounds that surrounded her.

Greta Zaretsky was out of uniform. She wore a colorful vest covered with Aztec designs, over black leggings, and some clunky shoes. She was a lot thinner out of her suit, shapely in all the right places, and sexy as hell. There was a mostly empty Collins glass on the oak in front of her. From the carbonation bubbles, the sugar residue, Juke guessed a Gin Cooler. It seemed Zaretsky's sort of drink. He wondered how many it took to get her in this condition. He guessed again: four or five.

Zaretsky turned, saw him coming, and smiled as Juke stepped up to her. But instead of a slurred *hello*, or a gamely *it's about time you got here*, Zaretsky started right in.

"Juke Miller," she said. "How come you never remarried? Or don't even have a girlfriend, for Christ's sake?" She certainly didn't sound drunk, just accelerated, a forty-five played at seventy-eight.

"This poor-pitiful-me routine is tiring. You're a good-looking man. Anyone ever told you that, Juke Miller? Dumb fucking question, Zaretsky. Of course, women have told him that. I can't believe I even asked. Don't you like sex anymore? Don't you miss it? I miss it. Shit, I miss it the morning after I break up with someone. You know what I mean? It's like, maybe I should have hung in there, at least for a few days longer, at least for the sex. It's a good release, Juke Miller. We all need a release now and then. Don't you know that?" She raised her shoulders as if feeling a tickle down her spine. "I would think you'd be exploding all over the place. It's been seven years, hasn't it? Seven non-fucking years."

Zoë, who was standing within earshot, shot Juke a curious glance, then said, "She's been like that for going on two hours."

Dominic Santorelli, who was sitting one barstool away, let out a little laugh. "Amusing as all hell," he said. "In fact it reminds me of a joke."

"Some other time," Juke said.

"But—"

"Some other time," Juke said again, and this time in his no arguing tone. He stared at Santorelli until the old-timer finally and reluctantly turned away. Then looking at Zoë, he asked, "How much has she had?"

"Her stomach should hold out."

Juke nodded his understanding that Zaretsky was leaning against the doorjamb of the slightly spinning room, one more and she'd be inside the spinning room, two more guaranteed a night cradled before the toilet.

Zaretsky called to Quintin James, who stood expectantly behind the bar waiting for an order. "Hit me up again," she said.

Quintin pointed at her. "You driving?" he asked. The one phrase he could enunciate perfectly.

The question caught Zaretsky off guard. She turned toward Juke suddenly, a few controlled breaths, tears coming to her eyes. "I'm cut off? Well, I don't need this place. And I don't need you, Juke Miller. I'll—I'll go somewhere else—"

"No," Juke said softly.

"No?" she said.

"Come home with me instead."

Zaretsky sniffled. "You mean it?"

Shaking her head, Zoë took a step back, heading toward a table which hardly needed service. "Funny," she said to Juke in parting, "I was about to ask you the same thing."

He held open the front door, and she walked past, a little shaky on her balance, floating back and forth between brash and insecure. Zaretsky had said little in the Saab, except, "This was your wife's car, wasn't it?"

Juke had nodded his reply, then asked, "How could you tell?"

"You drive it like you're afraid one day it's going to break down and you're not going to have it anymore."

Once the front door to Juke's house was securely shut behind them, Zaretsky stepped into the living room. She took in the details of the room, not like a cop, but more like a curious friend. The pen pal whose home you finally get to visit after all those years.

She picked up one of the framed photos off the mantel. "She was beautiful," she said, her voice unexpectedly sad.

"Yes," Juke agreed. "She was."

Taking the frame gently from her hands, placing it back in its spot, he steered Zaretsky toward the kitchen, and poured her a large tumbler full of water. Handing her the glass, she drank it down, never questioning the reason. It was as if she suddenly had a timeless thirst.

"What was his name?" Juke asked.

"Who's name?"

"The man you just broke up with?"

"Not just," Zaretsky said. "It was two weeks ago. And his name was Brian. Brian Luponte."

"A cop?"

She shrugged her answer, yes. Then made a face. "From New Haven."

"He hit you?"

"If he hit me, I'd be facing a murder rap right about now."

Juke cracked the slightest of smiles. "Why'd you break up then?"

"Usual reasons. Jealousy." Another shrug. "He was a jerk. All men are jerks, or they're married, or they're gay. Or—then there's you."

"How do you know I'm not a jerk?"

"You can just tell. Something in your eyes. You've got kind eyes, Juke Miller. And you've got big gentle hands. I've seen you pour drinks. I've watched you wipe down the bar."

"That's how you can tell?"

"Don't make fun. I can tell a lot that way."

He took her upstairs, to his bedroom, and once inside, Juke opened the door to his closet. Sorting through his shirts, Juke pulled out something old, something soft, cotton, and comfortable.

"You can sleep in—"

But turning around, Juke caught sight first of the shoes, kicked off most likely the moment he had turned his back. Then the leggings, now a black cotton ball on the bedroom floor. The vest, slung onto the closest headboard post. And Zaretsky, sitting on the edge of the bed, waiting patiently. The bra and panties were hardly a matching set. One white, with a lot of worn lace around the edges, the other a cotton print, a faded pink with equally faded blue flowers. Both pieces probably looked great in some lingerie catalog a few years back. Juke had to admit, they didn't look bad now.

As Zaretsky lifted her legs to slip them under the white sheets, Juke noticed a tiny flash of color on her outside right ankle. A tattoo. A heart, red, crying blue teardrops.

"What?" Zaretsky said, as she rested her head against his pillow, and turned on her side to face him.

He shook his head. There were probably a dozen reasons to explain it away, but they weren't important right now. The secrets behind Zaretsky's tattoo could wait, possibly forever. Stepping forward, to the edge of the bed, Juke took a seat. "There's something I need to take care of."

"Okay," she said. "Take your time." She closed her eyes. "I'm not going anywhere."

Juke stared at the woman in his bed for a long beat, then raising the sheet up to her neck, he gently tucked it in around her, wondering perhaps, if this wasn't how it was supposed to be?

Wondering perhaps, if he wasn't the biggest jerk of them all?

The ground was still soft, and a little damp from a late evening thunderstorm that came and went like summer blinking an eye. He worked by the light of the moon, one shovelful at a time, tossing it not too far, so as to not make a sound.

Tompkins Glen was asleep. The lights in the neighborhood extinguished, the nightmares running rampant, like children lost of supervision. Playing games of torture and crying heart tattoos in the minds of Anabelle and Sally and Neil. Disturbing the peacefulness of the neighbors beyond. Whoever said it was lonely at night was discounting the demons.

It wasn't long before the soil gave way to the hardness of the Rubbermaid lid. Juke opened up the hole, just wide enough so that he could get his fingers around the lip of the container, and then he lifted.

Refilling the hole, replacing the missing ground with potting soil from a bag he brought from his garage, Juke patted down the dirt, as he had seen Reggie do two evenings prior. Then he placed the shovel atop the coffin, and carried them both back to his garage, where he covered the casket with an old tarp.

He stood in his driveway a long time after that. Listening to the night. Inhaling the soft summer breeze that found life off some freshly mowed lawns, and carried it to this street, to these doorways of death and longing. He wondered about his Tompkins Glen neighbors. About the ratio of those who slept in someone's arms versus those who slept alone. And how it changed every night. A fight, a new romance, a one-night stand, a death. How to some, the arms mattered. And to others, like Anabelle, any arms would do.

Going inside, Juke took the cotton sheet he had brought with him from the second floor linen closet, and curled up, comfortable and quiet, on the dark green sofa in his living room.

Juke slept peacefully that night. He thought for a moment that perhaps it was the presence of a woman in the house. Her arms weren't around him, but still—

Or maybe it was because he was that much closer to solving this case. Or just really, he was that tired, dead tired.

So tired that Juke had never even felt her presence, as she watched him dig up the spot where Molasses was buried. Standing in the shadows beyond the other side of his fence, her face covered in darkness, wondering, worrying if this ex-cop knew too much. If he had figured it out, figured her out. Praying silently to no one that one more person, that he, Juke Miller, would not have to die.

wednesday

twenty-one

It was a quarter to seven when Juke backed the Saab out of the driveway. He had set the alarm in his bedroom for eight, and placed her pocketbook, a glass of water, and a note alongside the clock/radio. It was short and to the point, telling Greta Zaretsky there was something he had to do, and to make herself at home regarding matters of coffee, breakfast, a shower. Juke closed with the hope that she remembered where in Harmony she'd parked her car.

Driving down River Bank toward Wright, he made a left toward Centerville, toward the Harmony Veterinary Hospital, located in a simple windowless cinderblock building, behind a cigar store, and a fingernail emporium.

He knew Dr. Birnbaum got to work at about this time. He had accompanied Reggie on enough occasions: when Molasses was being neutered, when Molasses needed his shots, when Molasses just would not stop throwing up because he had swallowed a small rock and couldn't pass it.

The receptionist wasn't there yet, and Juke preferred it that way.

He carried the Rubbermaid coffin into the office, placing it atop a small bench where people could sit while waiting with their pets. Juke didn't sit. He walked around the waiting room, glancing at a display of flea collars, at shelves of specialized dog and cat foods, vitamins and treats, ceramic bowls with bones painted on their insides that cost a nickel under forty bucks—they could be personalized with the pet's name for twenty more, when finally, a bright yellow poster thumb-tacked to a bulletin board over on a far wall, caught his attention.

It read:

Free Lab Pups to Good Home. (Okay mostly Lab, 75%, the other 25% we're not too sure about, though German shepherd would be a pretty good guess.) The litter's all black, and will be ready to go by the second weekend in June. If you'd like more information, if you'd like to see the puppies, if you'd like to meet their mom, Phoebe, or if you'd just like some good homemade lemonade, give us a call at 286-8194. Not too late though.

"Is that what I think it is?"

Juke turned. He'd always felt that Dr. Birnbaum was born with a doctor's voice. So soothing, so soft, so honest and trustworthy. How could one doubt he'd do everything in his power to treat a rash, to cure kennel cough, to save a life?

"Probably," Juke said.

The doctor scratched at the back of his neck. He was a tall man, with a head that seemed too large for his lean physique. Maybe it was the rapidly receding hairline. All that forehead making his head seem so big.

"What do you want me to do with him, Juke."

"Cremate him," he said, pulling a small leather pouch from the pocket of his sports jacket, handing it to the vet. "Put the ashes in there. I'll pick them up later in the week."

"Should I ask why?"

"I'd prefer if you didn't."

*   *   *

The ride to Watertown, New Jersey was uneventful and not thoroughly unpleasant. The radio tuned to an all-news station which gave Juke traffic updates every ten minutes. Included with those updates was the weather. Another scorcher was on hand: hot, hazy, and humid, with a chance of evening thunder showers.

Juke was intrigued by a story, one he heard five times, every half hour, with little variation, on David Robertson's murder. It was attributed to a *New Haven Register* front page piece. Cross's work, Juke guessed, having not had a chance to so much as glance at the front page. It proclaimed Reggie's innocence, and said the local police remained baffled as to who killed the boy, and why. Though, and here Old Maid Marion was awarded with an uninspiring and clichéd sound bite if ever there was one, "we're investigating every avenue, and will bring the boy's murderer to justice."

Not *every* avenue, Juke knew. There were these few dark alleys and side streets which he preferred sneaking down first. He owed that much to Reggie, who'd been there the day Juke turned in his shield, and locked up his unmarked Caprice Classic for the last time. Standing out in front of the station house, leaning against the old pickup he drove back then. "Thought you might need a lift," Reggie had said. Anyone else, and Juke would have just kept walking.

And he owed it to the memory of Reggie's dog. And perhaps even to the Robertsons. Wasn't that what neighbors were all about?

Watertown City Hall loomed in the distance. One of those classic old buildings of stained marble and once-white cement. With a faded gold dome, and dirty leaded glass windows. Decrepit, it looked out of place, a little mortified, a lot tattered, amidst the industrial parks and strip malls, between the boarded-up shops on Main Street, and the rival establishments proclaiming, *We Cash Checks!* Once a rich man, Watertown City Hall was now a hobo.

The library was just next door. Its design fit in just fine with the rest of Watertown. Two stories, a flat-roofed rectangular with lots of dark glass and cinderblock. Architecture kindergarten.

Turning the first corner, Juke noticed a minivan pulling out of a metered spot. He waited, and the driver waved a thank-you for stopping traffic. Juke eased the Saab into the space. He had enough quarters in his pocket to buy himself two hours and twenty minutes. That would be plenty.

At the information desk, he ignored the older librarians, in their pastel-colored dresses and horn-rims, with their propensity to meddle and judge, and instead went right to one of the assistants. A petite woman, eighteen, nineteen, no more than twenty, Juke figured, with extreme red hair, that couldn't have been natural, and china white skin, which seemed to have never been exposed to the sun. She wore a little too much black, both clothing, a t-shirt tucked into an above-the-knee skirt, that made her appear wafer thin, and makeup, eye-liner, lipstick, and a beauty mark by the side of her mouth that Juke knew changed position at her whim. She had a few too many tattoos: a snake encircling her left wrist, a spider climbing the side of her neck just below her right ear, a stick-figure man reading a stick figure book titled "Everything Sucks" on her left calf—and those were just the ones Juke could see. And there were the piercings: her nose, right eyebrow, and of course ears. So many earrings that he could not have counted them without being accused of staring. So many, and so much, that the other workers, or the young moms with their children, seemed frightened of her. She stood by her lonesome at the far end of the counter, checking in a tall stack of hardcovers. Her name tag read: Ophelia.

"I was wondering if you might be able to help me."

The young woman looked up. She seemed surprised that anyone would be speaking to her. She seemed pleased and smiled, tentatively at first, as if he might be teasing her by asking for help. Those black-lined lips then opening finally into a full-fledged grin, her blue eyes wide and looming.

"I can try," Ophelia said. Nothing scary about that.

"I'm working on an article," Juke lied. "Unsolved murders. Children, teenagers in particular—"

"Natalie Sussman, right? Last summer," Ophelia said, not waiting for him to finish. She lowered her voice. "The police thought that fourteen-year-old boy did it. Her boyfriend. But they didn't have the evidence to charge him."

Juke nodded politely. "So I've heard," he said, thinking, God bless the lonely.

Ophelia pointed Juke in the direction of the newspaper archives, and explained that while the daily *Republican/American* covered the murder and investigation in detail, the best story was in the *CityRag*, an alternative weekly which was picked up mainly for club listings and personal ads.

"My ad's in there this week," Ophelia said. "Maybe you can take a look at it for me. Help me rewrite it, you being a writer and all. All the responses so far have been from creeps and jerks."

"There're a lot of them out there," Juke said.

Ophelia seemed to think about what she wanted to say, then stopped herself short as she glanced over at the other workers.

Juke followed her gaze. He figured they all wore wedding bands and had pictures of their children, or their grandchildren, behind some plastic flaps in their wallets. They had piercings as well, one in each ear.

"Mister," Ophelia said finally, shaking her head. "You don't know the half of it."

Natalie Sussman, a grade-A student at Saint Rita's Catholic Middle School, died the previous summer, on the fourteenth of June, between nine and eleven PM, three weeks shy of her fourteenth birthday. Her windpipe had been crushed. An inch-thick branch the murder weapon, or so the coroner had determined.

Juke sat alone at a table in the basement of the Watertown

Public Library. In his hands a copy of the Watertown *Republican/American*. Its headline: "Local girl found murdered." In front of him, stacks of local papers from the previous summer. Behind him, a year's worth of those same newspapers, and the *New York Times*—always the *New York Times*—piled high on steel shelves identified with handwritten labels. Anything older than a year was on microfiche. Juke was glad for having made their deadline. He hated those viewers.

He read every story, every written word, searching for answers, for clues that might—

Juke shrugged. "Might what?" he asked himself softly.

Natalie had not been raped, or sexually molested. Though the article in the *CityRag* claimed the coroner concluded that Natalie had not been a virgin at the time of her death. "She had been sexually active," was his attributed quote. Clues were nonexistent. No fingerprints, clothing fibers, hair, or footprints. There had been no struggle, leading everyone to assume that the girl had known her assailant.

The assault had taken place atop a boulder which sat in a secluded cove around a bend in the Dumont River. A stream really, which in the articles sounded much like the Mad, also called a *river*. A river which ran behind Juke's house, behind Reggie's house, behind the Robertsons' house—

It was on that boulder that Natalie's fully clothed body was found the next morning. Was it the rock upon which she sat in the photo on David Robertson's bedroom wall?

"Of course it was," he whispered to himself.

There were allegations that a classmate had been suspected in the killing, but because of his age—only a few months older than Natalie—his name was being withheld. Juke knew the classmate was David. He realized the excuse his mother had given him must have stuck with the police, because three days after the girl was found, the *Republican/American* noted that the only lead had turned into a dead end, and that both the local and state police were baffled, turning to the feds for assistance.

A few days later, a week after that, and nothing seemed to

change. The murder received less space, fewer inches, the stories buried deeper. Until days would pass with no mention, then weeks, then—

Natalie Sussman's murder fell to the bottom of the pile. Only a solution, a suspect, a conviction, could revive the interest of both the press and the public. She was a pretty teenaged girl who wandered out into the wrong place, on the wrong night. Juke could hear the file drawer slamming shut, the concern waning. Next.

Perhaps a short update would appear on the one year anniversary. He was pretty sure some intern at the *Republican/American* was readying that story just about now.

"Want to see the place where it happened?"

Juke turned.

Ophelia had pulled up a chair alongside where he sat. Sitting, she crossed her legs, and Juke noticed another tattoo high up on her right thigh. A wildly gyrating cherub—an angel doing the twist. A mischievous smirk on its face, as its wings fluttered from the dance, a few loose feathers floating free. What was it about angels? he wondered.

Catching his stare, smiling just slightly, Ophelia leaned forward, both elbows on the table, her hands together, pressed to the far side of her face.

"My lunch break's coming up," she explained. "And it's only about ten minutes from here."

twenty-two

More like fifteen.

The Dumont River was as shallow and dirty as Water-town. They walked along the rocky banks, about three yards from the beer can-littered water, before the river took an abrupt turn to the left, widening, deepening, opening and rushing. The transformation was sudden, invigorating. The grime giving way to a mostly fresh air scent, the sounds of birds, sunlight breaking through the leaves of the tall pines and evergreens that lined the banks.

"This way," Ophelia said, reaching for Juke's hand, and leading him up a steep incline, to what he knew, on first sight, was the place where Natalie Sussman had died.

The boulder had a flat, smooth top surface that measured a good eight-by-twelve feet. The size of a room. It was pitched at just the slightest angle, down and away from the water. Covered on three sides, and on top, by thick brush, and overhanging branches and vines. When sitting, or lying atop the boulder, privacy could almost be assured.

"I come here a lot," Ophelia said. "Especially since—" She shrugged. "When school's in session there's never anyone around at this time of the day."

"Or late at night?" Juke said.

"Or late at night."

She opened a pocketbook which she had carried with her from the library, and pulled out what appeared to be a small hand-rolled cigarette. But the moment she lit up and took a long drag, Juke knew from the sweet smell that it wasn't ordinary tobacco.

She took a long hit and reached out, offering him the joint.

He shook his head slightly, "No thanks."

"It's good," Ophelia said, her voice suddenly horse and husky. Leaning back on one elbow, she closed her eyes, and took another drag, holding the smoke in her lungs as long as possible, then exhaling slowly.

Juke watched her, thinking how peaceful this young woman looked, so relaxed in these surroundings, and because of that, how beautiful. What was it to close your eyes and give in completely to a drug, or a drink? To give in absolutely to love? He had known those feelings once, a long, long time ago—

"Do you think the kid did it?" Ophelia asked. "David Robertson?"

"Where'd you get his name?"

"Oh, c'mon. Watertown is home to a hundred and ten thousand of the busiest busybodies you've ever seen. Everyone talks. They talk about being in the worst city in which to live," she nodded proudly and sarcastically, "last on *Money* magazine's three hundred best places to live, three years running. One more and we break a record." She laughed. "They talk about who's fucking around with whom. They talk about David Robertson. And everyone says he did it."

"They happen to mention why?" Juke asked.

"Tall, good looking, and cocky. And he played football. That's all you need in this town. The girls are supposed to be a perk. Usually are, and you don't hear much about it. Until one says no."

"Talking from experience?"

"One bad experience," giggling, "in another galaxy a long, long time ago. A football player."

"Of course."

"Of course. He was tall, good looking, and—"

"Cocky."

"Very cocky. But I was gonna say, a creep. He was a creep. David Robertson was a creep. He had to be, right? Lot of creeps around here. Lot of creeps everywhere." An intoxicating smile came to her mouth. "Here a creep. There a creep. Everywhere a creep, creep. Old Ophelia had a farm—"

She shrugged, and took another long drag. There was a moment of silence as she let out a throaty groan.

"I met him once, y'know," she said. "A kegger out in the woods, not far from here. This was early August, last summer, just before they, him and his family, moved away. I was a little drunk, and by myself, and figuring, what the fuck, right? So, I went right up to him. Said, 'What's it feel like to kill someone?' Just like that. He looks at me. This faraway look in his eyes, like he's not really there. 'I'm innocent,' he says, like he's been practicing in front of a mirror, or with a lawyer, or something. Like you see in the movies, or on those TV shows. But he sounded so guilty. Like he couldn't live with himself anymore. Or like, I don't know, maybe he was planning on doing it again. So I say to him, 'If you didn't kill her, then who did?' "

"What did he say?" Juke asked.

"He shrugged and said, 'Someone I don't know,' and then he walked away. I didn't see him hanging around after that. I think he took off. Me, I just got drunker and drunker, thinking to myself how easy it was to shift the blame. Trying to figure out who I'd blame my hangover on the next morning."

Ophelia took another hit, smiling slightly at something in her head. Then she opened her eyes, turning, staring suddenly right at Juke.

"Wanna screw?" she asked.

Juke shot her a look.

"Whoa!" she said. "Never had anyone take offense before."

He stammered for the right words. "It's not—"

"I just like doing it up here," Ophelia said, cutting him off. "Since, y'know—I guess I'm just fucked up that way. And the pot—" she lay back, completely down, the back of her head against the cold, damp stone, and took another long toke, "—it makes me horny. What can I say?" She closed her eyes again, and was silent for a long time.

Juke remembered picnics in places just like this. A long drive on a weekday afternoon, when summer was taking over from spring, but the school kids, their parents, didn't know it yet. Wine would take the place of the pot, but was there really a difference? He could taste her still, so many years later. Her sweat mingling with the sweetness of the grapes. The freshness of her breath like an oxygen mask. So lost in one another, the tangled limbs, the release, the—

"I think I like going back to the biddies freshly laid," Ophelia said, laughing suddenly, hearty and long. "I'm fucked up that way."

"Sorry if I made you feel uncomfortable back there," Ophelia said. "Should have known better when you didn't want a hit."

"Not uncomfortable," Juke said. "Flattered. I'm old enough to—"

"You're not old," she said. "At least you don't look it." She turned away, a slight post-buzz blush flushing her cheeks. "You look good. Y'know?" A shrug. "For a cop."

"An ex-cop," Juke said, a small laugh. He knew he'd given it away. "It's been a long time."

"Rule number one," she said. "Next time you go undercover doing whatever it is you do: Writers never refuse pot or sex. It just ain't in their system."

"I'll remember that."

Ophelia turned back to face him, watching him for a long moment as he drove the Saab. "You don't seem like a creep," she said finally.

"I've worked on it."

"That's all most guys need to do. Then everything would be okay. The world would be a much better place." Ophelia nodded a few times, as if agreeing with herself. Then she said, "Let me make it up to you."

"Nothing to make up," Juke said. "You've been very helpful."

"My goal in life: here lies helpful Ophelia."

"Helpful, sarcastic Ophelia."

"Helpful, horny Ophelia," she corrected. "But really. I know where the Sussmans live. Don't you want to talk to Natalie's mom?"

twenty-three

The woman glared at Juke. She was middle-aged and a little overweight, dressed in old slacks and a t-shirt. Fresh from housework, chores. But her eyes. They were icy-blue bordering on death. Never had he seen such hatred pitched his way.

He was standing on the front stoop of her raised ranch. The Raised Ranch was to Watertown, what the Colonial was to Harmony. This one half-brick, half-clapboard siding, painted green. A leftover from the mid-seventies, he guessed. There was an old Toyota parked in front of the double-wide garage door. And a kid's bicycle lying on the lawn.

"You sick sonofabitch," Lillian Sussman said, tears welling as she began to shut the door. "If this is your idea of a joke."

"He poisoned my neighbor's dog," Juke said, hastily, making an effort to stop her. He didn't have the badge anymore. The black leather badge wallet to flip open, the gold shield which could keep doors open.

"He's dead?" Lillian asked. "The fucking little bastard is actually dead?"

Juke nodded. "Monday afternoon."

The tears came more freely now. And Lillian Sussman smiled. "Excuse me," she said. "I'm just—"

She sniffled, and wiped away some of the tears, but not all of them. She reached a hand up, a hand weathered by years of taking care of others, and pressed it against one side of her face. She looked first back into her home, then turned again to face Juke.

"Who are you?" she asked.

They were seated in the living room of her ranch home. He on a weathered forest green sofa with cushions wrapped in a pale green bed sheet. Juke wondered how worn the forest green material was underneath, how stained? Or was it shiny and new, the one untouched possession amongst the stale and used?

Lillian Sussman sat in a matching chair, leaning forward mostly, her hands folded atop her knees. "She was so small really," she began. "So precious. So blonde. She had long, curly blonde hair. And what beautiful blue eyes. A little angel, really. And he, he was—" She shook her head. "David Robertson was a monster. Oh, yes, he seemed like a nice boy at first. Even I was fooled. So tall, and that—that Goddamn smile of his. I'd watch my daughter every time he'd visit. She was completely under his spell. He'd flash that grin and I could see the effect, the goosebumps on her arms, the flush to her face. I had nightmares that she was—as a parent you worry about the inevitable. Do you have any children, Mr. Miller?"

"No," Juke said.

He caught her eyeing his wedding band. A simple gold ring which he still wore.

"Then you and your wife are smart," Lillian said. And when he didn't respond, "There's so much to worry about. Sex. Sure, we were doing it as teens. But your own kids. You want them to wait. There're so many problems today. Things we never faced. You think they'll wait. You think they're somehow smarter than you were. But you know, in your heart of hearts, they're not. She was

so young. Thirteen. That's—you read the reports, I'm sure. Not a virgin. My thirteen-year-old daughter was sexually active. You know how that makes you feel? The looks you get in the grocery store. You want to yell at every accusatory face. You want to scream. 'What are you looking at? Your kids are doing it too!' "
She stopped for a moment to catch her breath. "That bastard. He took her—He was bigger, he was stronger. I have to believe it was against her will. No matter how much she felt she loved him. Oh, yes. Natalie was going to marry David. She told me that on enough occasions. We'd be sitting at dinner. I always tried to have a nice sit-down dinner on Sundays. Natalie, her sister, Danielle—that was her bicycle I saw you notice in the driveway. And me. My husband, well—we're divorced. So it'd be just me and the girls. Natalie would go on and on about how David was the only boy she'd ever love." She shook her head. "Christ! How prophetic. Maybe she knew she was going to die. Maybe—do you have any idea how it haunts me? I've asked myself a million times, what could David have possibly wanted that night, other than to see her die? Did he bring her there just to take her life? Was he through with her? Was that it? Or did he feel he had such a power over my little girl that the only violation left was to watch the life fade from her eyes? She'd have done anything for him. I shudder at the thought. Anything. I see that now. So why kill her? Why—"

Lillian took a deep breath, lost for a moment in her uncertainties. "A dog, you say?" she said finally. "Your neighbor's dog? I have to wonder if some little girl in the town where you live was spared because of that dog. I have to wonder if some mother was spared. If some mother—"

There was a little shrine to Natalie Sussman atop the mantel of a fake fireplace, the centerpiece of the living room's fake brick wall. The sofa upon which Juke sat, the chair, they were positioned to face the fireplace, to take in its aluminum and red light bulb fiction. These photos were so different from the black and white shot of Natalie which hung over David's bed. They were Christmas poses, a child really, opening a brightly wrapped box. They were summer break, a swimming pool, a softball game. They were pictures of a thirteen-year-old girl doing thirteen-year-old things. Missing was the pain, in abundance, was innocence.

The house itself was so unlike the Robertsons'. A family lived here. Broken, but still, with memories, mementos, out-of-focus snapshots, unwound grandfather clocks, and toys in the yard. The works. Not perfect. Not even close. But this house at least felt like a home. Juke didn't get that feeling at one-three-nine River Bank Road.

"There was never any doubt in your mind?" he asked.

"Natalie didn't lie to me, Mr. Miller. There were some things I didn't ask. Looking back, maybe I should have. I don't know. I was embarrassed. Some part of me believed—I don't know what I believe anymore."

"What about that night?"

"She told me she was going over to David's," Lillian said. "They were going for a walk by the river. They did that a lot during the summer." A shrug. "That and afternoon movies. It was still light out, and Natalie was real good about being home before curfew. Nine o'clock. She even brought a couple of sodas. Pepsi's, I think. The Robertsons lived four houses down, a small yellow house, if you want to check it out."

"A raised ranch?" Juke asked.

Lillian nodded. "I didn't have any reason to doubt her. She was a good kid. She thought she loved him. She—I don't blame her for that. I'm not angry with her for that. I wish she could know that. I would have understood. I'd understand anything, if I could just have her back."

"But David's mother—"

The hatred flared in Lillian's eyes. But her words were controlled, even. "Please. Don't. Their excuses, their—they ran away, in the middle of the night. Just disappeared. Only the guilty run away. If you're innocent, you stand and fight for what's right." She took a few deep breaths. "What would you do, Mr. Miller?

Would you admit your son was a killer? Or would you cover for him? Or would you just run away?"

Juke didn't answer.

"Really," she said. "I'd like to know. Because I've given this a lot of thought. What if the situations were reversed? What if my daughter had somehow managed to kill David, and there was no evidence other than David's mom claiming they were supposed to have gone for a walk together, but no, she hadn't actually seen them together that night? Would I claim she'd been home with me all night? Watching a video?" She nodded. "You bet I would. A mother protects her children. It's a natural instinct. One we can't help. Do I believe Sally Robertson lied for her son? Without question. Can I blame her?" She shook her head, slightly, looking away. The anger had subsided, for now.

Standing, she walked over to the mantel and picked up a framed photo of her daughter. A brightly smiling girl dressed in a softball uniform. Juke wondered if Lillian once saw the promise of love, of success, of grandchildren in those eyes? If she had planned on one day getting to brag about her daughter the doctor, the lawyer, the judge, to those same grocery store shoppers? And now, just the memories. Those wretched reminders that you weren't there when she needed you most.

She looked past the picture, at Juke. It was as if she forgot for a moment that he was there, watching her. "What would you do, Mr. Miller?"

twenty-four

It had been a never ending battle to cross the George Washington Bridge, then to survive the one-lane horde of rubberneckers taking in the details of a three-car accident on Interstate-95, making the drive home take almost twice as long. But as Juke drove down River Bank Road, he became thankful for those delays, thinking of his days as a rookie cop, and how an old-timer—Fred Russo of all people in this small Disney world after all—told him solving a crime was all in the timing.

He drove past the Robertsons' house as Sally, Neil, and an elderly couple were just leaving, walking to their driveway, toward the blue Dodge. There was a scowl plastered to the old woman's face, a viciousness to her eyes, and the old man seemed distant, not removed, just not completely together. The in-laws, whose visit Sally was so dreading, and, from their body language, Juke could understand why.

As he pulled the Saab into his driveway, he noticed Sally breaking away from her family, and crossing over Reggie's lawn. She walked up to his car just as he was getting out.

"Mr. Miller," she said. "I just wanted to tell you David's wake will be tomorrow evening at seven. The funeral is on Friday, at ten."

"I'll be there," Juke said.

"Thank you." Sally was quiet for a moment. She looked back toward the Dodge, then hesitated. "Nine thousand, seven hundred, sixty-three dollars and seventeen cents," she said finally. "That's what it's going to cost. Ruth Sullivan told me I could round it off to nine thousand, seven hundred and fifty dollars, but I told her no. I didn't want any discounts for burying my son." She turned back to face Juke as if he were the only person who understood. "The price list. I've never seen anything—'there is no sales tax on these items.' That was the first thing that caught my eye. Then the fee for embalming. It cost four hundred, fifty dollars to embalm David. Tax free." She gasped. "The coffins, they were spread out like in a—"

"Car showroom," Juke said.

"Yes," she said. "Exactly.

"I wanted to run," Sally said. "I kept saying to myself, this doesn't matter. None of this matters." She shook her head. "Neil ended up picking it out. The Regency model. And you know what Ruth Sullivan said." She laughed. "She said, 'A very nice choice. Solid mahogany, with a tan velvet interior. Very stylish.' "

Juke nodded. He had vague memories of his dealings with Ruth Sullivan. But they'd been buried deep. He didn't need to go dredging them up—

A horn blared.

Juke looked over at the Dodge. Neil and his parents were already seated. He was behind the wheel, motioning for Sally to hurry up. His father sat behind him, his mother in the front passenger seat.

As Sally turned and looked, Juke noticed her hands. They were balled tightly into fists. "If I can survive this," she said softly, "I can survive anything."

"Ask her to get in the back," Juke said.

"No," Sally said. "I've got a better idea. She's always complaining how her back is killing her. And how uncomfortable our car is." She mimicked an old woman's cackle, "Vinyl seats." She shook her head, and let out a small laugh. "But y'know what? Tonight I'm in the mood for Rinaldi's. I think I deserve dinner at Rinaldi's."

"Where's Rinaldi's?" Juke asked.

"Greenwich," she said, taking a step toward dinner. "Over an hour away."

All in the timing.

Juke figured he had a good three and a half to four hours, perhaps more. And though it was still light out, one of summer's endless days, the answers that could be found in the Robertsons' house were well worth the risk.

The easiest way in would be through the basement. The metal Bilco doors, painted light yellow to match the foundation and the rest of the trim, were unlocked. Juke had never known anyone to slip the inside latch. The Robertsons were no different. He opened the top overlapping door, just enough to slip inside, and down the seven cement stairs that led to another door, this one wood, with a lock that a five-year-old could get past.

In darkness now, with the metal doors shut tightly behind him, Juke stooped down low, and withdrew a penlight from his back pocket. It was made of black aluminum, and supposed to last forever. It had so far.

Shining the small circle of light onto the latch, Juke was about to get to work, when he remembered the oldest breaking and entering trick in the book. *The unlocked door*. Bingo. And he was inside the Robertsons' basement, heading for the curtained off area, heading toward David's darkroom.

There were more negatives. The negative for the shot of Natalie Sussman which hung over David's bed for one. And probably others. Juke was sure of it. But where? And after the girl's death, would they still exist?

He started with the file cabinets, pulling out each drawer, checking for false bottoms, checking in boxes labeled: "photographic paper, do not expose to light." He flipped through manuals, under packets of chemicals, and finally reached in to pat down the empty shells of the cabinets. But nothing.

He turned to the enlarger, tilting it back, checking under its base. He looked under each tray, the drying rack. Nothing.

He checked for loose ceiling tiles. Or whether the carpeting could be pulled back in that corner of the basement. But again he came up empty.

Taking a seat on one of the barstools, Juke stopped, exhaled a long breath, then let his eyes go to work, scanning the small space. He let the old habits have their way: the nooks, dark corners, smooth surfaces and edges. The anything-out-of-place.

It was then that he noticed it.

The brown chemical bottles. Five in all. Two different developers, D-76 for negatives, Dektol for prints. One for stop bath. And two others: one labeled "rapid fixer," the other labeled simply "fixer."

One bottle of fixer too many.

He picked up the one marked just "fixer." But no liquid moved inside. No fixer, rapid or otherwise, slushed about as he turned the bottle over in his hands.

Running his fingertips along the smooth plastic surface, Juke found a slit along the circumference of its base. He pulled from each end, and two cylinder-like containers emerged, two bottles actually. One missing a top, the other a bottom. Forced together, the bottom pressed into the top, creating the appearance of one perfectly sized bottle, one perfect hiding place. And who, especially in the dim light of a basement, the dimmer light of a darkroom, would ever suspect otherwise?

Especially from a fifteen-year-old boy?

twenty-five

There was only one other item Juke wanted from the Robert-sons' home. But the Pentax K1000 was no longer in the dark-room, where he'd seen it last, the prior afternoon. Perhaps Sally had put it in the kid's bedroom. Perhaps she carried it with her now, in the bottom of her purse, wherever she went. Perhaps it was on its way to dinner in Greenwich.

Juke headed upstairs, into the kitchen, through it toward the living room, and up the flight of stairs that led to the second floor and David's bedroom.

The breath caught in his throat as he opened the door and im-mediately noticed it missing. The framed black and white photo-graph of Natalie Sussman which had hung over the kid's bed. In its place, a rectangular space cleaner than the rest of the walls, but not by much. If Juke hadn't known, hadn't seen the photo hanging there, only the empty nail hole would have given anything away.

Why move it? he wondered. Was it an act of a devoted mother who could no longer deny her son's depravity? Who no longer needed to face it, to be reminded of it on the day-to-day? Or was it just another reminder of a future which could never exist? Those Goddamn happily-ever-afters.

Juke began his search with the bureau. It was six drawers tall. He let his hands move through the layers of clothing, under and over and into the recesses of the drawers. He moved then to the closet. Everything was so in its place that spotting the black and brushed aluminum body would have been a cinch. But the camera, the lenses, were likewise not there. Not under the bed, not behind the few books in the milk crate night table. Nothing. Nowhere. No camera, at least.

Just—David's phone. A cheap Japanese knockoff that combined an alarm clock, with an AM/FM radio, and a phone. And there, at the bottom of the keypad, was a police officer's, if not best friend, then damn close. The *REDIAL* button.

Kneeling by the upturned milk crate, noticing that the mostly empty glass of water was gone, Juke lifted the telephone's receiver to his face, and pressed the button. Seven digital tones abruptly pushed aside the dial tone, and it was ringing. Once, twice—

"Hello."

The voice was female, decidedly young.

Juke knew it was her. The girl in the Catholic high school uniform from those last four pictures. The girlfriend David was too young for, wasn't ready for. There wasn't a doubt in his mind.

"Anybody there?" the voice asked.

"Yes. I'm, ah, wondering if you could help me," Juke said, figuring it was worth a shot. "I'm a friend of David's, and I was—"

He heard the gasp, and then a crisp click. And a few seconds later the dial tone. He held the receiver for a moment, then finally hung up. He could try calling again, but—

No. He needed a name, an address. Where was her phone number? Wouldn't a teenager as popular as David have an address book? He went through the desk drawer. Pushing aside the pencils, the ruler, the calculator, and compass. He found a small address book, one of those giveaways from the local oil company. Juke took a seat on the desk chair and scanned the mostly blank pages. He found Todd's number, and those of David's three other friends.

He noticed Lou Dixon's number, he was the coach of the Middle School football team. There was a Grandma and Grandpa. And Aunt Nancy. But no girls.

Putting the address book back, slamming the desk drawer shut, Juke stood and began pacing around David Robertson's room.

Looking for something, for that one bottle of fixer too many?

He came to a stop in front of the bureau. Leaning forward, resting his elbows on its top, folding his hands under his chin. His eyes coming to rest on the books. The used textbooks, the Math and English notebooks, and—

"Salinger," Juke said, softly.

He picked up the paperback and fanned the pages. Chapter two was circled. As was chapter eight. Page sixty-eight. And page one-ninety-four. Four circles in all. Juke flipped back, saying the numbers out loud: "Two, eight, sixty-eight, one-ninety-four." Again: "Two, eight, six—" A Harmony exchange. "Two-eight-six, eight-one-nine-four."

He ripped a sheet of paper from a pad on David's desk, and jotted the number down. He stared at it for a moment, wondering why it seemed familiar. Why it—no, he couldn't place it. But if his hunch was correct, it was the same number lodged in the telephone's redial memory. That he'd bet on.

He pocketed the slip of paper, placed *The Catcher in the Rye* back atop the bureau, then returned to the phone. Lifting the receiver, he dialed zero. He waited, listened for one ring, then hung up.

Zero was the number in the redial memory now.

Backing out of David's room, Juke moved across the hallway, and was faced with two doors. He guessed the one on the left would be the guest room, the one on the right the master bedroom. He chose the one on the right.

The walls to Sally and Neil's bedroom were painted a pale shade of pink, the decor was decidedly laminated. A faux-oak veneer and lots of it. Matching headboard, dresser, armoire, lingerie chest, as well as his and hers night tables. More cheap furniture which Neil's Corvette could easily replace.

He started with the closets. Neil's first, strictly by chance. His suits were mostly blues and browns. The shirts pale. The ties striped. The shoes wingtips and all flawlessly polished, spit-shined to almost military, or worse, police academy standards. And on the top shelf a couple of pieces of matching luggage, all empty except for a travel iron and a guide to restaurants in New York City.

Sally's closet was the larger of the two, longer by at least double. Her dresses ran the gamut, long to short, scoop neck to turtle neck, colorful to solid black. Shoes were lined two-deep on the floor of the closet, along its entire eight-foot length. Pocketbooks were stacked three high across the top shelf. At least Sally didn't skimp when it came to accessories.

Juke turned to the armoire next, with its stacks of neatly folded sweaters, sweat shirts, blue jeans, and—

"Bingo," Juke whispered.

—two camera cases, one black, the other dark green.

Smiling slightly to himself, Juke pulled both from the cabinet.

The first, the green case, contained a Sony handycam, one of those small 8mm video cassette recorders with the flip-out color viewfinder, and a stack of tapes marked "Disney vacation," "David's 14th Birthday," his fifteenth birthday, "X-mas '96," and '97, as well.

But opening the second, the black case, Juke found what he was looking for.

Gently removing David's 35mm camera, he checked the frame counter. It registered twenty-one. The remainder of the photo shoot which began with those four frames on the end of the roll he had developed the previous evening. David's Catholic high school girlfriend. Miss two-eight-six, eight-one-nine-four.

Turning the camera over in his hands, he pressed the rewind button, then manually returned the film to its cartridge. Opening the back of the camera, Juke popped out the roll of film, Tri-X, and pocketed it. Then he pulled a fresh roll of Tri-X from another pocket, loaded it into the Pentax, and clicked off twenty-one frames.

Juke was stepping through the kitchen, on his way to the basement, when he heard the key slip into the front door's deadbolt, and the decisive click as the lock slid open.

"What the fuck?" he muttered, taking a quick glance at his watch. They hadn't been gone one hour, never mind three or four.

Stepping through the basement door, closing it behind him, he quietly took the stairs, then listened. They were in the dining room, arguing. Angry voices cutting through the carpet, cutting through the oak floor.

"It's a terrible place. Just terrible. How you could have ever brought your son here, I'll never know."

"Mother, please. We've had this conversation before."

"I'm sick of this bullshit. Can we please get something to eat?"

"It's all bullshit to you, isn't it? To both of you?"

"It was my only grandson who died."

"It was my only son."

"A mother is supposed to protect her children, not lead them blindfolded into the valley of death."

"God damn you!"

Juke heard a crash. A dish, something made of glass, shattering to the floor. And footsteps stomping away.

"He already has," one of them continued. "He's damned us all."

Juke would wait, at least until dark. He had an hour, perhaps less to go. He would wait until there was no chance of being seen.

All was quiet upstairs for the time being. Just the smoldering remains of resentment. The participants silently skulking to their corners to await round two.

Walking into David's darkroom, making sure the black curtains were closed behind him, Juke turned on the swivel lamp, and took a seat. Lifting his right leg, he tugged up his pants, and lowered his sock. It wasn't an exemplary hiding place for negatives and proof sheets and what turned out to be a few choice enlargements, but while searching for the Pentax at least they'd been out of his way, and in his possession. He wasn't about to take the extra fixer bottle. It was just its secret contents that interested him.

Upstairs a loud slam caught his attention, making him look up before unrolling and flattening the proofs. He waited a beat for a second explosion of anger, more words, but it never came.

Lowering the lamp, Juke leaned in close, so he could examine the images. There were nine proof sheets in all, nine matching plastic pages loaded with negatives cut into strips of six. The enlargements he didn't count.

Focusing his eyes on the first set of images, so small, so barely visible, it took Juke a harsh moment to connect what he saw with some base in reality. But when he did it all made sense. A slap in the face, you stupid fuck, wake up and smell the inhumanity. Here finally were the rest of the Natalie Sussman photographs.

His heartbeat racing, his breathing ragged and enraged, he flipped a page, and one of the enlargements announced boldly that he had seen enough. Tasting the bile rise in his throat, he, as calmly as possible, but with slightly trembling hands, returned the negatives, proofs, and enlargements to where he had hidden them, in his sock, under his pant leg.

He switched off the lamp, and sat there, in the dark of the Robertsons' basement for what seemed like an eternity. That image, the barely inch-and-a-half wide photo which first caught his attention, burned now against his naked shin, like the eyes of Mephistopheles himself.

Juke had seen enough pictures of Natalie Sussman for one day. Pictures of her happy, pictures of her smiling. Pictures of her in her softball uniform. At birthday parties. On Christmas day. Those were the pictures he tried to remember. The shrine atop the mantel.

So why couldn't he get these heinous images out of his head?

He heard a shrill voice. "I detest you. I always have." And another slam. This time Juke was pretty sure it was the front door. He was positive the voice belonged to Sally.

He thought about Lillian Sussman. How she felt about Sally and Neil. How she despised David. "The fucking little bastard is actually dead?" she had asked.

If only she knew. If only she'd seen these photographs of her daughter. She'd surely have finished David off herself. Long before he ever got a shot at Molasses.

twenty-six

There was a knock at Juke's front door. He had just returned, creeping from the Robertsons under cover of night, the loathsome secrets eating away at his conscience. He had hardly the time to think, to weigh the evidence. Were the photos evidence if no one ever knew, ever saw? Wouldn't it be better that way? Better for Natalie Sussman? Better for—if only he knew her name.

To weigh the consequences. David Robertson was dead. The tormentor of these two girls murdered. There were no punishments beyond that. No guilty verdicts. At least in this life. Hopefully David was suffering his due now, that God didn't shake his head, not this time, and look the other way.

Standing silently in his kitchen, the negatives still wrapped around his shin, the undeveloped roll of film in his pocket, Juke waited a moment, pressing the balls of his hands against the countertop. Pressing with such pressure until his palms hurt. And he stepped back suddenly and finally, then went to the door and answered.

"Got any more of that coffee?" Wilbur Cross asked.

*　　*　　*

"So Anabelle's being looked at seriously as a suspect," Cross said. They were sipping it black and hot.

"You asking or telling?" Juke said.

"Asking and telling. As a longtime member of the fourth estate, I have that prerogative."

"Other than a hefty insurance policy, what do they have?"

"You haven't talked to Piccerillo?"

Juke shook his head. "Had a busy day."

Cross cracked a smile. "And I guess you and Zaretsky have better things to do with your time."

He shot Cross a look.

"C'mon, Juke. The pretty detective spends the night at your place. Word gets around fast. What'd'ya expect? I'm happy for you."

Christ! Juke thought, wondering where it started. Probably Piccerillo. He'd be sure to thank Tom personally for that one. And from there—by day's end everyone on the Harmony force would know. And by week's end, every cop in the state. The biggest gossip network of them all. A psychic heartbreak line for those who should know better.

He took a deep breath, "Get to the point, Wilbur."

"Piccerillo seems to think a two million—"

"Old Maid Marion seems to think."

"Either way, that policy is a shitload of—"

"Yeah, yeah, yeah. They have anything else?"

"Fingerprints."

"They matched Anabelle's fingerprints to the crime scene?" Juke asked, more than a little surprised.

"Piccerillo wouldn't say for sure, but he was leading me down that golden path."

"I find that one hard to swallow," Juke said. "Anabelle may be a lot of things—"

"To a lot of guys."

"But she's not a murderer."

"Maybe she had a partner?" Cross suggested. "A younger lover?"

The cop, Juke thought. Brett Genovese's rival for Anabelle's attentions. If such a person really did exist.

"Piccerillo told me there were two unidentified sets of prints found in the Robersons' living room," Cross said.

"There you go," Juke said, not believing the implications himself. No, it was a wrong way turn down a dead end. "How could I have missed it?"

"Your killer instinct, Juke," Cross said. "It ain't what it used to be."

Juke was on the horn the moment he heard Cross's car start up and pull away from the curb in front of his house. He sat in the kitchen, the receiver cradled between his shoulder and face, while he tugged up the pant leg, rolled down the sock, and finally pulled free those images which had been rotting his soul from the leg up.

Piccerillo answered on the second ring. "Hey, partner," he said, picking up. His words a little garbled as he swallowed a mouthful of something.

It dawned on Juke. Piccerillo had a caller ID box. Zaretsky must have called her new partner this morning using Juke's phone. And it wouldn't have taken Piccerillo more than a heartbeat to jump to a dozen perverse conclusions.

"You rely too much on technology," Juke said.

"Don't knock it. You'd be surprised at the benefits," Piccerillo said.

"You mean nauseated," Juke said.

"Hey. Can't a guy have a little fun?" He snickered, "So," then sucked in the snot, "I know where you were last night. You believe I couldn't squeeze a Goddamn detail out of Zaretsky?"

"There are no details," Juke said.

"Whatever you say," Piccerillo said, then, "So, where the hell were you all day?"

"Watertown, New Jersey."

"Sounds like a story I want to hear."

Juke wondered if he should tell Piccerillo about the murder of Natalie Sussman? And the implications and suspicions surrounding David Robertson? Was there a reason to bring Natalie's name into this investigation? Or her mother's? Was there a reason that Lillian Sussman ever needed to know about the photographs? Was anything worth the risk that she might possibly see one of them? Or what about the new girl? Miss two-eight-six, eight-one-nine-four— the number etched forever in his brain as he repeated it in the darkness of the Robertsons' basement, anything to take his mind off those images. And her family? How could a parent live with such knowledge? How could they ever—

But she was alive. She had survived David Robertson.

"Not much you haven't heard already," Juke said.

He wouldn't say a word. Not unless he was willing to tell his ex-partner about the photographs, a leap Juke was not at this moment prepared to make. He didn't want to turn the pictures in, not unless he had to. He didn't want to see those images blown up and examined, possibly leaked, passed from hand-to-hand. On the slim chance that there was some sick fuck who'd find pleasure in them, as David Robertson obviously had. Natalie had suffered enough indignity.

"Great," Piccerillo said. "A lot more of the same. A lot more of nuthin.' Just what I need."

"Lot of dead ends?"

"All dead ends. Seems Reggie got his Walther by way of the Salvation Army."

Juke laughed. "Didn't know they were running guns now."

"I guess secondhand suits and dresses weren't paying the bills," Piccerillo said, explaining how he and Zaretsky had spent a good part of the day in the northeast corner of the state, interviewing Anthony Troviano, Jr., and his mom Victoria.

"The Walther was registered to an Anthony Troviano, Sr.," Piccerillo said. "But when he passed on about five years back, his wife tossed the pistol in a box headed for the Salvation Army. Guess she took the name literally."

"Probably didn't know what to do with the thing," Juke said.

"That's what she said," Piccerillo said, then, "You, um, happen to know if Reggie was friends with anyone by that name?"

"Troviano? No, it doesn't sound familiar," Juke said. "Of course I never heard him say he was going to the Salvation Army, either."

"Yeah, talked to the grieving widow. She told us the same thing," Piccerillo said. "You know, we got her to give up her prints today?"

Juke nodded. Not that Piccerillo could see that response. "Anabelle," he said, finally, "she put up a fight?"

"You kidding? We walk in there, and right away she asks if it's about the insurance policy. Zaretsky tells her two million dollars is a lot of money. I tell her it's a lot of motive."

"You were trying to get on her good side," Juke said.

"Something like that," Piccerillo said. "So, she gives me the sob story." His voice became an absurd whine. "I don't have a thing to hide. I'm not proud of some of the things I've done. Yeah, me and Reggie, we used each other. But we both got more or less what we wanted. Yadda, fucking-yadda, fucking-yadda."

"I'd say Anabelle got more, right about now," Juke said.

"Yeah, but guess what? Your insurance buddy was holding out on you. Ol' Reg had the same policy written for him."

"Another two million?" Juke said. That was something Reggie had never shared. Maybe he was embarrassed. Maybe he just felt it was none of Juke's damn business.

"Yeah. It was like a promise the love birds made to one another. Y'know, If Anabelle went first—"

"Like that was a reality?" Juke asked. "She's thirty—"

"One."

"Whatever. She's got a lot of time left."

"Still, she tells us, if she went first, Reggie would have had enough money to keep him supplied with whatever he'd need for the rest of his life." He laughed. "I had to explain to Zaretsky that Anabelle was talking about hookers. That Reggie liked the pros."

"And with Reggie going first," Juke said, "what does that two million keep Anabelle supplied with?"

"She don't have to pay for what she needs," Piccerillo said. "All she has to do is shake her little tail feathers, and what'd'ya know? Wood grows on trees."

"You tell her as much?"

"Right to her face."

"What'd Zaretsky say?"

"She chewed me a new asshole," Piccerillo said. "Told me I was being rude."

"She was right."

"Hey, we're talking about Anabelle DeLillo here, not Mother Teresa, God rest her soul."

Juke could just imagine his ex-partner making the sign of the cross. He had to laugh. "How'd you get her to give up the prints?"

"You're gonna love this. She gets a glass, puts her prints all over it, then drops it into an evidence bag for me."

"Christ!" Juke said.

"She told me she preferred that to me swiping the glass when her back was turned," Piccerillo said. "I told her, she's watched too many bad cop shows on TV." He coughed, not covering his mouth. "She told me, she's known too many bad cops."

"So what's the outcome?" Juke asked. "Wilbur Cross seems to think you've got a match."

"That guy sure gets around, which brings me back to you and my new—"

"Stay on the subject. Anabelle the doer?"

"No," Piccerillo said, letting a half-breath escape his lips. "At least her prints didn't match up. But still—"

"Old Maid Marion keeps harping on the two million."

"The guy's wetting himself."

"I'll send him some Depends."

Piccerillo laughed. "We ran the prints we found at the scene through the NCIC and DOJ computers," he said. "We even ran Anabelle's."

What sort of technological advances had been made over at the

National Crime Information Center and the Department of Justice since he'd left the force? Juke couldn't even imagine the scope of their data banks. The sheer number of names, crimes, evidence, and prints. The ability to cross reference every minute detail. He couldn't help but wonder now if he could find the sonofabitch? Would these advances lead him down a path that didn't dead end with Johnny Marciano?

"Nothing, right?" Juke asked.

"Not a fucking thing."

"Talk to the ride yet?"

"Yeah, Todd's mom. A real looker. Divorced and stacked. Shit, if I weren't—"

"What'd she say?"

"Nothing unusual. Dropped David off like she did every Monday and Thursday. Didn't notice any other cars. Didn't notice squat."

"What about the toxicology tests? The kid doing anything illegal?"

"He's clean. No drugs. No booze. The little bastard didn't even smoke. He was a Goddamn angel."

"Yeah," Juke said, the black and white images coming back. Some fucking angel.

"Me and Zaretsky are gonna hit up the school again tomorrow. Talk to everyone if we have to. Care to join us?"

"I think I'll pass, this time around. Maybe you'll get farther if you ease up on the elbow grease."

"Ease up?" Piccerillo said, "The way I'm feeling about this case right about now, they start that street lingo shit with me, I'll smack the little fuckers upside the head."

twenty-seven

The call came a little earlier on this night. A quarter to eleven, the hump-night regulars bitching about the past three days, praying to high heaven that the next two would slide past unnoticed. It had been a tough week for Tompkins Glen, and the funerals had yet to come. A game was probably entering its final innings on the TV over the bar, no one paying it much attention. Talking instead about David Robertson. Talking about Reggie DeLillo. Asking the same question that was tormenting Juke, plaguing Piccerillo and Zaretsky. The bug up Old Maid Marion's ass. The question that ate away at the parents of Harmony. Destroying Sally and Neil Robertson from the heart out. No matter what she said, that knowing the killer's identity could not bring her son back, deep down, and Juke knew this as well as anyone, Sally Robertson wanted to know. Like everyone else in town. *Who killed David Robertson?*

He picked up on the third ring, wondering perhaps if he should bother picking up at all. It had to be important. The important calls at home always came late at night. But two nights in a row?

"Yeah," he muttered, two nights in a row. It was that sort of week.

It was Zoë Gilmore, and a quick, no nonsense: "Get down here now." Nothing amusing or amused about her tone.

Juke was walking through the front door when he heard the shouts. Zaretsky in some guy's face. Her jaw set, teeth clenched. Her voice angry. She was saying, "One more time. Get your hands off me."

The guy was tall and muscular, with one of those military-style buzz-cuts and a moustache—Juke could have picked him out as a cop from a football field away, in dense fog, in the dead of night. What was it with cops and buzz-cuts? Did it make them look tougher, meaner? Or was it something more practical? In a fight, the bad guys had no hair to grab onto? Juke figured it was the latter, though he doubted anyone wearing the style would admit the truth. Of course, back when he was in uniform, he'd have never given the bad guys a chance to get that close. But the rookies had changed over the years, a lot of them now seemed in it for the blood, to make a point, to get in someone's face and bust ass.

Buzz-cut had his right hand around Zaretsky's left arm. He was pulling her toward him. But she stood her ground, trying to pull away.

Zoë, Quintin and a handful of regulars, were standing back, at the edge of a half-circle that had formed around the couple. It was the curious human version of crime scene tape. Before the fact.

"A riot at the popsicle stand," the bartender told Juke, who noticed a couple of chairs had been overturned, a couple of beer bottles smashed—hardly a riot, the violence mostly limited to words, to looks that could kill.

Nodding, Juke stepped forward. He clamped a hand around buzz-cut's right wrist, and squeezed. "You heard the lady," he said, taking an educated guess, "Brian."

The scorned ex-boyfriend laughed. Hearty and a lot drunk, his brown eyes going wide in mock terror. "Well, what do you fucking know? Here he is now, your fucking knight in shining armor."

"That's enough, Brian," Zaretsky said. She shot Juke a glance filled with apologies and regrets.

It was the first time he'd seen her since that morning, when he left the note near the alarm clock then snuck away. He had thought a lot about her during the traffic jam on the GWB, his mind numb from trying to put the David Robertson pieces together. He pictured her lying on his bed. So soundly asleep. A beautiful woman who wanted to be in his bed. So what was wrong with the picture? Only one thing really. And he kept coming back to it. Greta Zaretsky carried a badge. And that dulled the attraction. It turned it inside-out. Her badge hit too close to home. It was his crying heart tattoo.

Glaring down at the hand gripping his wrist, Brian let go his hold on Zaretsky, and pulled away with a snap from Juke's grasp. He turned toward him, getting into his face.

Juke could smell stale booze and the hair gel that gave his buzz-cut that spiked glossed-over look.

"Stop by for your nightly piece?" Brian asked. "Huh, Mr. Two-bit Bar-keep?" He looked back at Zaretsky, his baby browns glassy with lust and hatred.

Juke could see that Brian wanted to fuck her and wring her neck in the same instant. And he could feel himself slipping. He could hear the *snaps*. The Johnny Marciano snaps. His fists balling themselves, all white-knuckled, always white-knuckled first, a chain re-action, and the first domino was down.

"What'd you see in this guy anyway?" Brian asked his ex. "Was it pity? Did you wanna know what it was like to end a seven-year dry spell? That it? Everyone knows about fucking Juke Miller. The man who couldn't fucking cut it as a cop. Well, he couldn't fucking cut it as a husband either." He turned back, poking a fingertip in Juke's chest. "Tell her, huh? Tell her what happened to your last fuck partner. Tell her—"

His first punch broke Brian's jaw. The words trailed off in a slow motion dribbling dance to painkillers and the miracles of modern surgical techniques, as Brian crashed onto the nearest table, the wood splintering, the legs collapsing with the violence.

Grabbing him by his throat, Juke lifted Brian, threw him against the closest wall, and just started wailing. He hit him for his wife. He hit him hard for Zaretsky. He hit him for Natalie Sussman, for Lillian Sussman. For his friend next door, and the dog. And he would have kept on, taking out all the inhumanity, all the injustices of the world on this idiot beat cop from New Haven. He probably would have beat the life out of him, probably would have sent him to asshole heaven, if it hadn't been for the hands pulling him off, pulling him away.

He never heard the sirens, the shouts of the officers, but he felt the cold slap of the cuffs, the pressure of the billy club against the back of his neck as he was held to the floor by eight struggling hands, four of Harmony's finest. He could see the glint of the steel gurney used to wheel the unconscious Brian out to the awaiting ambulance, the heels of Zaretsky's shoes following, as he knew she would. He could sense the anger in Zoë's eyes, the fear in Quintin's, as they watched silently while Juke was led out. The confusion in Piccerillo's face as he arrived on the scene a lot too late. He could hear the sucking in of his own breath as he braced himself for the flat of the hand against the top of his head as he was pushed into the back of a squad car. And he could imagine the laugh boiling in Marion Bradbury's gut when the Chief of Police heard the crisp clang of steel bars as Juke's cell door slammed shut.

twenty-eight

It was all a sickly beige. Faded and rubbed, chipped and bruised. The mattress an inch and a half thick. It smelled of urine and sweat. The blanket, dark brown and tattered near the edges, remained tucked in, doing its damnedest to contain the stench. The walls were barren except for the most recent graffiti: names of girlfriends, snitches, some phone numbers, the face of Jesus Christ, and a few obscene drawings.

Juke sat at the head of the bed, his knees pulled to his chest, his back pressed against the cement wall. His hands aching, his eyes closed, he tried to ignore the smell. He managed to ignore the squalor of sounds that echoed down the corridor of the Harmony lockup. A dozen cells, six to each side, only half filled with prisoners, and those at the opposite end from where Juke now settled. Was he being segregated because he was an ex-cop and his life was at risk? Or because he had just beat up a cop, and Old Maid Marion didn't want him getting a hero's treatment?

He pressed his hands against the meat of his thighs, cramping. How long had he been sitting in that position? Stretching, yawning. And a crinkling, his left pocket. He reached inside and pulled out the one thing he'd forgotten to hand over with his wallet, his watch, his keys, his wedding band. A small slip of paper. Half a deposit ticket from a checking account at the First National Bank of Watertown, New Jersey. The account was in the name of Ophelia Yegyazarian. A street address was printed under her name, and handwritten in slanted blocks was her phone number. She had pressed it into Juke's hand when he dropped her back off at the library. "If you ever change your mind," she said, and was gone.

He returned the slip of paper to the same pocket, knowing he'd never call. Ophelia was minus the badge, but still—Juke shook his head, no. I guess I'm fucked up that way, he thought, smiling, despite everything. Smiling despite that Goddamn question which would not go away. He remembered all the faces, kept hearing their statements of hatred, of contempt. But who, really, would want to kill the Robertsons' kid?

Reggie, of course. And that Salvation Army gun. It would almost be like his old friend, now that Juke thought about it, to go shopping for firearms at the Salvation Army. But it could never have been a secret. No, Reggie would have been too proud of his bargain. He'd have bragged to Juke. "Hey, neighbor! Look at the Walther P-88 I just picked up for three bucks!"

But it would have made everything so easy, and Juke could have forgiven his friend, especially now, after seeing so much. Even if Reggie hadn't known about the photographs, he knew firsthand about the evil that lurked in David's soul. The violence that's really just kept on pause within us all. Just push the play button—David might have killed Natalie Sussman just to watch her die. He probably killed Molasses for the same reason. And couldn't Juke just as easily have ended Brian Luponte's life? Sent that wise-assed smirk to hell, where it probably belonged? But there had been provocation. Brian Luponte had pressed the play button. Did Natalie Sussman do or say something that sent David reeling over that edge? Did the dog? Or did David Robertson's propensity for violence float at the surface, high above his soul? Mingling with his day-to-day in slow motion? Always a snap away?

Lillian Sussman could have killed him. Her anger was as real. But could a mother take the life of a child? Yes, if protecting her own. Without doubt, breath, or hesitation. But afterwards, as vengeance? She'd say emphatically yes, but he'd guess no.

Juke ruled out the friends, Todd and company. They were all-talk, and minus the balls. Kids, nothing more. Drugs or something gang-related was always a possibility, especially with David's high school in such close proximity to the edge of the inner city. But his corpse tested negative, and his quarterback image was squeaky clean, but then the teachers, his friends, didn't know about David Robertson's hobby, the sort of photos he liked to take. Photos of—

Perhaps the new girlfriend. Her phone number now a bad commercial jingle in his head.

He shook his head. The undeveloped roll of negatives. So much lay with those latent images, disclosure and closure, perhaps. All he had seen so far were shots of her walking along, and standing by, the banks of the Mad River. Those four images. But there was something in her body language. The way she stood. The fear. Undeveloped fear, as if she knew what was ahead. As if she knew that all things would change with a fresh roll of film. But would that make her kill? Would that press her play button? Perhaps. If there were indignities on that undeveloped film to match Natalie Sussman's.

David's parents hadn't a clue. Neil on the road half his life selling auto parts. Tweaking the Vette the other half. Sally, the perfect PTA sort of mom, with the job as a bank teller. She probably made great Christmas cookies, and kept the house meticulously clean. Yes, Juke thought, remembering the boy's bedroom, their bedroom. So clean, so—

"Y'know what your problem is?"

It took a long while for Juke to answer. He probably wouldn't have bothered, if he could have walked away. But that wasn't a possibility, and he knew Old Maid Marion would tell him, whether he wanted to hear or not.

"Immediate problem?" Juke asked, opening his hands toward the bars. "Or are you speaking generally?"

"Generally," Bradbury said, leaning into the bars of Juke's cell, holding them with clenched fists as if he were on the other side wanting to get out.

Juke looked at the Police Chief. A lot of sarcastic mumbo-jumbo passed through his mind, including something about Bradbury's wife giving the Chief permission to leave the house at this unGodly hour, but he was too fucking tired, and it was too fucking late.

"Why don't you just tell me."

"Okay. You're a walking corpse, Miller," Bradbury said, no sarcasm, just the truth as he saw it. "You died that night, in the alley with—" He looked away. "That's why I came down on you so hard when I was with IAD. I knew you couldn't do it anymore. Your life as a cop was over. Christ! Your life period." He turned back. "You knew it as well. You wouldn't sleep, you wouldn't eat. You were just this ball of anger. The other cops on the force. They respected you for going after Marciano. For what you did. You got a dirtbag off the street. But it was the *why* of it that bothered me. You were like a machine. There was no stopping you once you got it in your head that Marciano was your guy. Once," and he paused, shaking his head, choosing different words, "you were a good cop. An honest cop. But after—" He shook his head. "You just wanted to put the fucker who did this down—"

"Can you blame me?" Juke asked, picturing Marciano, the slick, sick smirk on the fucker's face. The laugh. Marciano read Juke's pain like a comic strip. Fed on it. An intravenous to his soul. His little shop of horrors projected in his eyes. *She was a pretty girl,* the bastard had said. *"A pretty girl,"* reaching a hand under his shirt. A flash of silver. The snap in Juke's head. Quicker to the draw. Juke was always quick on the draw. The first shot hitting Marciano in the gut. *"A pretty girl."* How was Juke to know? The next hitting Marciano in the throat. How was he to know? The last blowing off the side of his face. How the *fuck* was Juke to know the pretty girl wasn't his wife?

"No. No, I—" Bradbury got to the point. "You're not a cop anymore, Miller."

"Meaning?" Juke asked.

179

"Meaning, leave the police work to Piccerillo and Zaretsky. They'll find out who killed the boy. This ain't seven years ago. I know Reggie was your friend—"

"Is that what this is all about?"

"No. I just like repeating myself. Want to make sure my warning to stay away sunk in."

"I haven't been—" But the lie was too feeble. Juke knew even Old Maid Marion could see right through it.

"Be a good neighbor, Miller. And butt out."

Bradbury pulled an oversized key from his pants' pocket, and slipped it into the lock of Juke's cell door. It slid open with a riled squeak instead of a clang.

"Now go home."

"I get a lecture, and you pay my bail?"

"No bail, Miller."

But Juke didn't move off the bed. Something wasn't right here. Why wasn't Bradbury busting his ass? Reveling in the notion of Juke Miller behind bars?

"Sort of hard to hold you, Miller, when every witness we talked to said you were just defending yourself. That the other guy threw the first punch."

The nod was slow, and he wasn't sure about the realization: why do we cover up when we see supposedly good people do bad things? Why do we lie, or turn away, or make like it never happened? So willing to make that leap of faith, are we all so fucking frightened of the bigger picture?

"He's a cop," Juke said.

"One with a history. He's banned from half the bars in the state, including yours now, I assume. Seems alcohol turns Brian Luponte into an even bigger asshole."

"If you were still—"

"—with Internal Affairs? Hell, Brian Luponte would have been history a long time ago. He's not the sort that should be going around carrying a gun."

"Like me."

"Nothing like you, Miller. Nothing like you at all."

And the conversation, the lecture, was over. Bradbury waved at freedom, a flourish of his arms. "C'mon. Your ride's waiting." The Chief again caught Juke by surprise, and smiled. "And when a woman is that good looking, I've learned from experience, she won't wait around long."

twenty-nine

"**D**on't know about you, but I'm starving."
They were in her 1967 MG Midget Mark III, racing green, original paint, original interior. Juke in the passenger seat, his knees just about blocking his view out the windshield. And thankfully the roof was down or he'd have never fit. Cars like these were built for speed, not comfort.

She just drove, her platinum hair whipping in the wind. Speeding toward Harmony's only twenty-four-hour eatery, the Betsy Ross diner. It was located over in the shopping plaza, a stone's throw from the also always-open Super Stop & Shop. Anyone else would have turned and apologized about the cramped conditions. But not Zoë Gilmore. It was her car and she was giving the ride. What the hell did she have to be sorry about?

They both ordered breakfast and cheap American beers. It was a bar worker ritual, a solid chunk of fat and cholesterol, some hops and wheat to wash it down, not long before the sun began its stretch and yawn. What better way to end the day?

"So," Zoë said, "no one knows about Hope?"

Juke shrugged. It was as much a statement of fact as it was a question. "You do," he said.

"That's it?"

"That's it."

"What about Reggie?"

"Never told him."

"Wow. You're as good at secrets as I am."

Hope was a mistake. Juke's belief that perhaps it was time to move on, too fast, too soon. They only had a few dates. A movie at an art house in Hartford. A few dinners at her place. "It's been four years," Hope told him, trying to get him to relax. They made love once. Or at least had sex once. Juke afraid that he'd hurt her. She was petite. Maybe five-four. And blonde. But it was her eyes. Her eyes definitely reminded him—

She had come into his bar just once. Scribbled her number on a napkin, and pressed it into his hand. "If you don't call her, I will," Zoë had warned at the time. It took him three weeks to convince himself, but finally he did call. And finally, after those few dates, meeting her anywhere but in Harmony, he invited her over to one-four-seven River Bank Road. They were sitting in the living room. Each with a glass of wine in hand. Making small talk. Nothing but small talk. When she looked over at one of the framed pictures of his wife. It was from a vacation in Key West. She was standing on the balcony of their hotel room, looking out at the sunset. She was so radiant, the sunset didn't stand a chance, even with Juke behind the camera.

"Three's a crowd," Hope had said, lowering the photo, face-down on the end table. Then she lowered her wineglass, stood and took each and every photo of Juke's wife, and turned them over, or lay them down, or removed them from the wall altogether, placing them facedown in a pile on the living room floor.

"That's better," she said, returning to the sofa.

Juke didn't respond at first. He stared instead at the backs of the frames. He would never have turned his back on her. How could he—

"You really should leave now," he said.

Hope thought he was joking. "Don't be silly."

"Please," he said, softly. His voice catching in his throat. "Get out of our house."

"*Our* house?" Hope said. "There is no *our*. Your wife is dead, Juke. She's—"

"Just go," he yelled, his anger frightening them both.

Hope glared at him for a long while, never saying a word. Then she picked up her purse from the coffee table, and left.

Juke sat there, on the green living room sofa, all that night, his hands folded in his lap, his eyes straight ahead, staring at the back of what he knew was one of their wedding photos. A shot of two mostly empty wineglasses in the foreground, in focus, seemingly the subjects. And in the background, all blurred, splotches of a white dress and a black tuxedo, the bride and groom, kissing softly.

It was her favorite picture from the wedding. None of the others even came close.

"You sure know how to pick 'em, Juke."

"She picked me, remember?"

"Very well. But you didn't have to call."

"Don't remind me," he said, then, "And you should talk."

"I've been with some very fine women over the years," Zoë said.

"Most married."

"Most unhappily married."

"But they always go back."

"Think Greta will go back?"

"Hmm." Juke thought for a minute. "Yeah," he said. "I made him irresistible."

"You really believe that crap about women wanting to mother their men?" Zoë asked.

"Let's say I believe that the mothering instinct is a hell of a lot stronger than we give it credit."

"I give it tons of credit. I'm as nurturing as all fucking hell. And so is Sally Robertson. I mean, from what I hear."

"What do you hear?" Juke asked.

"She loved her kid. He was all she ever talked about. Had pictures of him taped up to the inside of her teller window. Every stage of life. David as a just-born. At three. At eight. At fifteen."

"Guess it stops there," Juke said.

"Um. You know Vicki Lefcourt? Tall, lanky, cute as hell. Got long straight brown hair, looks like that model in the Chanel commercials."

It took Juke a second. "Matt Lefcourt's wife?"

Lefcourt was the freshman Congressman from the sixth district, the Tompkins Glen district. A real up-and-comer in the Republican party. A slightly moderate conservative, who said all the right things, pushed all the right buttons. The kid seemed to have it all. The local hero running back for the Yale Bulldogs—came in third his junior year in the Heisman voting. A Rhodes Scholar. He had the style. He had the gorgeous wife. And he won by a landslide. It was a perfect package the voters could not resist. Except for Juke. Lefcourt's public persona was a little *too* perfect in his eyes. He knew the other Matt Lefcourt. The regular customer back when Juke had just bought the bar. The drunk who'd gone home with a different woman at the end of every night. Who twice puked all over himself and fell asleep in the men's room, only to be discovered by Juke when he was cleaning up. He was always a little too loud, and a little too cocky. A bad drunk by anyone's definition. Juke voted for the Democrat instead.

Zoë nodded. "Vicki's the manager of the branch where Sally works."

"How old is she?" Juke asked, thinking she looked rather young to be a bank manager.

"Twenty-four," Zoë said, then added, "But you don't want to know how she got the job."

"How do you know this?"

"You really don't want to know that either."

Juke took a swig off his beer and waited.

"So, anyway, according to Vicki, Sally never mentions her husband. There are no pictures of Neil. If someone asks, she cuts the conversation short and brings up David. It's almost as if Neil doesn't exist."

"Problems at home or just a proud parent?"

"Don't know about problems," Zoë said. "The Robertsons don't seem to socialize much. No one ever sees them out together. Not at the movies. The grocery store. Dinner. Nothing. He's working all the time."

"Could he have a lover in some other city?"

"He's male, isn't he?" She smiled. "And oh, so studly."

"Sally told me he was a good husband."

"A real provider, right?"

"Something like that."

"You live two houses down, what else is she going to say: he beats me, beats the kid, has a lover in every port? C'mon," Zoë said. "Neighbors have to keep up appearances."

"So, that's your theory?" Juke asked, "David's an abused child, so in turn he abuses?"

"I don't know about that," Zoë said. "And I don't know about Sally being all that proud either. Blind? Now we might have something there."

"I've been thinking the same thing," Juke said. It had been dogging his imagination. Didn't Sally ever question what her son was doing in his darkroom? Or did those photographs of frogs and plants provide such a realistic cover? When did a hobby become an obsession in a parent's eye?

"I mean, and this is just coming from drunks—"

"Such high regard for our clientele."

"When they start tipping."

"A sexy smile beats intimidation any day."

"Not in the bars where I hang out."

"You and Vicki?"

186

"You want details, I'll give you details," Zoë said. "It'd be a bonding experience. And I'm pretty sure I can make you blush."

"Anyway," Juke said. He wasn't going there.

"Anyway." She laughed. "You've got two groups here. Those who think the little SOB got what he deserved for what he did to Molasses—"

"You're in that group."

"Better fucking believe it," Zoë said. "I don't buy that boys-will-be-boys shit. Kids will be what their parents allow them to be. If I pulled something like that when I was his age, I'd have been grounded for life. If I lived that long. But of course that's just my opinion."

"Is it still the majority?"

"People don't know what to think. They're scared, Juke. Drinking more than usual. You can see it in their eyes. Especially now that Reggie's been cleared. It's like, what the fuck's going on in Tompkins Glen? Y'know? Is there some deranged killer out there lurking in the shadows? Are we living in the middle of some horror movie?"

"Nightmare on River Bank Road."

"Something like that," she said. "And a lot of people are beginning to wonder just what the hell Reggie was doing. What was he thinking? Going in there with an unloaded gun. If he didn't mean to kill David." She shook her head mostly in disgust. "And suddenly the little—"

"SOB?"

"Yeah. He's being talked about like he was the next Heisman trophy winner. Y'know, the grade-A student shit. My son will be President one day. Amazing what some nice words in the paper will do. They forget all about the dog. Talking about the kid like he was the second coming of Ronald Reagan, for Christ's sake."

"Or at least Matt Lefcourt," Juke suggested.

"At the very least," she said. "Makes my skin crawl."

"Could be a rash."

"Yeah, I'm allergic to assholes."

"That'd be debilitating."

"I'd need fucking life support."

"You don't buy—"

"Good kids don't poison dogs," Zoë said. "Just to see them die, or whatever the fuck his reason was."

Juke nodded. Good kids, good people, keep that violent impulse on pause. They lock that fucking pause button down forever. Hammer it down. Break it off. So as to never be tempted.

"That's cult," Zoë said. "That's some sick Mexican voodoo black magic shit."

"Santeria."

"Whatever. And Heisman trophy winners, future Presidents, don't do it. Or at least, I sure as fuck hope they don't."

"You even know what the Heisman trophy is?"

"The John W. Heisman Memorial Trophy, awarded each year since 1935, to the best college football player. Usually a running back."

"I'm impressed."

"Don't be. Football wives are the easiest marks."

thirty

His hands weren't shaking. Not this time. They clipped the trimmed end of the roll of negatives to the center of the stainless steel reel and wound. Smoothly, slowly, the edges of the film sliding into the grooves. The reel fitting in the tank. The rubber top securely on. The chemicals in, timed and temperature controlled. Washed and hung out to dry.

Juke was tired. Beyond that and then some. But he had to develop the film. He needed to see her face clearly. Her fear, anger—had the body language lied? Her innocence, would it be shattered, or intact? Could she, perhaps, pull a trigger? Could she stop what Natalie Sussman had not foreseen? Did she put a stop to it, not taking the chance, not taking it anymore?

The twenty-one images were there. A sequence continued from the previous roll, twenty-five frames in all. Nothing like Natalie Sussman, but on the same road to her hell. Clearly defined and humiliating and, why was she wearing her high school uniform on a Sunday night? Was that part of David Robertson's fun? And what would Zoë say about that boys-will-be-boys shit? What would she say about these? Nothing, Juke knew Zoë would have simply strangled the life out of the little SOB herself. Damn the consequences.

Perhaps David Robertson got an easy out. If there were such a thing. No guilt on his part, no time for remorse. No heartbreak, no credit card debt, no cancers, no SATs. No looking over his shoulder thinking that one day it would all catch up. One day a Lillian Sussman would be around the next corner, pistol in hand, ready and eager to pull the trigger, a dream come true of watching him die.

The sun was on its second cup of coffee by the time Juke got to bed. Another hot and hazy, another full of questions. He set his alarm for noon, and lay back against his wife's pillow. Using a small fan to speed up the drying process, he had printed one of the negatives. Just part of it really. Following the procedure in the basic guide book. Watching it come to life in the tray of developer under the dim amber light. A close-up of the girl's face flushing in from white. The details in a gray scale. The next Natalie Sussman in David's Robertson's life. He closed his eyes and memorized the look in her face, the sharp, focused anger staring right at him, right at the lens, right at David Robertson. The hardness in her mouth, frowning slightly down at one corner. The angle of her nose and chin, pointing not down, but defiantly to the side.

What made the kid press the shutter just at that moment? Was it something in his sadistic nature? A portrait in loathing. Was it planned? Was that the look, the emotion he wanted from his model? And what had he done off camera to elicit such hatred?

The details of Natalie Sussman's death came to mind. What had David Robertson done, more than once, if the coroner could be trusted? What had his smile allowed him to get away with? His good looks, his charm. And for how long? Was she, or this new victim, so enthralled, so enamored? What could he have possibly told them? He loved them? Needed for them to do these things for him? Or was there a threat? A little innocent playing around with his camera, a few seductive poses that got out of hand? And now he'd show their parents the pictures if they didn't play along? Or was it something more than that? That these girls believed in their hearts that they could save David Robertson? That he would love them forever, if only they could save him? The mothering instinct again.

Juke wondered about the photographs. Were they souvenirs? Trophies? He doubted David had shared these images with anyone, let alone Todd and company. They were for his use, and his alone. And that thought made Juke shudder. The vileness of humanity. The point of violence was that there was no point.

No, Juke could never believe that. The point was to dominate, to frighten, to prove what a big person you were. Whether looking into the eyes of a dog as it ate your poison. Whether looking into the eyes of a girl as you shattered her innocence. Whether looking into the eyes of a woman as you stole her life away. And for that you deserved to die. You David Robertson, and those like you.

He turned onto his stomach, pressed his face into her pillow and inhaled deeply, as if her scent was the only thing that could make it all go away. But it wasn't working. Not this time. Sleep would be uneasy, and there'd be no dreams. He was too close to evil for dreams, and what Juke had seen in those photographs would haunt his nightmares till the day he died.

thursday

thirty-one

At the hot, hazy edge of an investigation. Piccerillo and Zaretsky and Old Maid Marion, their voices, other voices, filtering to his ears. Something about a necklace. "I can't believe they took my necklace." But that voice so much louder than the others, so much—

Juke was talking to them, telling them what they were missing, telling them of the horrors that old 35mm camera had seen. The lens, if only the ghosts of pain remained, trapped forever between the aperture and the ground glass. If only the shutter were too fast. Too fast to allow its escape. One-one-thousandth of a second. How fast was that really? Could humiliation travel at such speeds? Couldn't it all be in there? The answers. David Robertson's guilt. His victims' release. Their freedom from the scars that ran the length and breadth of their souls. It's in the camera, he was telling them. In the fucking camera.

*　　*　　*

It had been one of those bottomless pits of sleep. Juke's head was heavy and numb, separate from the rest of his body. He was still waking up, still clearing, pushing the muscles in his neck back toward responsibility, when he took a look out one of his open bedroom windows, and the voices he dreamed were on the Robertsons' lawn, along with the squad cars and commotion to go with them.

He threw on yesterday's clothes, and caught up with Piccerillo on the front stoop.

"What's going on?" Juke asked.

Piccerillo shook his head annoyedly, grabbed Juke by the arm, and led him around the corner of the house, away from the other cops, away from where anyone might see or hear them.

"Old Maid Marion drilled me a new one this morning. He wants you to have nothing to do with this, nothing to do with us. Period. Until this is over. He mentioned a departmental hearing, for Christ's sake. Desk duty's one thing, but, oh Christ! He sees me talking to you—"

"Then get to the quick of it," Juke said, pulling his arm away from Piccerillo's tentative grip.

"Mrs. Robertson was laying out what she was going to wear to the funeral. She went to her jewelry box to get a necklace the kid gave her, but it was gone. She's all broke up about it too. Crying about how the kid gave it to her for her last birthday. How it was the last thing she had from him." He shook his head. "Then she lost it. Just fucking lost it. Went off on Zaretsky, saying what the fuck good are you people? Meaning us, the cops."

Juke knew a little too well about keeping memories alive through objects. "Only the necklace was taken?" he asked.

"No, everything. All her jewelry. The husband's gold watch. Her diamond earrings. The box was wiped clean."

"I thought she reported nothing missing."

"The box was there, so she never bothered looking inside. Guess she was too upset at the time about her kid being shot dead."

"You can drop the sarcasm."

"Yeah, like you dropped Brian Luponte."

196

"What? Suddenly he's your best friend."

"Fuck you. He was an asshole. But one with a badge. You broke his jaw, his nose, and three ribs. The guy's gonna be sucking down his steaks through a straw for the next month. And that's why Old Maid Marion's got this new bug up his ass. He thinks you're headed off the deep end again, and he doesn't want you anywhere near this when it happens. He ain't as stupid as he looks, Juke. He knows your connection to this case is through me."

"Read me the fucking riot act already, and move on."

"All I'm saying is—"

"I know what you're saying. Move the fuck on."

"Yeah. Sure," Piccerillo said, his voice cutting and matter-of-fact, "So now it's looking like the kid might have walked in on a burglary in progress."

"But there were no signs of a break-in."

"The cellar door was unlocked, and neither Sally nor Neil remembers opening it recently. We're dusting it for prints now. Same with the bedroom. You remember the routine."

Juke nodded slowly. He knew he could explain away any prints in the bedroom—he'd been all through the house the day of the murder. He'd been in the basement, as well, with Sally Robertson. But were his prints on the outside cellar door handle? Or on the Bilcos? He was pretty sure he'd find out soon enough.

"They take anything else?"

"Yeah," Piccerillo said, softening finally, shaking his head. His nerves letting up on the gas. "A couple of things." He pulled out his notebook, and glancing at the list, was about to begin reading them off, when the Chief's voice cut through loud and clear.

"Don't you have work to do, Detective Piccerillo?"

Marion Bradbury was standing by their side. His steely smirk aimed directly at the overweight cop, who now buckled under the slightest pressure.

Pinching his nostrils and sucking in loudly, Piccerillo nodded, a little of the color draining from his face. He flipped the notebook shut, slapped it a couple of times against the palm of his hand, and turned, heading back toward the house, heading back inside.

"How high?" Juke said.

"What was that?" Bradbury asked, turning back from watching Piccerillo's retreat.

"You tell him to jump," Juke said, himself taking a step back, going home.

"I'm sorry about the other night."

Her voice stopped Juke in his tracks. He didn't turn around, not at first. He didn't want to see her. He didn't want to face her. There was too much swirling around in his head, and he didn't need the—

"I'm sorry about everything." She was right behind him now. He could feel the warmth of her fingertips just hovering over his arm. As if she were reluctant to touch him. Or afraid. "I just didn't want to be alone. I just—"

Her hand gave up. He could feel the heat retreat, and hear her turn, the soles of her shoes rustling against the grass.

Then he turned.

"Anabelle," he said.

When she looked back, there were tears in her eyes. "What?" she said, sniffling, brushing them away, and a little laugh at her embarrassment.

"Do you have enough pallbearers?" Juke asked.

"Um—" Anabelle shook her head, unable to find the words. Then she nodded. "Reggie would like that."

"So would I," Juke said.

"Yeah," she said, taking a step back, then, "We really did love each other, Reggie and me. In our own fucked-up way. We fought sometimes, but everyone fights. Everyone argues. Everyone thinks they made a mistake. It's just natural, y'know? We were good for each other—"

"Yeah," Juke said, rubbing at his eyes. Hearing the snap. The call. Why couldn't he just leave things be? Why couldn't—the answer was Reggie. He had to find out for Reggie.

"It was better than being alone, Juke. Anything's better than being alone."

"Yeah, well, you've never had that problem, Anabelle," he said. "As far as I could tell, you were never alone."

"Not now, Juke," she said, a hurt coming to her voice. "Can't you just let it rest?"

"Why don't you tell me about the cop first. The one you were seeing."

She nodded a few times, setting her jaw. "You won't want to hear this," she said.

He laughed once, then looked away. "I don't doubt that for a minute."

thirty-two

The kitchen looked as if it belonged on the pages of one of the better home magazines. A spread about dream kitchens. It was another of Reggie's ongoing projects. The whole house was a project. If he could no longer build for others, then he'd build everything for himself. And when he was done, he could start over again at square one. The joys of home ownership.

They were both standing, leaning really, against the countertop. A little too angry to sit. A little too antsy. Juke found himself staring down at Molasses's water bowl. It was over in a corner, by the side of the stove. Ceramic, with bones painted on the inside, and the name *Molasses* around the outside, it was about a quarter filled with water. Which would dry up in time, he thought.

"Just say it, Juke," Anabelle said. "Just get it out of the way. We're not going to be neighbors that much longer. I'm getting out of here, you probably know that."

"I figured as much," he said.

"So ask me. Just come out with it. Did I have anything to do with Reggie's death?"

He glared at her for a long moment, then said, "Did you?"

She shook her head. And Juke understood that despite the prodding, despite their words, she still couldn't believe he'd actually asked.

"No, Juke," she said bitterly. "Y'know," and the tears started up again.

Juke wasn't sure if they were angry or sad. He didn't really care. "Two million dollars," he said.

"Now you're sounding like your ex-partner," Anabelle said. "I thought you were a lot smarter than that. This wasn't planned. I'm no master criminal. I didn't have Reggie knocked off to collect the insurance."

"Where are you going with the money?"

"Got a sister in Phoenix. You met her at the wedding."

Juke nodded.

"Gonna spend a little time out there. Get reacquainted with my family, and then, well—" She shrugged.

"Whatever, right?"

"Yeah," she said, sadly. "I liked the old guy. And I felt like shit when the dog died. You think I wanted that to happen? You think—Molasses was like part of the family. He'd lie at my feet, too, y'know? Sleep with his head on my lap. Kind of hard not to love him." She rubbed at her eyes with her fingertips. "I know you won't believe this, but I miss Reggie a lot. It's not the same not having him here. Cracking wise. Or grabbing me every time I walked by. We, um," she sniffled, "we had a lot of fun together. If you'd have opened your eyes, you might have noticed."

"I was too busy noticing other things."

"Like what, Juke? Like how Reggie still liked calling in the pros every once in a while?"

Juke was silent.

"Oh," she said. "Guess Reggie didn't brag about that. He didn't—y'know I'll bet there are a lot of things he did, things I did for him, that you don't know about after all."

"I'm not buying it, Anabelle."

"Christ, Juke. You want to see the American Express receipts?

Full body treatments from the Silk and Lace Agency. Two hundred, twenty-five bucks a pop. What the hell do you think that was for?"

"But you put up with it?"

"It made him happy," she said. "And if he was happy, I was happy." She laughed. "You know those peanut butter bones he was always making for Molasses?"

Juke nodded. It was a simple enough treat. A hollowed-out, sterilized bone that Reggie would load up with peanut butter, then freeze. The dog could spend hours suckling, getting out every last taste.

"One of the girls showed him that. Heather. She was Reggie's favorite. Bred weimaraners on the side. They were always gabbing about dogs. Before, after," a small laugh, "during."

"What about all your lovers, Anabelle? You've been with—"

She held up a hand to stop him, then looked away. "Because," and she said the words slowly, turning back, watching how he'd react, "it turned him on, Juke."

"What are you talking about? Reggie couldn't stand the fact that you were—"

"What would you expect him to say? That he got off on it? That he encouraged it? Then it wouldn't have been fun for him, Juke. He had to bitch and moan. Otherwise you'd have known something was up."

Juke remembered the conversations. The bitch sessions, Reggie would call them. He never understood why Reggie didn't just ask for a divorce, if the infidelities bothered him so. Was it that batting .300 wasn't so bad in Reggie's eyes after all? Or was he batting 1.000 and keeping it all to himself?

She took a step closer to where Juke stood. "He wanted to know every detail from the time I got there. He'd even pick out the panties he wanted me to wear."

Juke began shaking his head.

Another step closer. "I could never take a shower after I was with another man. You want to know why, Juke?"

"This is—"

"No, probably not." Another step. "You probably also don't want to know what Reggie really wanted. But that I'll tell you this one anyway. He wanted me to be with you. You, Juke."

"Stop."

Another. "But he knew you'd never. Not unless it was dropped into your lap. Not unless it was an offer you couldn't resist."

"No."

Anabelle was right in his face. "But you did resist." She leaned up. "You always said no." Her lips so close to his. "Up on your high and mighty." So close. "You resisted—"

"Enough!" Juke said, his voice shaking the room.

He grabbed Anabelle's shoulders and pushed her back. Then Juke stepped away, turning, leaning over the counter. Slapping a palm hard against the countertop.

"Reggie was the one who sent me to you, Juke. He wanted you to get on with life, and he thought that, well—" She shook her head. "The other night. That was the only time I ever came to you on my own."

"Please," he said softly. "Stop."

"Not what you wanted to hear?"

He was quiet for a time. Breathing, just breathing. He didn't want to think, to picture, to—he let out a loud groan. And when he spoke, his voice was even, controlled. "Tell me about the cop."

"The cop was a playmate. He had a uniform, and a lot of fun toys hanging from his big black belt. You remember those toys, don't you? Reggie certainly did. It was his idea."

"He picked the guy out?"

"Nope. He left that up to me. He just liked the after the fact. He thought a cop would be fun. He was bored with hearing about Brett Genovese. He was bored with the things Brett would do with me. I was bored with the things Brett would do."

He looked at her. "Then why go back?"

She seemed to be caught off guard. "The other afternoon?"

He nodded.

"Figures," Anabelle said, then, "I was alone, Juke. I didn't feel like being alone." She laughed. "This is such a small fucking town."

"Every town's the same."

"You're probably right." She took a deep breath as if trying to hold back an onslaught of tears, then she continued, "Reggie, um, he—Christ! Juke. He wanted to hear about handcuffs. He wanted to hear about billy clubs, about—" She shook her head, then walked over to a cabinet where Juke was sure Reggie kept the booze. "I'm beginning to wonder if you knew Reggie at all."

Juke was wondering the same thing. Did we all have secrets and secret lives, the small white lies and the darker side that kept everything interesting? Were they real, or just invented out of boredom, taking on a life of their own? A runaway train of greed, or lust, or drugs, or violence, or power.

Juke had his one secret. And it seemed so insignificant now. He had never told Reggie about Hope. He would have, eventually, if—but that *eventually*, *if* never came to be. And what he was hiding from was his own guilt, his own suffocating remorse. It had nothing to do with keeping things interesting.

"Something to drink?"

She was standing by the kitchen table, two rocks glasses in her hands, and a bottle of Johnny Walker Gold Label. It wasn't Macallan, but as far as Scotch went, it was damn close.

"Sure," Juke said, nodding.

She poured two drinks, and held one out to him. He walked toward her and took the glass.

Anabelle clinked the lip of her glass against his. "To Reggie," she said.

"Yeah," Juke said softly. "May he rest in peace."

thirty-three

Zoë and Quintin had done a fine job cleaning up, reworking the placement of the tables, nine to fill the space of ten. They left a note, taped to the cash register. It read: "Thursday? Please." Scrawled on the bottom, in Zoë's handwriting, was a translation: "Q needs Thursday night off. I'll be in around two. Please try to stay out of jail."

I will, Juke thought. Working, tending bar actually sounded like a vacation after the past few days. Jesus, after the past few hours. He could loose it in the splash, the foam, the clink of the ice. He could polish a shot glass for hours, like they did in the movies.

"Yeah," he muttered, cracking a laugh.

A radio was playing softly while he ran through the inventory check list. The same all-news station. Regular half-hour updates about the break in the Harmony murder case which was leading authorities to believe that the Robertson boy had walked in on a robbery in progress, and was shot by the perpetrator. Police were supplying every pawn shop and jewelry store in the tri-state area with descriptions of the stolen property, in the hopes that the thieves might have tried to hock any of the items.

Tuning the voices, the stories out, Juke focused on counting bottles. Judging from the inventory, the liquor order he was preparing to call in, Juke's Place had had a record-breaking week. And Juke figured with two funerals in the next two days, the town, or at least Tompkins Glen would be looking to drown a lot of sorrows. Something bothered him about that, making a profit off the deaths of two neighbors, off Reggie. But Juke knew that if he ran out of alcohol, the next bar was just a quarter mile away. The booze would always flow.

"Don't be a chump," Reggie would have said anyway. "I prefer you making the cash over some joint in Centerville."

Or at least that's what Juke imagined he would have said. He wasn't sure anymore.

Juke smiled, remembering his friend's excitement when he announced he was going to purchase Patsy's. An insurance policy Juke never even knew his wife had. Not two million dollars, not even close. It went along with her health benefits, and in the case of accidental death it doubled. She bought him the bar. A new shield. She took care of him when she knew he'd no longer be able to do it himself.

"No shit, huh?" Reggie had said. "I love Patsy's." He had helped Juke get used to the change. Bottles instead of a service revolver. A cash register instead of a cruiser. Bringing Molasses along on lazy afternoons. The dog falling asleep behind the bar, a little buzzed from licking the alcohol residue off the bar mats. Reggie making up a new bunch of fortunes to put in the mechanical genie. Handwriting the cards. Laughing his head off. Things like: *"Your lover is screwing your best friend."* Or: *"Plastic surgery is a viable alternative."* Or: *"Your breath could kill a garlic plant"*—Reggie told Juke he put that one in solely for Piccerillo's sake. They were all mixed in with the usual, *"Your luck is about to change."* It made them seem more authentic that way.

"Yeah, Reggie," Juke muttered, thinking about Anabelle, and everything she had said. That last question as he was stepping out the door. The one he'd been afraid to ask. *"Do I know the cop?"* He laughed now in disgust, shaking his head. His gut instinct had been—well, he was working on that gut check now. He was working on keeping the pause in place, the pause button down, the snaps in his head at bay. Nothing like paperwork to put everything in perspective. It was like an antacid for anger, distracting you from the pain. Making you think at least twice before wringing someone's neck.

He headed into the walk-in cooler. It was where the champagne, the kegs of beer, the wine for people who liked their wine chilled, was stored. All stocks were low. Especially the Pabst. Reggie would have been proud.

As Juke ran his hands over the cases and kegs, he thought about how the customers in the bar, how Zoë and Quintin, had covered for him, though he'd obviously been in the wrong. He'd obviously thrown the first punch. Was that what he'd been doing for Reggie? All along covering up for his friend's weakness? His addiction to—

Juke wasn't sure what it was an addiction to. Just that it started after Reggie's wife passed away. Maybe a year after, maybe a little less. Reggie boasted that "the girls," as he called them, made him feel less lonely. All he had to do was pick up the phone and order a blonde, or a redhead, an eighteen-year-old student, or a forty-year-old housewife, or anything in between. A-cup, B-cup, C-cup, D-cup. Whatever he was in the mood for that night. But Juke said he didn't want to hear about it. Told him that more than once. He realized now that just because Reggie stopped bragging, didn't mean he'd stopped calling.

Finishing up, Juke scratched a note on the inventory pad to have the draft system flushed next week. Nothing worse than sour-tasting beer. Nothing worse, he thought, repeating the phrase in his head, realizing there were a million things in life worse. Then, taking his check list with him, he passed by the genie, and popped a coin into the slot.

Juke watched the genie's mouth move a few times in mock speech, wondering what it was trying to say. Some internal gears whirred, and a fortune popped out.

"*You're wrong about everything,*" the handwritten card read.

"Christ, Reggie," Juke said. "Couldn't you tell me something I didn't already know?"

The door swung open, filling the pub with sunlight, and a blast of heat from outside. Juke looked at the clock. A little early, even for the Thursday afternoon regulars. But then the silhouette stepped forward, pulling up the first barstool, placing her purse atop the old oak bar.

"A Coke," she said.

"Nothing stronger?"

"I'm working," she said.

Juke aimed the soda gun into the tipped, ice-filled glass. He hit the "C." The sticky mist of cola coated his hand, as he tilted the glass back to its upright position, just a little foam, then placed it down on a cocktail napkin, right in front of her.

"Thanks," she said.

"So," Juke said, leaning forward on the bar, watching her with such intensity that it made her blush slightly, then turn away. "What's on your mind?"

It took her awhile.

Juke knew the feeling. The search for words when you know nothing you say can possibly sound right. That it was all so fucked-up why try in the first place? Why live in the first place? Why anything?

But she made it easy on herself, tossing the ball back into his court. Turning back with a shrug, she said, "You."

Juke wasn't about to mince words. Wasn't about to play games. He was too out of practice. Too out of the loop when it came to—

He asked the obvious. "What about Brian?"

Greta Zaretsky's face flushed. Her mouth twisted with anger. She looked as if she wanted to slap Juke across the face. Instead, she grabbed the raised rounded edge of the oak bar, and after taking a few deep breaths, lifted the soda to her mouth and drank.

"I told you the other night, we broke up."

"I figured now—"

"You figured wrong. And it's going to take his ego a hell of a lot longer to heal than the rest of him. That won't be any fun to watch. I'm not his mom. I'm not his lover. I'm not even his friend. He came here last night because he was feeling sorry for himself. He heard through the grapevine about me and you. He heard— Goddamn, Caller ID." She laughed pathetically. "Too bad he didn't hear the truth, that would have given him something to laugh about. He wanted to see if he could get me back into his bed for one night. That was it. That ego thing. He had a little too much to drink, and he got a little too loud when I said no. I'm handling the situation. I'm taking care of it. But what happens? He gets all busted up by an ex-cop who might just have the only ego bigger than his in this very fucking-small state. And now Brian's laid up. There's something funny there, but I ain't laughing about it. I don't find any of this amusing, or valiant, or—I don't know what the hell I find it. But the joke here, there's probably a dozen bimbos lining up right now, ready to spoon feed him. Ready to breast feed him, for all I know. For all I fucking care. Brian's going to need a traffic cop on his front lawn. Christ!"

She finished off the soda, and slammed the glass down atop the bar. It didn't break like Juke figured she'd have wanted it to. It just made a very loud noise.

"What the fuck is wrong with you anyway?" Zaretsky said, grabbing her purse, slapping a dollar onto the bar, standing, then walking out.

thirty-four

Saint Thomas High School was one of three seemingly identical two-story cinderblock buildings set up high on a hill and across Ardmore Street from Saint Thomas church, the oldest church in Connecticut, and undeniably the most ornate. Its copper dome towered above Harmony. Its thirty-foot high stained glass windows, fourteen in all, each depicting one of the stages of the cross, ancient cruelties in all their glory, shimmered in the midday sun. As in most of the great churches of the world, it was hard not to feel awe, reverence of some sort, or perhaps anxiety at the waste, when sitting in one of the solid mahogany pews in Saint Thomas.

But none of that splendor had been transferred, or wasted, on the schools. Aside from the large aluminum cross and their names in raised lettering, there was nothing to distinguish the three buildings from any others, anywhere. They were as generic as the school day, to the students, was long. They'd fit in well in Watertown, New Jersey.

To the right of the high school, halfway down the hill, was the middle school. Beyond that, and closest to the church and its adjoining rectory, was the grammar school, grades one to five, as well as kindergarten and preschool. Get them while they're young seemed to be the principle behind the location, when placement was made back in the early seventies. Each let out at a different time of the day. The high school first at two-thirty, followed by the middle school a half hour later, and lastly the grammar school, a half hour after that.

The Saab was parked up at the top of Ardmore, in front of the high school building. The street itself was more of an extended driveway, a place for buses and parents to park, which jutted up from Wright, at about the nonexistent border between the Wrightville and Tompkins Glen sections of town. No one lived on Ardmore except the priests and sisters of Saint Thomas. It was that sort of street.

Juke had a clear view of the high school's entrance. Each of the students would need to walk past his car to get off the school property and on their way home. In his hand was the enlargement, the photo of the girl's face. With a little over six hundred students enrolled in their grades nine through twelve, three hundred, sixty-seven of those female—Juke had a very helpful Sister Eustacia to thank for that information—he hoped he'd be able to spot her.

Now all he had to do was wait.

Back when he was on the force, Juke used to love the serenity of a stakeout, of that wait. Unlike Piccerillo who'd fidget and twitch, sweat and itch, coffee runs and donut runs, and anything to get out of the Goddamn car, Juke used the time to his advantage. A quiet time, away from the hustle of the squad room, away from the passions of home, to think, to replay the details of the crime at hand and connect their dots, find the missing pieces, or just shake his head realizing he wasn't even close.

But now he was feeling a little like his ex-partner. The self-doubts creeping in, what the fuck was he doing here? Was he that bored? That tired of being a corpse, the walking dead, as Bradbury put it? Did he miss the force, the job, with such ferocity that he needed to be involved? Was it for Reggie, the best friend that he hardly even knew? Or was he just a fool? Did he need to be a hero now, finally, seven fucking years too late? To discover what happened to his friend, when he was impotent to find out who murdered his wife?

His wife. In April of her twenty-ninth year, she had been beaten, raped, and shot dead in an alley behind a parking garage in downtown New Haven. Spitting distance from the bright lights of the theaters and nightclubs and restaurants, a little farther than that from the center of Yale's sprawling campus.

She'd been shopping. A credit card receipt from one of her favorite boutiques was found in her pocket. She had bought a lamp. Pewter based, with a beaded glass shade. She'd been eyeing it for months. If it went on sale, only when it went on sale. The clerk at the boutique told Juke that, yes, it had just been marked down.

But the lamp was missing, and would forever remain as elusive as her killer. Apart from the semen sample and the single .45 caliber bullet, the evidence was fuzzy, no one saw anything. No one heard the gunshot. There was nothing much clear and cut, no open and shut, except for the MO. And a few weeks later there was another rape, this time in East Haven. Brutal, bloody, but the woman lived. She lived.

Juke shook his head, remembering her face, the frightened look in her eyes as she picked out Johnny Marciano from his mug shot. Then she looked up, blanching suddenly, gasping and covering her mouth with her hand, as she caught Juke's stare. Seeing the face of her attacker again was nothing compared to what she saw in Juke's eyes.

"Christ," he said softly. Johnny Marciano did not murder his wife. Of course he didn't know it until after, after the blood and ballistic tests proved he wasn't the one. Yes, Marciano had raped and shot the woman from East Haven. He'd raped others. His list of crimes was never ending. But as far as Juke was concerned—

Was that it? The reason? To at least be able to solve Reggie's case? And if so, wouldn't it be the final nail? To know he could do it now, he had done it so many times before, brought cases to closure. But not then, when it really mattered.

"What the fuck is wrong with me?" he asked out loud.

The ringing bell could probably be heard for blocks. Was it a warning: restless teenagers on the loose? Or a challenge: we've done all we could for one day, they're your responsibility now?

In the still heat of that early June afternoon, they came in droves, zooming by the Saab. Boys pulling off their clip-on ties, unbuttoning that top shirt button, or removing their shirts altogether, girls wishing they could. A sea of blues and whites, the boys in navy pants, and white short-sleeved shirts, the girls in dark blue plaid skirts, and proper white blouses. Knee socks and penny loafers for girls, wingtips for the boys. Nothing like the fashion statements of Harmony High. Heading for their school buses, their cars, their rides, or just heading home. Walking, running, anything to get away. Only a week more till the freedoms of summer, only a handful of years till the restraints of adulthood. For some, less than that. So much to look forward to.

Juke watched the faces, every face. The photo was recent, from the Sunday evening after Molasses died. So her hair would be the same. Light in color, blonder even than Natalie Sussman's. Though shorter, chin-length and straight. Her mouth was full, her nose a little rounded at the tip, with a tiny bump at the bridge. And the eyes— there was something about her eyes. They too were light, gray, or perhaps green. Large and set far apart, her lashes full. Her eyes had been burned into his memory. The look of hatred. The anger, the—

"Resolve," Juke whispered now, staring down for a moment at the shot. That's what it was. Her sheer will to survive, to seek revenge, to—

Movement brought his attention back. They were tall, short. They were fat, thin, and somewhere in between. Many were developed beyond their years, others still looked like children. They were blonde, brunette, a few Asians with jet black hair, and a few freckled redheads. It was the United Nations of teenaged girls, smiling, laughing, many sweltering from the heat, some seeming not to give a damn. But none of them, not a solitary one, so much as made Juke look twice.

He waited a little longer, and then a little longer after that. The last few students straggling out. Another redhead, this one without freckles, and an African-American girl.

Had Todd Scilila lied about the Catholic high school girlfriend? Was she from some other town, some other catholic school with an identical uniform? Were all Catholic school uniforms identical, and Juke just never noticed? Why would he?

Was she a product of Todd's imagination, or David's bragging teenaged ego? Did she even exist?

"Yes," he said. She had to. He'd heard her voice on the phone. That had to have been the girl. And her number, hidden as it was in the Salinger. David's double life, what he didn't want his mother to know. Reggie's double life—

Juke nodded. The proof was in his hands. The photograph. Miss two-eight-six, eight-one-nine-four. He stared into her eyes trying to connect, trying to read her mind. Where was she? Did he scare her away by calling? What had she done?

The proof of her existence was on those negatives. There was a girl, somewhere. David Robertson's girlfriend. His new girlfriend. Someone to take Natalie Sussman's place. Someone to—

"Resolve," he said again, nodding, glancing up, away from the picture, as brunette twins walked past.

He tapped at the bottom of the steering wheel, and started to get excited. The pieces of the puzzle were starting to fall together. They were starting to form a picture. An ugly picture, but still.

"Fuck the burglary," he whispered. "Fuck the theories. Fuck Piccerillo. Fuck Old Maid Marion."

Juke would bet the ranch that this blonde girl was the one who pulled the trigger. That she was the one who killed David Robertson. And rightfully so, he thought. A quick end, a quick out. A little retribution, a little penance, for the little SOB.

He glanced over at the church and mumbled, "Thanks be to God."

thirty-five

After the perch on Ardmore Street, Juke swung home, picked up his garment bag, and checked his messages. He figured Piccerillo would call with the rest of that list, the items taken from the Robertsons'. He spotted the red blinking 2 and pressed *PLAY*.

"Juke," came the shaky voice. "This is Brett. Brett Genovese."

Juke sighed loudly.

"She did it again." He was crying now, into the phone. "She left me. Said it was over for real this time. Said she, she, she just needed company the other day, 'cause of Reggie and all. And that it was a mistake. Oh, God. A mistake. How am I gonna live without her, man? How am I gonna—"

"Shut the fuck up," Juke said, punching the *DELETE* button, wondering who was the bigger fool: Genovese for thinking Anabelle cared, or he for thinking Reggie did?

There was the sharp *BEEP*, then a pause. An audible breath, then the voice. High pitched and tentative. Very nervous and angry. Juke recognized it instantly, though he'd only heard her speak once.

"You're not a friend of David's."

Then the click, and another *BEEP*.

Zoë Gilmore whistled, then clapped her hands together a few times, nodding her head in approval. "Very nice," she said, looking him up and down.

"You through?" Juke said.

He had changed in the office, waiting until the last minute to put on the dress shirt, the suit, the polished wingtips. He could have waited another lifetime before tying another necktie. It seemed like it took him about that long to get the damn thing right.

"I've just never seen you like this," Zoë said. "It's another side of you, Juke Miller. The suave, the sophisticated, the—my—" And she raised a wrist to her forehead, faking a swoon. "My knees are weak. I'm getting hot flashes. I—I do believe you've cured me, Juke. One look at you in a suit and the evil lesbian spirits have been cast out. My parents will be so happy."

He stood on the other side of the bar, waiting. The sweat already building up around the collar, at the armpits. He'd be swimming in sweat before the night was up. A black suit in this heat. But it was the only one he owned. His wife had bought it for him, a thirty-fifth birthday present, and it still fit nicely. She had told him he looked sharp. Handsome. He wore it out to dinner that night, that birthday celebration, and then they went dancing. The way it made her smile, he'd have kept it on forever.

"I'm through now," Zoë said, laughing, enjoying her joke. "God, that felt good."

"Can you manage by yourself for a couple hours?"

"Only if you promise to return in the suit."

Ruth Sullivan greeted Juke at the entrance. A stoic mountain of a woman in her fifties, she asked how he was, then pointed out the guest register. He signed his name, wondering why. He had never looked at his wife's register. It was in a box in the attic. One he'd never open. He doubted the Robertsons needed such a box. And he was sure that like him they'd never open it, never go near, for fear of what it might reveal. For the ghosts it might unleash. The truths buried deep, or forgotten, or never realized.

David Robertson's wake was held in Sullivan's Funeral Parlor's largest *viewing room*—Juke could hear the snap echoing in his head from when Ruth Sullivan had asked him seven years earlier what size *viewing room* his wife would require.

He thought this was the same room. It was just as cold. And still decorated in pale blue. Very cold. Very blue. Like the furniture in David's room.

There were flowers everywhere. So many damn flowers. Like a nursery, a rain forest, a botanical garden. And sprouting from the center, a mahogany bloom, David's casket. The Regency, Juke remembered.

Piccerillo, Zaretsky, Old Maid Marion, and about half the force had turned out, sitting in back, respectful and quiet. Juke nodded at those he knew as he walked past. At Bradbury, at Piccerillo, who in turn rolled his eyes in the Chief's direction. At Fred Russo and—

Zaretsky turned away before. Could he blame her?

He caught Peter Castagnetti's glance. The rookie was seated beside his wife Robin. They both looked as if they'd been crying, as if this were some big mistake, some curse on their young lives. Juke held the cop's look for a moment before turning away.

The press was there in full force. The local news TV crew had been held outside capturing the mourners as they came and went. But Wilbur Cross made it past Ruth Sullivan, as had many of his contemporaries. They took notes, made lists, and racked their brains to come up with suitable adjectives to describe the Robertsons' sorrow. A thesaurus would be their next stop.

There were a lot of neighbors. Regulars from his bar. Dominic Santorelli, Malvina Washington, Sam Ehrhard, Mary Simson and her four kids. A lot of others. People whom he noticed when walking to work, people he'd usually see mowing the lawn, or taking their dogs for a walk. All here now, bonded by dark suits and sorrow, joined in this curious ritual to say goodbye to a child they barely, if at all, knew.

And many students. Todd, Marvin, the pair of medium/regulars, and others, tears streaming down their faces. Not nearly as tough, no street lingo to get past this harsh reality. Parents holding hands, the looks, the fear in their faces. The questions of, How can we ever be sure? How can we prevent this from happening to us?

"You can't," Juke wanted to say, waiting his turn to step up to the casket. "We're all helpless. We're all innocent. We're all guilty as fucking sin."

He stepped forward, but didn't kneel. There was no one left to kneel to, not after. Not anymore. He looked at the child before him. That's all David Robertson was, a child, a teenaged boy. He seemed so frail now, that Juke wondered what Lillian Sussman would say? Would there be a good riddance, all spittle and loathing? Or would she run, crying, no evil left to hate? Just closure? And what good was that when you weren't ready to move on?

Juke touched the boy's hands. They were cold, folded, a rosary wrapped around his intertwined fingers. It was different for Juke, standing there now. No rush of emotions, just the pieces of the puzzle floating in his mind, coming together, then breaking apart again. You could put the pieces together, David. How do they fit? How does it all come out in the end? Would it be worthy of one of your photographs?

Stepping back, Juke turned toward the receiving line. His heart went out to Sally Robertson, trembling as she sat there. Her eyes the only visible scar for the pain held inside. She didn't understand. Perhaps she never had to. Bury the pain, the evil. Bury the monster with the boy.

"I'm sorry for your loss," he said softly, squeezing the woman's hands. He remembered the hand squeezing, the hugs, vague, slightly removed. Everyone had been sorry for his loss.

"Thank you for coming, Mr. Miller." She touched a hand to her throat, and let out a small burst of breath.

Juke nodded solemnly, watching her hand. Was she feeling for the missing necklace? Covering her throat so that her son, so that no one, would realize she didn't have it on?

He turned toward Neil and shook his neighbor's hand.

"I'm sorry, sir."

"Thank you," Neil said. "I appreciate the concern. I know you're not a police officer any longer—"

"Reggie was a good friend."

"Yes," Neil said. "I understand. I just wish this whole thing never happened. This thing with his dog."

"So do I," Juke said.

Neil nodded, then looked over at the casket. "Funny," he said.

"What's that?"

"Huh?" He looked back to face Juke, then shook his head. "Oh, nothing. Nothing. Just, ah—" Neil turned then toward the elderly couple sitting to his left. "These are my parents."

And to his parents he said, "This is one of our neighbors, Mr. Miller."

"A terrible place," the old woman said softly.

"Excuse me," Juke said.

"Get out while you can."

He held her look for a moment, then stepped away. There were a few empty seats in the back. Juke chose one, lowered his frame into the chair, and sat back. He looked around, catching Peter Castagnetti's eye once again. The rookie nodded once. It was a friendly gesture. One Juke ignored.

He looked around instead, at the faces of the mourners, at the backs of their heads. Little tidbits of conversations floating to his ears, riding the waves of muted sobs and heaving chests.

But Juke wasn't interested in what anyone here had to say. Instead he was looking for a sign. A marker from someone above that he was on the right track. All he wanted right now was to catch a glimpse. To know she was more than just an image captured by David Robertson's camera.

Just a flip of her light blonde hair would do.

thirty-six

He could breathe again. Hanging up the suit, tossing the shirt into the hamper. Did he have enough clean white dress shirts? Especially with the heat showing no signs of letting up. "Record-Breaking," was the front page headline of that morning's *Register*, already pushing David and Reggie below the fold. With more heat to come. A triple-digit high was expected for Friday, the same for Saturday. Relief finally on Sunday. Mother Nature knew.

Juke checked his closet. They were hanging, wrapped in clear plastic. How long had they just hung there wrapped that way? How long could they remain, before the material finally rotted off the hanger, and the buttons fell to the closet floor, leaving only the plastic bag?

He'd need one of the shirts for David's funeral Friday morning. Another for Reggie's wake Friday night. Then Reggie's funeral the morning after that. How many shirts, how many creased dark suits? The dry cleaners in town would be cleaning up. He laughed, and thought, *no pun intended*.

He cooked a little pasta before heading back to work. Angel hair with red sauce, a small salad on the side, and some Italian bread. Back during his days on the force, the others, Piccerillo, the guys in the squad room, would tease Juke about the way he ate, what he ate, as they chowed down their greasy cheeseburgers and cream-filled donuts. They'd joke that his wife had him wrapped so tightly around her little finger, that he couldn't eat like a man anymore. And the gag would continue on and on, until, inevitably one of the younger detectives would say something to the effect of: "I'd give up cheeseburgers and donuts, too, if I could be married to his wife." And one by one they'd reluctantly come around: "Yeah, okay," or, "Good point." Except for Piccerillo who said he wouldn't give up his donuts for no one, for nuthin'.

Juke tried to imagine what it would be like working this case with his old partner. He was pretty sure the photos would have racked him up pretty bad. Over the years Piccerillo had seen just about everything, in every configuration. But despite the breath, the wrinkled suits, despite seeming at times as if he just didn't give a damn, when it came to kids—Juke was pretty sure his ex-partner would have lost it. He was pretty sure Piccerillo would have gone home every night and cried himself to sleep in his wife's arms.

So why settle for this burglary theory? Because Piccerillo hadn't seen the pictures? Because he hadn't talked to Lillian Sussman? Or simply because it was a lead, the only lead, the only avenue, at this point in the case, and he was tired of having Old Maid Marion breathing down his back?

That sounded about right to Juke. To Piccerillo the pressure was always personal—You don't like the job I'm doing, then step down off your high horse, and do it yourself.

The pressure never bothered Juke. Reprimand went with the territory. It was the Chief's job. He was a cheerleading and firing squad all wrapped up into one obscene package. He got what he dished out, only from the Mayor, or the feds. The detectives, the patrolmen, were supposed to think he was an asshole, otherwise he wouldn't have been doing his job. Pretty plain, pretty simple. Nothing personal, just business as usual. The chain of command. Of course, Old Maid Marion took that calling to new levels—

Juke thought more about the burglary aspect. How it fit with his theory. Would a fourteen- or fifteen-year-old girl seeking revenge on David Robertson try to cover up his murder by making it look like the house was being robbed? No. That didn't work for Juke. This would have been a crime of passion, raw emotion, payback for the ultimate sin. Quick, violent, get it over with and run. The consequences would have been an afterthought, just like covering it up.

He brought his plates to the sink, rinsed them off, and poured one last cup of coffee. Doubts clouded his mind. *What if* David *had* walked into a burglary in progress? *What if* the kid tried to be a hero? *What if* he tried to stop some perp from stealing his mother's jewelry?

Something didn't play right with that. This neighborhood—a safe neighborhood despite what Neil Robertson's mother might believe. The time, middle of the afternoon. Any crook worth his lock picks would have been staking out the house. He'd have known what time David came home from school. And he also would have known that Reggie, living right next door, was home most of the time, usually lying out on the deck with his dog—

"Who died the previous day," Juke said, finishing off the coffee, letting his words hang in the air, letting his imagination have a field day.

The crowd seemed tame compared to the previous three evenings. Juke believed David Robertson's wake was mostly responsible. It was real now. More so than before. There was a corpse on view. There'd be another tomorrow. It wasn't just a headline, a news story, anymore. It wasn't another town's problem.

There were small pockets of conversation at every table, in every booth. And at both ends of the bar. People stopped by for one round, two at best. No one was drinking hard tonight. Maybe the hangovers seemed real as well.

When the booth across from his end of the bar cleared out, Zoë pocketed the tip, removed the glasses, the couple of beer bottles, and returned with the empties.

Looking up, Juke caught Dr. Birnbaum's eye as the vet walked into the pub, part of a party of six. They headed straight toward the empty booth. Zoë waited a beat, then was right on their trail.

Juke watched her as she took their orders, each face turning, smiling politely. First Birnbaum's wife, Melissa. Then Birnbaum. Then a younger man Juke recognized as a doctor who worked in a walk-in clinic across the street from the Harmony Veterinary Hospital. Soby. That was it. Dr. Walter Soby. The woman he was with ordered next—they were newlyweds, if Juke remembered right, still holding hands. Then an older gentleman who asked Zoë a lengthy question. He looked familiar, but Juke could not place him. And lastly—

"Christ," Juke said, barely a whisper.

The hair, it was a little longer than in the picture, but just as blonde. The face. The eyes so wide. The thick lips, but now they looked sensuous. Even the little bump on the bridge of her nose.

It was the girl. David Robertson's replacement for Natalie Sussman. Only older. He figured she was—Goddamn, he had no idea. He didn't care. She was beautiful. She was timeless. He could feel the warmth of her smile from across the room. This was the future. Years in the future. And she had survived her ordeal. She could radiate. She could—

"I'll flip you for her."

"What was that?"

He turned and looked at Zoë. She was in the waitress station, leaning on the drop-gate, order in hand.

"You're staring," she said. "You never stare. You never even look twice. Keep that up and the women in town are gonna think they have a shot. You're going to give them—"

"Don't go there."

"Hope."

"Thank you."

"You're welcome," she said, then, "And where's that going to leave me?"

"What are you talking about?"

"Blonde at three o'clock," Zoë said. "My three o'clock. Your nine o'clock."

"What about her?"

"You tell me."

"I just, um," Juke stammered. He wasn't sure what to say.

"Wow," Zoë said. "This is scary."

Juke nodded blindly, turning away from her as he filled the order. Trying to concentrate on pouring into a glass. Why was he drawing these blanks? Did the ice come first? Did—

"You look like you've just seen the bogeyman," Zoë said.

"No," Juke said, "It's just that," he shook his head, "I'm tired. Didn't get much sleep."

"I picked you up, remember?"

"And if I didn't thank you," he said, hoping to change the subject.

"You did."

He placed two bottles of beer onto her tray, then a Manhattan, and a Vodka Sour. He owed her two glasses of house wine: one white, one red.

"She's drinking the red," Zoë said.

Not acknowledging her, Juke turned and opened the temperature-controlled cabinet where he kept his wine stock. After running a fingertip across the labels, he selected a Pinot Noir that went for forty bucks a bottle.

"But she only ordered the house," Zoë said.

"This is better."

Juke placed the glass of red on her tray, then poured a glass of good Chardonnay.

"On the house," he said.

"We're entering the twilight zone here," she said, shooting him a concerned look.

"I owe Birnbaum one."

224

"Sure," Zoë said. "Whatever you say."

He watched her take the drinks to the booth. They made small talk as Zoë placed each drink onto the scarred tabletop. Birnbaum shot Juke a small friendly wave of thanks when he got the news about the round being gratis.

Juke nodded back, mouthing the words, "You're welcome."

Zoë stayed a moment longer. She must have cracked a joke, because everyone at the table laughed suddenly. Then looking back at her employer, she moved on to another table.

Juke tried to appear busy, wiping a wet bar rag against the old oak, pouring the odd beer, but he was watching the woman. She was wearing a black t-shirt and jeans. Casual. Very casual. But he hadn't seen a black t-shirt and jeans look that good since—

She was lifting the glass to her lips now. Sniffing at the wine, then taking a small tentative sip. Closing her eyes. Getting lost in the taste. Something small playing on her lips. Something more. She beamed. And it seemed to Juke as if the temperature in the bar rose twenty degrees.

"Okay, Juke. You haven't heard this one."

He looked up. Dominic Santorelli had commandeered his usual seat at the bar. "I'm not gonna wait for Zoë this time," he said, rapping his knuckles against the oak for a drink, "she never gets them anyway."

Juke mixed the rum and Coke.

"Okay," Dominic continued, unaware that he was being ignored. Completely. "Carrying this adorable little puppy home for his wife's birthday, Jimmy runs into one of his neighbors. 'Hey, Bob,' he says. 'Wha'cha think of the dog I got for my wife?' 'Hmm,' Bob says, examining the pooch. 'Great trade.' " He laughed. "Get it? Great trade."

"Yeah, that was funny, Dom," Juke said, handing him his drink.

"Really? You liked it?"

But before Juke could answer, Zoë had returned to the waitress station. "Her name's Eva Wechsler," she said, placing some empties onto the bar, grabbing his attention. "She's an MD. Does one day a week at the clinic. The rest in private practice. My guess

would be that she's thirty-two, give or take a year. And single—
she ain't wearing a wedding ring."

"How'd you find this out?" Juke asked.

"Met up with Deanna Soby in the bathroom."

"Walter's wife?" Juke said, glancing again at the table. Deanna
was just returning, sliding in next to her husband. A beautiful smile
on her newlywed face.

"Yeah," Zoë said. "She and I go way back."

They only stayed for one drink, and were gone by nine-thirty.

"Thanks again," Birnbaum said, as he led his companions from
the booth toward the bar. He shook Juke's hand, then added
knowingly, "I'll see you soon."

"Yes," Juke said.

Eva Wechsler was at the back of the group. Giving Juke a small
distracted smile as she walked by. He returned it as best he could,
wondering if it weren't all in his head. The pieces playing tricks
with his mind. Not coming together after all, but multiplying in
their complicity.

He had stared at the photograph for so long, burning it into his
memory, that maybe he was projecting. Seeing the blonde girl's
face on that of a woman. On that of Dr. Eva Wechsler. Halluci-
nating. Wishing for both the girl's sake, and for Natalie Sussman's
sake, it had all been a nightmare. And they could wake up now,
and go back to being children. They could grow up now. And one
day their smiles could light up a room.

thirty-seven

Tom Piccerillo showed up at Juke's Place around midnight. He shook hands with a few of the locals, made a pit stop, hit up the mechanical genie with a penny, then pulled up a stool at the bar and ordered a beer. His eyes looked as if he'd spent the last week filling out paperwork. His hands shook as if his second wind was gone, and his third was calling in sick.

"Surprised to see you here," Juke said.

"Yeah, well. What's he gonna do, demote me for having a drink?"

"Probably not."

"Yeah."

"You okay?" Juke asked, placing the beer bottle atop a cocktail napkin in front of him, then waving off the five. It's on me.

"I'll be okay when this is over," Piccerillo said, his voice low, a staticky whisper, his shoulders hunched forward. He was talking to Juke, no one else had better dare listen. "The dog. Reggie's dog. It's missing."

"One more time," Juke said, himself leaning in close, his eyes stinging for a moment at that first shot of Piccerillo's breath. *Scope*, he remembered one of David's friends saying. Industrial-strength, he thought, if such a thing existed.

"The grieving widow," Piccerillo said, "this afternoon she paid some kid to dig it up. Figured when she went to sell the place, it might spook off some prospective buyer if they knew a Tupperware container of dead dog was buried under the old oak tree." He shrugged. "Something about it giving her nightmares."

"It was Rubbermaid," Juke said, wondering why Anabelle hadn't mentioned the nightmares, or whatever they were, to him earlier.

"What?"

"Not important."

"So, the kid digs and digs and he comes up empty. No dog."

"Anabelle's problem is solved."

"You'd think, huh? But no. She calls us, just in case. Y'know, there's a clue here somewhere. But we're out grilling Todd and his friends. Finally got over to the high school after all that commotion this morning," he held up a quick hand, "Don't ask. The tough guys have turned into babies. They all of a sudden came to the brilliant realization that dead is forever."

"I could see that in their eyes at Sullivan's."

"Yeah, that was a fun scene," Piccerillo said, pinching at his nostrils hard, shaking his head in disgust. "So, Old Maid Marion, he takes the call. But instead of telling Anabelle not to worry. Instead of chalking it up to some mischievous kids. Or that maybe she didn't remember the exact burial spot. Or who the fuck knows what? He's got this conspiracy theory brewing in his head. He says to us, what if the kid was done in by one of these animal rights extremists?"

"David Robertson?"

Piccerillo nodded. "Y'know, those nuts who spray paint fur coats, and, ah, blow up laboratories? Shit like that. He thinks that maybe the kid was killed as a warning, and now the dog is going to be used as a symbol for, oh, I don't fucking know what? And that Reggie's going to end up being a martyr. He actually wants me to ask Anabelle if Reggie belonged to any animal rights groups. He wants Zaretsky to run another check on the Trovianos. Maybe there's this animal militia movement right here in Connecticut, and no one knows about it, he tells us. A fucking animal militia movement, can you believe it? I'm telling you, Juke, he's driving me and Zaretsky nuts."

Juke stared at his ex-partner for a beat, waiting for the punch line, waiting for that crack of a smile, the *got'cha*! But it never came, and Piccerillo only shook his head again, then downed about half the bottle of beer.

"This is a joke?" Juke said, finally, trying to get him to give in.

"We've been on the horn since three this afternoon. Only stopped to go to the Goddamn wake. Calling every one of these fucking animal groups. And now Old Maid Marion's talking about bringing in the feds. The feds keep track of shit like that. There was a bombing at some medical research place in Stamford last year, maybe it's tied in. Shit, the feds'll take this thing right out of our hands, and fast."

"Maybe it's better that way."

"Yeah, well. I don't know what the fuck's better anymore. Just, um, make sure you keep this to yourself. This gets out—"

"You kidding? Wilbur gets holds of this, he'll die of a heart attack from laughing too hard."

"Yeah," Piccerillo said, finishing off the beer, wiping a hand across his face, covering his forehead and eyes with the cool condensation from the bottle. "Reggie wasn't—"

"No," Juke said, thinking about the avenues Piccerillo and Zaretsky had to travel. All the hairpin curves, all the roadkill, all the dead ends. The stop and go, never knowing what's around the corner. He shook his head. That was one part of the job he would never miss. "Reggie wasn't. He ate a hamburger every afternoon, steak and potatoes every night. And barbecued ribs on Sunday."

But even as he spoke the words, Juke had to wonder. He had joked with Piccerillo and Zaretsky about David Robertson's double life, but what about Reggie's? The secrets which Anabelle had revealed. All the grumbling just Reggie's way of covering up secrets which he did not want Juke to know. So why couldn't he be an animal rights extremist? Was that so far off the mark? Juke didn't know anymore. It was just another piece whose slots and edges matched none of the others. Hardly a rarity in this case.

"That's a relief," Piccerillo said with a smile. "Fucking Old Maid Marion."

"What about the robbery angle?" Juke asked. "Turn up any prints?"

"Nothing off the cellar door," he shook his head. "I keep thinking I'm missing something here. I keep wishing you were working this one with me."

"I am in spirit," Juke said.

"Yeah," Piccerillo said, standing up. "Better get home to the wife."

"Give Cathy my best."

He nodded, finally looking at the card he pocketed after dishing out the penny. He tossed the fortune face-up on the bar. "What'd'ya know, my luck's about to change."

The detective had to laugh at that one, taking a step away from the bar, then, as if remembering, turning back. "Oh, yeah," he said, "Better check the paper towels in the men's room. You're running low."

Pulling a package of folded paper hand towels from a top shelf in his office, Juke headed to the men's room. It was empty, no one in the stall, no one at the urinal. He noticed that the local sports page usually held in the acrylic frame over the urinal had been replaced with the front page of that day's "Today's Woman" section from the *Register*. An article titled, "Your Sexual Self: What's Going On Down There?" Zoë's way of enlightening the clientele.

He popped the cover on the wall-mounted towel holder, and swung it back. But it was just as he thought, the regulars weren't that up on their personal hygiene, the thing was three-quarters full.

Just a stack of folded paper towels, and one white, number ten-sized envelope. Juke took the envelope, topped off the stack of towels, and closed the unit. He tucked the envelope into the mostly full package, and returned to his office. The extra towels went back onto the shelf, the envelope into his safe. He'd open it later, when there was time, when he was alone.

Right now it was last call. The night before David Robertson's funeral. And though he wasn't sure about anyone else, Juke knew he could use one final drink, to help him make it through the long day that lay ahead.

thirty-eight

There was a knock at the door. Juke was seated at the bar, counting out the receipts, making out a deposit slip. The TV was on low, one of the twenty-four hour news stations. Zoë had knocked off early, Juke telling her to get some rest. He'd mop up, wipe down, handle the paperwork. He'd take care of updating the reading material over the urinal.

And now he figured she, or some customer, forgot something. Car keys, a purse, a wallet, whatever. But when he turned to face the door, taking a few steps toward it, unlocking and pulling it open. Neither Zoë Gilmore nor any of his regular customers were standing there.

"Can I come in?"

Juke heard the snap—echoing, but still not that far off. Feeling the sweat suddenly covering his palms, the pause not so secure. He took one step back, out of the way.

"Sure," he said, glaring, thinking, so much for the fucking mother lode of self-control.

"It's killing me inside. I keep thinking there was something I could have done. Or maybe if I waited. A little hesitation. A little— I . . . I . . . I . . ." stuttering for the right word, "I want to think it was instinct. But I keep asking myself, what the hell is instinct? Instinct comes from experience. I don't have any experience. I know that. I know—instinct comes from—it was fear. I was scared shitless. A flashing in front of my eyes. My wife in black. Crying. That's always been my biggest fear. I couldn't bear leaving her alone. I couldn't—"

Peter Castagnetti stared into the glass of beer Juke had poured him. His head bent forward, reading his future in the foam. He'd yet to take a sip, and just held on to it, like a frothy security blanket. Rolling his hands around the glass, pressing the stubs of his chewed-off fingernails inward, holding the damaged cuticles against the cold.

The rookie looked bad, Juke thought. Worse than before. There was an age now to the remorse. His eyes, puffy and red and lined in black. Maybe it was a symptom of something dangerous going around, an epidemic that took hold of their town. Everyone stricken. Maybe it was guilt.

He'd been talking for going on a half hour. Rambling, a sentence or two, then fragments, half-baked thoughts, insecurities. His wife Robin played a large role. The only role in a production Juke was sure she could do without. Castagnetti had come to believe that he shot Reggie to protect her. That if he hadn't pulled the trigger, Robin would be a widow now. Robin would be alone.

How many times would Castagnetti replay that afternoon? How old would he be before the feel of that one shot, the pressure against the underside of his index finger, the backlash of the gun, faded finally into something fuzzy and unsure? How long before he could turn down River Bank Road, pass by the Robertson home, without blood suddenly covering his hands?

Juke wondered what *he* had looked like to others back then.

What excuses had *he* muttered? What misery had *he* drowned. What happened to those days that disappeared from the wall calendar, from his life. Days that never existed? When were the seconds that haunted him forever finally going to go away?

"I've talked to my priest, Father Torre," the rookie said. "He told me I was only doing my job. That Reggie's death was part of God's bigger plan."

Juke nodded a few times, then leaned forward, onto the bar so that his face was only inches from Castagnetti's. His tone was full of self-control. The quintessence of the fucking mother lode.

"What about you fucking Anabelle?" Juke asked. "Did the good Father happen to mention what part that played in God's big plan?"

Stunned, Castagnetti stared at Juke. He stammered for words, lost, looking as if he might fall from the stool. "I never. I don't know what—"

"Cut the shit," Juke said, slamming a fist down onto the oak. "Anabelle gave you up."

"But that's not why I shot him." There was such a panic in his tone. Not guilt, just disbelief.

"It ever run through your mind that Reggie knew?" Juke asked, grabbing hold of Castagnetti's collar, pulling him closer. "In that split second when you supposedly were imagining your wife in black, could you maybe have been thinking that Reggie had been waiting for this? Could that have crossed your mind instead? That Reggie knew you were fucking his wife. And now he was going to get even. Now he would take you down—"

"Stop it," Castagnetti said, pulling away. Standing back. Pacing. His hands frantically searching for a purpose. "It wasn't like that," he cried, running one hand through his hair. Putting the other in his pocket. "I was trying to help. I was doing Anabelle a favor."

"A two-million-dollar favor," Juke said, pushing the envelope a little.

"I didn't know anything about that," Castagnetti said. "She never told me about the policy."

"She never whispered in your ear how she was getting tired of the old bastard. How nice it would be—"

"No," Castagnetti said. "I went to help. She asked me to keep an eye on the kid. To help her keep Reggie under control. She didn't want to see him go over the deep end. She loved him, y'know?"

"Yeah. I know," Juke said.

And she had the American Express statements to prove it. Anabelle had insisted. Juke knew she wanted for him to believe her. And he did, regrettably. But still, he could have never guessed at the dollars spent, at the frequency of the visits. He had asked her again if it didn't bother her. "You don't actually think we met in the hardware aisle of the Super Kmart?" was her response.

Juke glared now at Castagnetti. Hating him, despite knowing his words rang true.

Figuring he owed her one, Anabelle had asked the rookie to intercede, to go easy on Reggie. That her husband didn't mean any of the threats. That he wasn't going to burn down the Robertsons' house. And that maybe if Castagnetti stayed on top of the situation, it would eventually blow over. It would eventually—

Anabelle didn't know Reggie had a gun.

Juke shook his head. It was still a mistake. Castagnetti should have stepped back. He should have never intervened. There was too much at stake, all too fucking personal. Fucking the perp's wife, for Christ's sake. Even if it were Reggie's idea. How would it look if it backfired? How would it—

But Castagnetti never expected that scene in the Robertsons' living room Monday afternoon. He never expected the boy would be dead. Or that Reggie would be packing. But the gods felt it was time for a little payback for the little pleasures. The gods made the rules. And payback was the bitch.

"Your wife know?" Juke asked.

Castagnetti shook his head. "It only happened a couple of times. It was—"

"Once was enough."

"It'd kill her if she found out."

"That's on your conscience, kid," Juke said. "It's none of my business whether she knows or not."

"Thank you," Castagnetti said.

"But Bradbury's another story."

The rookie blanched, his hands falling to his side. Limp and lifeless. "You want me to tell the Chief?"

Juke nodded.

"I can't." A panic setting in. "It'll—this won't—" He swallowed hard, raising a hand to his mouth, sucking in the breath from his palm. Pressing a nail between his teeth. "He'll take my badge away."

Juke stared at Castagnetti for a long time before speaking. "Better him than me."

thirty-nine

Piccerillo's envelope was on the kitchen table. Still sealed, it rested alongside Juke's keys, his wallet, and some pocket change. Juke was leaning against the counter, over in front of the sink, a bottle of ice-cold beer pressed to his lips. The bottle tipped up, the cold burning on the way down his throat, ripping off the heat like wax.

He finished off one bottle, and looked out the open window for a moment. No breeze stirred, just the cries of crickets, the trickle of water from the Mad River beyond. Even the moon seemed to be taking a break, resting behind clouds, laying its weary head, or not bothering to show up at all.

The door to the screened-in porch was open. Juke moved past it now, returning to the fridge for another. Twisting off its top, bottoms up as he walked over to the table.

Taking a deep breath, he stared at the envelope, wondering if he should bother now? Would it be a bust, or would it only keep him awake, turning, appraising, battling the demons? He had seen enough for one day. Heard enough.

He picked up the envelope, holding it up to the wrought-iron light over the table. Wanting to see into it, through it, to know if there was something Piccerillo could possibly tell him about this case. About who shot David—

It was the pop that he heard first.

Like backfire from a small car. The muffled ping of a softball blasted to the heavens by an aluminum bat.

The window above the sink shattered.

The bullet whistled past Juke's ear. He fell to the kitchen floor. Flat. Instinctive. Rolling away. Away from the open door. To the wall. The light switch. Reaching up. The switch at his fingertips—

Another gunshot.

A planted pot on the windowsill. Shards of clay. Sand. Leaves. Blasted into some flora eternity. The whoosh. Crack of wood. A dull thud.

And darkness—

The sounds of night. Of death and dying. Echoing in the room. Bouncing off the countertops. Bouncing on the floors. Slicing through time against the hard edges.

Juke, his breath slow and ragged. His back against the cabinet doors. Mind reeling. Why didn't he keep a spare gun under the sink? Or in a drawer. Anywhere, any gun. Any fucking gun would do.

"Shit!" he muttered.

There was an old service revolver upstairs. Closet, top shelf. Inside a fireproof box. With a trigger lock. And the fucking bullets in a fucking box in the fucking basement, with his fucking nightstick, belts, and shoes—a lot of fucking good they'd do him now.

He lay flat, then counted to three in his head. One—two—rolling. Hoping to get a look out the open door. Through the screening of the porch. Staying low. Praying invisible—

A third shot.

The blast. The sparks. The bullet ripped through the screening, not two feet from Juke's head.

"What the fuck?"

The shooter was on the lawn. Ten yards. Maybe not even that far away.

He heard the running. Breaths, heavy, frightened, panicked. A pant. An adrenaline surge.

And a small shriek—

Then silence.

He counted off in his head. One—two—three—four—it started again.

Careful now. Quiet. The breathing calm.

A sniffle—he was sure he heard a sniffle.

Crunching—dry leaves.

Slurping, sucking—footsteps in the mud.

Splashing.

Silence.

It had been a long time since Juke held a gun. The balance of it felt unfamiliar at first. Heavier than he remembered. The cold wooden grain of the grip deadweight in his right hand. Even loading it was a second-cousin he hadn't seen in years. Slipping a bullet into each chamber. The crisp clicks of metal against metal. The finality as he slapped the cylinder back and flipped off the safety. But he left the house now armed with that old Smith & Wesson model 36 service revolver—a five-shot .38. Along with his eternal penlight, not yet turned on, not unless he needed it.

No one was awake in Tompkins Glen. No neighbors stirred. No one questioned the noise. He doubted if anyone heard.

Just sound effects in the night, a TV too loud, or engine trouble. Toss once, turn, and go back asleep. Real gunshots were never as loud as they were in the movies, unless you were on the wrong side of them.

Crouched low, walking alongside his garage, Juke made it to the fence. Following along, the gate open. Shining the beam cautiously. Broken twigs. An indent in the leaves. Someone had been sitting. Waiting. Someone—

He spun around.

A thick branch, thigh high.

A flash of—

Pink.

"What the fuck?" he cursed, bending, brushing back some leaves.

Mostly hidden. Under a thick covering.

Thrown. Or perhaps, ripped off while running.

Holding it into the beam of light. Holding on to it. Taking it with him. Moving forward. Down the bank.

Broken branches. Terrified steps rearranging the earth. Then a few footsteps where the ground leveled out. So clean. Forever preserved in the mud.

Juke leaned close to the first. Fresh. Such a perfect imprint.

No more.

Stepping onto the footprint. His size-fourteen wiping it away.

Then the others. All the other tracks. Wiped clean. No one would know.

The long strides. Running fast. Away.

Into the water, finally.

The river would take care of those prints. The river would wash those sins away.

Into the heart of Tompkins Glen.

A thousand homes.

Ten thousand nightmares.

friday

forty

He chose a maroon tie, with soft splotches of color. Standing now before the oak-framed mirror mounted on the wall over his dresser, their dresser. Tying it slowly. Yesterday's Windsor knot had not been perfect, but today's would be.

Closure, Juke thought, and lies. The stench his ex-partner anticipated. "Something's got to stink somewhere."

He glanced down at the items lined atop the dresser. From left to right: his Smith & Wesson, loaded, safety off, tucked into a black leather shoulder holster; the three .38 slugs, one pulled from a can of pitted black olives, another from the wall just behind a battered can of tomato basil soup, the third from the frame of the cabinet located just under his sink. Though he had not seen the ballistics report, the markings on the bullet pulled from David Robertson's body, he was certain these would match.

He had made an early morning sweep of his lawn, looking for casings, finding none. There were no casings found in the Robertsons' home either. And in both incidences, Juke would have guessed a single-action revolver. The *same* single-action revolver. Another match.

Next: a pink leather fannypack. The belt set for a twenty-two-inch waist. The pink faded from what must have been bubblegum brightness. The buckle broken, yellowed Scotch tape stuck to the larger plastic piece. The zipper to the main compartment open, the compartment itself empty. Its inside lining mostly torn. The smaller compartment, zipped shut. Inside, an ID tag. If found please return to. A name. An address. A phone number. He had guessed that one right. Two-eight-six, eight-one-nine-four. And as for her name, well, perhaps the pieces had come together after all.

And lastly: Piccerillo's envelope. Slit open. Its contents unfolded and laying atop the bureau beside it. Four photocopied sheets of paper. An official Harmony, Connecticut police report on the burglary at the home of Neil and Sally Robertson. It contained the alleged time of the crime—Monday afternoon, at approximately three PM; the names of the officers present—Piccerillo, Zaretsky, Bradbury, and too many others; the areas in the house dusted for prints—the bedrooms and the basement door. It was filled with Piccerillo's inept typing, a lot of useless information which no one would ever need, or bother to read, until the last page, an inventory of what was taken.

Jewelry topped the list: the pearl necklace given to Sally by her son, diamond stud earrings, gold hoops, a tennis bracelet, Neil's gold watch, his high school graduation ring, various other necklaces, earrings, and rings, miscellaneous pins and brooches. More jewelry than Sally could ever wear.

Then there was the rest: a crystal candy dish, a CD player/boom box, a Mont Blanc fountain pen, an old 386 IBM-clone laptop computer, and lastly, a handycam. One of those 8mm video cassette recorders with the flip-out color viewfinders. It was in a dark green camera case, along with the Robertsons' collection of tapes, tapes from vacations, tapes of birthday parties, tapes of Christmas cheer.

It was the kicker. That something taken in a robbery on Monday afternoon could have been so clearly visible in the armoire of the Robertsons' bedroom on Wednesday evening.

And though one tidy explanation went through Juke's mind—a little innocent insurance fraud—they seemed secondary to speaking with the blonde girl from the photographs. The owner of the pink fannypack. She held the answers. She was the last person to see David Robertson alive. Of that, Juke was certain.

Sitting quietly in an aisle seat in the last row at David Robertson's last viewing, Juke watched the proceedings.

The turnout was larger. More press, more cops, more neighbors, more students. The Mayor had deemed this a day of mourning canceling classes in all of Harmony's public schools. The private schools had followed suit.

An unfamiliar dark-haired woman in her early forties sat with the Robertson family now. The grandparents separated her from Neil and Sally, but still the resemblance was remarkable. She had Neil's eyes, his nose. She must have been the sister Sally had mentioned. The Aunt Nancy from David's address book. The Aunt Nancy whose body language said so much. How she leaned away from her parents. Averted her eyes. It wasn't a casual dislike, but loathing, and perhaps fear. As if she felt violated just sitting there.

But there were tears in the woman's eyes as she looked over at the casket. As she stared at her nephew. Would she have felt the same way, would the tears be present, if she knew? If she had seen the photos of Natalie—"

"Mr. Miller."

Juke couldn't place the voice at first, though it triggered a gut clenching mechanism of contrition. Turning, his mouth dropping open just a bit, the shock of seeing her here.

"I would have thought you were beyond surprise."

"I can still be caught off guard," Juke said, standing, shaking the woman's hand. "Every now and then."

Lillian Sussman nodded. She was dressed in dark brown, and seemed younger than before. Her eyes a lot less tired.

"I had to see for myself," she said. "I had to know it was true."

*   *   *

Juke watched her walk to the casket. Kneeling before it, Lillian made a sign of the cross, her mouth seeming to move in prayer.

But Juke knew Lillian Sussman wasn't praying. She was speaking to David Robertson, telling him what went through her mind when she first found out he was dead. And everything since. She was describing her relief, her gratitude. Or how she had visited her daughter's grave, bringing fresh flowers. Probably telling him, "I told Natalie that you were burning in hell now, and that her soul could finally rest easy." Juke had had similar conversations a million times in his head.

She crossed herself again, then rising from the kneeler, reached out and squeezed David's hands. Juke understood that Lillian needed to know that David's hands were cold. She needed to feel his death, rejoice in it, praise God for it.

Walking slowly to where the Robertsons sat, she reached out first to Sally. It took a moment, but finally David's mother raised her glance, and tentatively reached out, her own hand trembling, as she shook Lillian's. A few words were exchanged. Seemingly polite enough.

Juke saw it as a transferral of grief, more closure. This time for Natalie's mother. While the chasm in Sally's life continued to expand. To deepen. To grow bottomless and hungry. She had to be wondering now, when would it end?

Lillian then turned to Neil. They shook hands as well, as he stared at her glassy-eyed and angry. The grandparents next. Neil's father nodding politely, his mother turning away.

The sister, though, Aunt Nancy, seemed not to notice Lillian Sussman. She seemed not to care, staring still at the coffin, at the face of the young boy within. Juke wondered about their connection. They couldn't possibly have been close. Not with the gaps that obviously separated her from the rest of the immediate family. Was it something else? Beyond blood? Something that intrinsically linked David Robertson to his aunt?

Juke hoped to God, no.

forty-one

Saint Joseph's Roman Catholic Church was a block and a half from Juke's Place. Smaller in both grandeur and congregation than Saint Thomas, the church had more of a local feel, a Tompkins Glen feel. The faces that attended were familiar to Juke when he happened to drive past just as mass was letting out. These were the faces of his neighbors, his customers, the people he once swore to protect and serve. These were the faces of those who sat in the pews behind him, the last time he entered the portals to this house of worship.

He was in the back now. One of the many paying their lasts. Sally and Neil Robertson were in that first pew, right side, just off the aisle. Only a few feet away, their son's casket, draped in a simple white linen cloth. And across the aisle, the pallbearers. Six men, Juke assumed, from Sullivan's. None of David's friends could have, nor should they have. He'd be sitting in that row tomorrow morning. With five others chosen by Anabelle.

The priest, Father Torre, was a fixture in Harmony, seemingly as old as the town itself. As wide as he was tall, with a bald head and a short-cropped white beard, the priest swung a metal ball filled with incense around the casket. A gesture wasted on Juke. A gesture, he was sure, wasted on most everyone attending. The smells wafted through the church, accompanying the sounds of sobbing, of sniffles, the occasional cough. The dirge of the church organ, something sounding remotely like Bach.

Father Torre eulogized the boy. He spoke of innocence lost, of suffering, of sorrow. He willed David's soul toward the gates of heaven, praising God's wisdom, God's greater plan, God's greater good. He quoted a few different passages from the Bible. Juke remembered that same priest once asking him if his wife had had any favorite biblical passages. The sixth commandment was all Juke could think of at the time.

And when communion was passed out, the flock divided into two groups. The sinners—cops and reporters—on one side, seated, eyes cast downward. The blessed, the meek, the holy on the other, walking down the aisle, as a vocalist sang "Ave Maria," tongues out, hands folded in prayer, on their way toward inheriting this earth.

The procession moved slowly. Down Wright Avenue into Centerville. A right onto Harrison Street. A half mile to just before the North Haven line. A left onto the one-lane drive. Past the stone archway, the sprawling hills stretching out, the greens yawning with monolith teeth. Juke had spent so many hours walking the paths between the tombstones and grave markers at Mount Olivet Cemetery. His thoughts scattered as rain fell, snow accumulated, the sun rose, or darkness engulfed all around. There were moments when he wondered if he'd ever leave. There was never a doubt as to how soon he'd return.

He stood at the edge of the group, waiting.

"We've got an opening, if you're interested."

"What's that?"

Juke turned to face his ex-partner, his suit a little less wrinkled than usual. Perhaps Cathy Piccerillo had helped that morning. *"You're going to a funeral,"* was what she probably had said, *"You've got to look nice."*

Zaretsky was standing by Piccerillo's side. She wore black, her hair pulled back. She nodded this time, first.

"Morning," Juke said.

"You can once again become one of Harmony's finest," Piccerillo answered. "Castagnetti turned his badge in this morning."

"You don't say," Juke said.

"Something about him and his wife moving out of town," Piccerillo said, glancing back and forth between Juke and Zaretsky.

Juke figured Piccerillo was looking for sparks between the two of them. "Getting on with their lives?" he suggested.

"Running away from something," Piccerillo said, shooting him a questioning look. "If you ask me."

Juke answered with the slightest of shrugs. Peter Castagnetti wasn't worth the energy, or the breath. Juke got him to turn in the badge, got him off the force. Hopefully guilt would take care of the rest.

"We're, ah, off to talk to a pawn broker in Bridgeport," Piccerillo said. "He thinks he might have some of the missing jewelry."

Juke nodded. There was no missing jewelry, as far as he was concerned. At least no missing handycam.

"What happened to—" he stopped himself short.

"The animal rights thing?" Piccerillo said. "She knows I told you." He nodded at Zaretsky. "I was so pissed off, she knew I'd tell somebody."

"He always tells somebody," Juke said.

"Thanks for the warning," Zaretsky said, then, "Old Maid Marion—"

"She's learning quick," Juke said.

"Got me for a teacher," Piccerillo said.

"Despite that."

"—he, um, got off it—the animal rights kick. Thought the idea might be a little far-fetched."

"A little," Juke said. "That was a stretch even for him."

"I guess sleeping on it wised him up."

"It'd take more than a good night's sleep to wise him up," Piccerillo said. "Years in this place, maybe." He smiled. "Now there's a thought."

They watched in silence as Father Torre blessed the coffin. Sally and Neil stepped forward, each with a single rose. They placed them atop the polished wood. Sally turning first, burying her face against her husband's shoulder. Her hands covering her eyes. Then palms turning, pressing against him. Pushing away. Holding each other's gaze for a moment. And walking away.

"What'd'ya say we blow this dump, Zaretsky?"

Zaretsky looked up at Juke for a moment, then without turning to face her partner, "Give me a minute, will you?"

Piccerillo held his hands up, *nolo contendre*, and walked toward his car. He was whistling something. The tune carrying just far enough for Juke and Zaretsky to hear. It was an old Beatles melody, one of their cornier love songs, a little out of tune, a lot out of place, but his message unmistakable.

When Piccerillo was finally out of earshot, when the serenade was over, Zaretsky said, "Can we, um," she corrected herself, "Can I start again? Fresh. Forget those—" She exhaled loudly. "I like you, Juke. I find you attractive. Very attractive. I think you're sweet. And, well, Goddamnit, I—how about dinner some night? I'll cook. You bring the wine. We can sit around and talk, just me and you, no prying eyes, no ex-boyfriends, no customers, no—" She shook her head. "Maybe that's all we'll do. We'll just see what happens. I'd like to at least have that. To give it a shot. I'd hate to think that I had a shot, but I blew it completely, because I—" She stopped herself short. "I'm doing it again, aren't I? I always do this. Talk too damn much. Go on and on. Ramble." She turned away, a little red faced. "You make me nervous, I—aw, shit."

But when she turned back to face him, Juke knew it had to have been obvious. He could tell from the look in her eyes, the blush fading to embarrassment. He went to speak, but she held up her hand, nodding. She took a step back, a step away.

"You don't have to say anything," she said, turning finally, hurrying to Piccerillo's car.

Juke let her go. He watched her walk away. He knew there was a pawn shop owner in Bridgeport waiting to be interviewed.

forty-two

Juke was standing at the outer edge of the mourners, when Sally and Neil Robertson walked by. Stopping, Sally turned back, stepped up to her neighbor, and squeezed his hand.

"Will you please stop by for something to eat?"

"Of course," Juke said.

"Thank you," she said, holding his gaze for a moment, then taking a step away, moving on.

Juke looked then to Neil, standing as he had been, a half-step behind his wife. He'd yet to move, to follow Sally, instead holding Juke's glance for a heartbeat, not really looking at him, just past him. Juke figured he was gazing into a future, perhaps, when all this would seem a distant memory. When this day would fail to elicit tears. Looking to Juke as an instance of survival. A record that we can persist.

Bad example, Juke thought, watching him walk away finally, following his wife into the limousine. The grandparents a few steps behind. The sister walking to another car. Its Florida license plate. The schoolmates and teachers in orderly fashion to a yellow school bus. The reporters pulling up roots, on to other stories. The other cops on to other crimes.

"Always the last to leave," Wilbur Cross said, stopping by Juke's side, flipping the perpetual notebook shut, tucking it into his jacket pocket. Even he was ironed to almost perfection.

Those Tompkins Glen dry cleaners, Juke thought, giving the old news hound a half smile, before stepping not toward his car, but deeper into the cemetery.

"Unfinished business," he said.

The grave was on the crest of Mount Olivet's highest hill. A lovely cascading view of the towns that surrounded them. The richness of North Haven, the family neighborhoods of Harmony, the monuments of East Rock and the high-rises of New Haven beyond. Everything looked safe and clean. Even the Mad River looked serene.

And there was always a breeze, even on the scorchers. It evened out the humidity, and carried with it the scent of flowers. It was a lovely last resting place. The reason Juke bought it for her. It was the sort of place they'd have picnicked at. A bottle of red wine, some cheese and fresh bread. And her falling asleep, her head propped against his thigh, as he brushed the hair from her face, or scratched softly at the back of her neck. Her peaceful, sleepy look turning to a frown the moment he stopped. Her hand tapping his to continue please.

The stone was gray marble. Wider than it was tall. Decorated with an engraving of the two contemplative angels from Raphael's "Sistine Madonna." She'd always loved angels, always loved that picture.

Under the right angel, its hands crossed at the wrists, the following words were engraved: "Good night, sweet darling, and flights of angels sing thee to thy rest. Margaret Larrgieu Miller, born August 2, 1961, died April 20, 1991."

His Maggie.

Juke knelt in front of the monument. Eyes closed, his fingers tracing lightly over her name. This wasn't a moment of grief, but one of contemplation. Like the two angels, he was looking skyward for guidance. Not to a god he doubted and distrusted, but to Maggie.

The muffled sobs came to his ears on the breeze. Juke listened, wondering for a moment if they were echoes lost in time. This place had seen so many tears, heard so many cries, including his own, perhaps a few got trapped. Or maybe they felt comfortable here, haunting the hills, bouncing off the monuments. Finally a place sorrow could call home.

He stood, following the sound, just down the hill a row of monuments, and to the left. It came from the other side of a statue of the Virgin Mary. She towered over the grounds, protecting the loved ones buried there. Her arms spread wide for all the children of God.

She didn't notice Juke at first. A tall lanky girl who couldn't have been more than fourteen. She wore dark green shorts and a white and beige striped t-shirt. Her light blonde hair cut into a chin-length bob, pushed mostly back behind her ears. A few strands falling free. She was seated on the grass at the base of the statue, her head bent forward, hands pressed to her eyes. Her tears flowed freely, a sob which moved in time to her breathing, all hiccups and sniffles.

"Megan Wechsler?" he said, as softly as possible.

It was the name on the fannypack's ID tag. The last name of the woman in his bar. Dr. Eva Wechsler, no wonder she looked familiar. Zoë had noticed she wasn't wearing a wedding ring. Too bad she hadn't asked about kids.

Megan sniffled one last time, loud and definitive, then wiped at her eyes. She looked up to face Juke. Her green eyes courageous, despite her obvious fear.

Juke knelt close to her. There was the same hardness in her

mouth, still frowning slightly down at one corner. The angle of her face, so defiantly to the side. Could Megan Wechsler hate Juke as much as she had hated David Robertson? Did she feel he represented the same threat?

"I won't hurt you," he said.

She reacted as if it were a lie she'd heard a hundred times before. "What do you want?" she asked, pulling back, pressing against the statue. "I can't—" Her eyes watered back up, and she covered her mouth with one hand.

"To talk to you," Juke said. "I need to know what happened. He was my friend."

Her voice was loud. Angry. "David wasn't—"

"Not David," Juke said. "Reggie."

forty-three

They were seated in Juke's kitchen. The ride had been silence mostly, punctuated by small outbursts of tears. Juke glancing over at the girl as she stared stone-faced out the window. Only once did she look at him. Only once did she speak.

"What could you gain by killing me?" he had asked.

"Freedom," she had said.

Juke had poured her a glass of soda which sat untouched now on the table in front of her. Megan wouldn't look at it, she wouldn't look up.

He was on his second cup of coffee, his jacket off, tie off, the top button open, the shoulder-holstered service revolver placed on the top shelf of a cabinet over the fridge. Tired of the silence, the unanswered questions, Juke stood abruptly. Heading upstairs, his size making the stairs creak, both coming and going. He returned with the pink fannypack, placing it down on the table in front of her, then reclaimed his seat.

"You dropped this."

Megan raised her glance only enough to take in the fannypack.

She nodded, then raised a hand out to touch the old leather. When she spoke, her tone was soft, a whisper, almost as if she were speaking to herself. Comforting herself with memories of a time before.

"I was nine and I just really wanted this. More than anything." She lifted the fannypack off the table, pulling it onto her lap. "My mom bought it for me at the North Haven fair. It was like, I never took it off until the buckle broke." She was wringing the pink leather with her hands. "David's the one who told me all about you. About you being a detective, and all. How you solved every case. And then," Megan shrugged, "your wife."

"Yeah," Juke said. "That changed everything."

"You went crazy," Megan said.

"We all go crazy sometimes," Juke said. "Especially when we can't explain things."

"I know that."

"Yeah. I know you do," he said, then, "What happened to the gun, Megan?"

"I was so scared my mother would find it. I had it hidden in the attic, in an old box of toys. In the bedroom of my Barbie Dream House."

"Is that where it is now?"

She let out a long breath, and said, "No. I got rid of it."

"And no one'll ever find it?" Juke asked.

"No one'll ever find it," she said.

"Are you sure?"

"Yes."

Juke nodded a few times, then let out a small laugh. "Good," he said.

Megan finally looked up.

"You don't understand," Megan Wechsler said, the floodgates down, the tears rushing out with the words, her sounds, her soul laid bare. "I've been watching you. Since that afternoon. And that night when you dug up the dog. I knew you had it all figured out.

And that you must have had the pictures. Especially after you called from David's room."

"How'd you know it was me who called?"

"Who else could it have been?" she asked, rubbing at her eyes. "It had to be you."

Juke nodded. "Why were you wearing your school uniform in the pictures? It was Sunday night, right?"

"He wanted me to wear it," she said. "He liked it. He—oh, God, I didn't want my mom to see those pictures. She could never see those pictures. You understand? It would kill her. She'd be so mad at me, so disappointed. She'd never speak to me again. I'd prefer to die first, I'd prefer to—"

Juke watched the fourteen-year-old as she tried so hard to keep it together. A little dignity, whatever strength she had left. It ripped his heart that she'd even need to, ever need to. That she'd been placed in this situation. Boys-will-be-boys. Bullshit, he thought.

"What makes you think I'd ever show those pictures to your mother?" he asked.

But Megan didn't have an answer. Just more tears. The whimpering that takes the place of breathing.

"Come with me," he said, standing, taking her hand gently.

He led her toward the living room, then motioned toward the Stickley chair.

"Have a seat."

Megan sat at its edge, the sobs subsiding for now into hiccups and gasps, watching as Juke squatted before the bottom shelf of a built-in bookcase. He retrieved a coffee-table book of paintings, cracked it open, and from it pulled the plastic sheets of negatives, the proofs, the enlargements. Everything he'd taken from David Robertson's darkroom.

"Are those?"

"Yes," Juke said, standing, turning back, and finally handing them to her.

Megan's pictures were on top of the pile. She held up the sheet, the twenty-five negatives, toward the window. The sunlight streaming through the blinds giving her more than enough light to help her relive. She didn't cry now, but instead shook her head a number of times, angrily.

The sound caught her attention. One loud clang.

Juke was kneeling in front of the fireplace, its screen pushed aside. His hand reaching in, opening the flue. He struck a match to some kindling, which ignited the firewood he kept on the grate year-round. It looked nice, and in New England the temperature could always drop to fireplace time.

Then Juke stood back, taking a seat opposite Megan in the old wooden rocker.

"Your call," he said to the girl.

Megan stared at him for a moment, looked over at the fire, then back. "Really?" she asked.

"Yes," he said.

"Thank you," she said, moving off the chair, dropping to her knees in front of the fireplace.

She turned the pile of negatives and proofs and enlargements over, and placed them down on the floor in front of her. Starting now at the bottom, the oldest photos first, she lifted one sheet, and glanced at the shots of Natalie Sussman. Her eyes displayed confusion, and then pain, as she stared at the images.

Juke wondered exactly what was going through the girl's mind as she lowered them onto the flames. The photographic paper cracking and curling, the negatives *whooshing* to ashes. What had David told her about her predecessor? Did he tell her how Natalie Sussman had died? Did he tell Megan she was next, if she didn't—

She got into a rhythm. As soon as one sheet was destroyed, it would be followed by the next, an enlargement, or more negatives, more proofs, more negatives. She no longer stopped to glance at the photos. Juke could tell she had seen enough, watching her as the last remnants of Natalie Sussman's horror crinkled to dust, and only two plastic sheets of negatives remained: those of Reggie and Molasses, and those of herself.

When Megan spoke again, it was to the flames. It was to the ashes. "I was so scared he was going to show these to my mom," she said, holding on to the hellish images a moment longer, then inching them finally into the fireplace. Side-by-side. A promising grace note to such wretchedness.

Both she and Juke watched the pictures ignite. As Megan's hell, her torment, burned away. Dissolving before both their eyes.

They stayed that way, Megan kneeling in front of the fireplace, Juke watching her from the rocking chair, until the embers faded, and finally died away. He didn't care what Old Maid Marion would say, or Piccerillo, or any of the others. If and when they'd ever find out. It'd been his call. As far as he was concerned, his case. Only he'd seen the photos. Only he'd met the girl. And Juke was quite certain Reggie, his dear friend Reggie, wouldn't have wanted it any other way.

He broke the silence finally, offering Megan advice he wished he one day would be strong enough to heed. It was a variation on the same theme he'd heard a thousand times over during the past seven years. Perhaps she'd be wise enough.

"Move on with your life, Megan," Juke said. "Forget about David Robertson."

Megan stared into the fireplace, the finality seeming to set off another round of tears. No sobs this time, and her chest wasn't heaving, just the wetness rolling down her cheeks onto her knees.

"But," she said, turning to look at Juke.

He wished he could stop her from crying. That there were some secret words to alleviate the sorrow.

"What?" he asked.

"I loved David."

Juke could feel the walls crumbling. The fingers snapping off rounds in his head. One for anger. One for stupidity. One for *What the fuck was wrong with the human race?*

He dropped to his knees in front of Megan, and grabbed her shoulders. He shook the girl, looking into her eyes.

"How could you love someone who'd do that to you?" he yelled. "How could you love someone who'd poison a dog just to watch it die?"

Her tears stopped abruptly, and Megan began shaking her head, muttering a word over and over again.

"No," she said. "No."

Juke let go of her shoulders, and fell back. Sitting on the floor, he rubbed at his face with his hands. Breathing deeply, evenly, he needed for this to subside. He needed—

"You don't understand," Megan said, her voice surprisingly calm.

Juke couldn't look at her. Fourteen and already the excuses for abuse. Already the denial. "Then why don't you explain," he said, disgusted.

"David didn't take those pictures," Megan said.

The words stung. And Juke spun back around to face her. "What?" he said.

"I thought you knew. I thought you were the one who had figured everything out," she said.

"What are you talking about?" Juke asked.

"David didn't take those pictures," she said. "He didn't poison Molasses either."

"But—"

"He loved dogs," she explained. "Our dog Phoebe just had a litter. I was going to give David one of the puppies."

Juke could only stare in open-mouth shock.

"What happened to Molasses was a warning," Megan said. "The puppy would have gotten it ten times worse."

forty-four

The slam of the car door shattered what remained. The splinters of logic coming apart at the seams. The question had never been who killed David Robertson, but who killed Natalie Sussman? Who took those photographs? Who killed Reggie's dog? Juke had let the obvious blind him, the open and shut of it all. That David was guilty beyond the reasonable, and someone would want him dead. Someone would want for the humiliation to stop. He had bet on the same question that plagued Piccerillo, Zaretsky and Bradbury, but for different reasons. And still he lost. David Robertson had been a victim. Like Megan. Like Natalie before her. Like Reggie and his dog. He was the good kid after all. The football hero with the all-American smile. And he had suffered the greatest embarrassment of them all, and at the hands of—

Juke rushed from the house, toward the sound. Megan's voice, a repercussion in his mind, *David didn't take those pictures.* The look in the girl's eyes, *I was so scared he was going to show these to my mom.* The *he*, not David—Christ! She loved David. The choking in her voice as she said it. The emotion so Goddamn real.

Why hadn't Juke seen it? Why? he screamed in his head. Blind, he had been blinded by his perception of evil, of what he thought David was capable of. Of what he knew we were all capable of. And he had turned away, too soon, not needing to see more. What the fuck was wrong with him?

Neil Robertson was standing by his car, loosening his tie, undoing the top button of his pressed white cotton shirt. He noticed Juke walking toward him.

"Just dropped my parents off at the train station," Neil said, mountains of relief in his voice.

Juke responded with a hand wrapped around Neil's throat, lifting the small man off the ground, pressing him back against the side of his Dodge. His other hand balled into a fist, pumping air.

"Give me a reason, you fuck," Juke said, through clenched teeth. "Give me a reason not to kill you."

But Neil couldn't speak, he could barely breathe.

"I've seen the pictures," Juke said, his voice pinched with strife. "All the pictures. I know about Natalie Sussman." He slammed Neil hard against the car door. "About Megan." Again. "I know you killed Reggie's dog." Again. The Detroit metal buckling under pressure.

"No." Neil spit out the word, clawing at Juke's hand. But he was overpowered, overmatched. His eyes darted back and forth in a panic. Darted right and left and—

He stared over Juke's shoulder in shock.

Juke turned to see what his neighbor was looking at.

A flash of blonde hair. A lanky girl standing on Juke's lawn. The look in her face, the slightest hint of relief. She was watching, nodding. Taking a step back, another, and another, then turning, and running down the street.

"Fuck," Neil muttered.

"That you, Neil?" The voice came from behind the front screen door. Sally calling out, tentative, worried perhaps.

She had lost so much already, Juke thought, and now she was about to lose what was left. He let up his hold on her husband's throat, and took a step back, a beat into civility, just for show as Sally stepped onto the porch.

"Oh, Mr. Miller, what perfect timing," Sally said, smiling at Juke. "Dinner's just ready. Won't you please join us?"

They were in the dining room. Neil sitting at the head of the table, Sally to his right, and Juke, the added place setting, to his left, across from Sally. There were just burgers, some grilled peppers and onions, homemade steak fries, potato salad. Beers all around.

Sally, an apron protecting the black dress she wore to her son's funeral, was talking about the service, the mass. About how Ruth Sullivan had delivered everything she promised. With her voice catching in her chest, Sally said she felt good about the way her son was buried. It was proper, proud. He could rest in peace now.

"I wouldn't have wanted it any other way," she said.

Neil seemed to be avoiding conversation. His gaze aimed downwards, he finished one burger, then started in on another. Only a few potatoes gone from his plate, he was already on to his second beer, drinking it quickly.

Juke stared at him as the pieces of the puzzle fell together in his mind: Neil faked a burglary to make sure the investigation strayed as far off path as possible, and collected a little insurance money in the meanwhile. Nice, and break your wife's heart yet again. That necklace. Neil could have let that necklace slip through. He could have found it behind a bureau and brought a smile to Sally's face. Yeah, that was the least he could have fucking done. Juke hated him now even more for taking that necklace away from his wife.

A nauseous look crossed Neil's face. He pressed one hand to his stomach, the other to his mouth. Juke forced himself to turn away. He didn't understand the needs, the havoc these sort of demons wreaked on one's soul. All David wanted was a dog. He wondered about Neil's rationalization. What he told his son on one of the last days of his life? *"Who the fuck has time for a dog?"* or, *"I'll show you what I'll do to your dog."* And how killing Molasses set everything in motion.

Juke looked at Sally.

"This seemed like such a perfect place to raise a child," she said, turning, looking to her husband. "Don't you agree, Neil?"

But instead of answering, Neil lowered his second burger back onto his plate, and pressed a hand to his mouth as if to cover a belch. He looked pallid, and seemed to be sweating.

"Something's not right," Neil muttered at a barely audible clip.

"You okay?" Sally asked.

Neil looked at her with a start. "No, I—" He went to stand, his legs shaky, his hands trembling as they held on to the tabletop. "I need to get to the bathroom—"

"I really don't think so," she said.

Juke and Neil turned to face Sally Robertson at the same moment. There was something numbing about her tone, a little too calm, a little too congenial. The glint caught their attention. She was holding a gun. A cheap .38, a Saturday Night Special. And it was aimed directly at her husband.

"What are you doing?" Neil asked, his voice dry as he swallowed back the retch rising suddenly in his throat.

"Sit down, Neil," she said. "And finish your food."

"We were supposed to have started over, Mr. Miller," Sally said, then, "May I call you, Juke?"

"Yes," Juke said, staring at the gun, his hands flat against the tabletop.

"Good," she said. "Call me, Sally."

"Stop this," Neil said, "Stop this now." He was clutching at his stomach, pressing hard into it. His breath coming in short spurts. He screamed at Juke. "Do something, for Christ's sake."

"I told you to eat," Sally said.

"Fuck you," Neil screamed.

"No," Sally said, calmly, so matter-of-factly, lowering her aim and shooting once.

Neil cried out as the bullet sliced into his thigh. The tears streaming suddenly down his face. His fist smashed hard against the table, breaking a small plate, sending a butter knife flying to the floor, its sound dampened by the rug.

"Eat," she said, raising her aim just a little.

Neil held up a trembling hand. "Okay," he said, "okay, okay," repeating it a few times more, just mutters fading away. Then, picking up the burger, he raised it to his lips, and took a small nibble, then another, never taking his gaze off his wife, his hateful—

"That's better," Sally said, and turning to Juke, explaining matter-of-factly, "They're poisoned, the burgers. Same thing he used on that poor dog." She shook her head, then added quickly, "Not yours, of course."

Both she and Juke looked down at his plate. The burger was untouched.

"But I'll understand if you've lost your appetite," she said.

"He's going to die," Juke said, turning slowly to look at Neil, who continued to eat, forcing a swallow as a convulsion racked his chest. His trembling a counterpoint to the rhythmic dripping of blood from his thigh to the puddle that was forming below.

Sally nodded. "Such a sorry excuse for a human being," she said, her voice repulsed, watching her husband for a moment, then turning back to Juke, her tone switching back, the cordial host once again. "I bought this gun back in New Jersey. After what he did to Natalie," a half-laugh at the ludicrous, "what he did to David."

There was a long pause, and Juke could only imagine the images in Sally's head. Were they that much worse than the images Neil had preserved on film?

"How'd you get it back?" he asked.

"Megan, she, um," but Sally shook her head, as if she'd told a secret. "You know about Megan?"

Juke nodded.

"Of course you do," she said, then, "I should have killed Neil then, Juke. Back in New Jersey. I should have, but we moved. And he promised that he'd changed. That he'd never again—I believed him. Or at least I wanted to believe him. I wanted to believe that we could be a happy family. I truly wanted that more than—And then David, poor David." She took a deep breath, and then another. "Those pictures I showed you. In his darkroom. They were all his. He loved to take pictures. But then his father stepped in. He asked to borrow the camera. How to develop the pictures. He took everything that was important to David. Everything! Just took it away—Christ!"

She covered her face for a moment, not breathing now, not moving. When she spoke again, her voice was flat. "Neil took the photo of Natalie that hung on David's bedroom wall. I think David hung it there just to spite his father. Can't say that I blamed him."

"Why let it go on?" Juke asked.

"Because I was a fool. Because I thought it would get better. Because I was afraid that it was somehow my fault. That we, David and myself, were also to blame for what happened to Natalie. For what happened." She shook her head, then added softly. "All he wanted was a puppy."

She glanced over at Neil. "I was going to kill him myself. Kill my husband. Get it over with on my lunch hour. After what he did to the dog, what he did to Megan later that night. I wasn't going to let it go on one more day. Not one more—but he got called into work. Work saved his life."

She raised a steak fry to her mouth and took a bite. "When I told David I'd take care of everything. That I wouldn't let what happened to Natalie happen to Megan, he must have figured it out. He was a smart boy, Juke. He found the gun."

Sally turned back to her husband. "You were supposed to die, not my son. You!" Her voice raised in volume with her anger. Years of reprehension, of private humiliation. "How many families can you destroy? How many, Neil? How many?" She screamed now, the thoughts fragmented and disgusted. "How fucking stupid do you think I am? That poor little girl, and her mother. They blamed David and you didn't even care. You didn't even care."

She looked to Juke again, the switch not as complete. Shakes, and her tone a little too loud, the words coming a little too fast. "I waited too long," Sally said. "Too long."

"Do you know how your son died?" Juke asked.

Sally nodded. "David was showing the gun to Megan. Such a sweet girl. Showing her how to hold it. How she didn't have to worry. How he was going to kill the sonofabitch. Stop him. When your friend Reggie came in." Sally's voice started to fade out. Her tone became listless, her eyes glossed over. "He scared them, that's all. She pulled the trigger by mistake. She—"

"Mrs. Robertson," Juke said.

"Sally," she corrected.

"Sally," he said, his voice even, not soothing, not angry. Just conversational. "It's not too late. We can save your husband if we get him to a hospital now. Let the police handle this matter. He'll spend the rest of his life in jail. I promise you that. Please." He held out a hand, stretching it across the table. "Let me have the gun."

She looked over at Neil. He was pressing his fists into his stomach, groaning. His skin had turned a pasty white, his eyes rolling back slightly into his head.

"He could live through this?" she asked.

"Yes," Juke said. "If we hurry."

Sally nodded her understanding. Raising the gun, she took aim at her husband's face, and shot once. The side of his head exploded against the far wall, his body falling backwards in the chair, lying immediately still, immediately dead.

She watched Neil for a moment, as if to make sure that he was dead. Then turning back to face Juke, Sally raised the gun to her own temple. "This really seemed like such a nice place to raise a child," she said, pulling the trigger.

saturday

forty-five

Dr. Birnbaum handed Juke the small leather pouch. It was filled, its contents soft like the insides of a pillow. A draw string held it shut, double knotted.

"And there was this," the vet said, giving Juke a folded-in-half yellow slip of paper. "Found it under the bedding."

He unfolded it and read. A receipt. Dated a year earlier. A pawn shop in Maine. Juke remembered when Reggie and Anabelle took the trip. He'd taken care of Molasses, letting the dog sleep over at his place, up on the couch. He was pretty sure they had watched a ballgame together.

According to the receipt, Reggie had paid one hundred, seventy-five dollars for a used Walther P-88 9mm automatic pistol. Juke was also pretty sure Reggie bought it while Anabelle was herself shopping elsewhere, or taking a nap, or—so much for the Salvation Army gun shop. Anabelle would have known. She'd have said something.

Nodding to himself, Juke wondered if we can ever truly know

anyone? Or are there always secrets, little asides, mistresses of truth? Mistresses—yeah. Reggie hadn't seemed like the gun type, what was that anyway? *"He didn't seem the part."* The cliché of those who have done wrong, and their neighbors, their good-natured, good-hearted, well-intentioned neighbors, saying he seemed like such a nice man. So quiet. Never bothered anyone.

And why had Reggie kept the gun a secret? Was it the one thing he could hold back from them both. From Anabelle, from—

Christ! Juke wouldn't have cared. He wouldn't have pressured Reggie to get the damn thing registered. That wasn't their relationship. Reggie was old enough to know what he wanted, old enough to know better.

Putting the receipt in his pocket, knowing there were no easy answers, that there'd never be any, Juke looked up at the vet.

"What do I owe you?"

Birnbaum held up a hand, and in his soothing voice said, "An explanation, one of these days. I think this is a story I'd like to hear."

The turnout surprised Juke. It would have astonished Reginald Michael DeLillo. He'd have beamed at the thought that this many people cared. That he had this many friends, even if many of them were just curious onlookers. "They came, didn't they," he'd have argued, a Pabst Blue Ribbon in one hand.

Juke sat this time at the end of the receiving line. That first row which began with the widow at the side of the coffin, and curved around, leading, blending in with the other rows, mingling those closest to the deceased with the other mourners.

"You were his best friend," Anabelle had insisted. "He'd have wanted you here. I want you here."

Juke didn't argue. He greeted the mourners, many people he had never seen before. A few beautiful young women who hugged Anabelle dearly. He wondered which one was Heather, the breeder of weimaraners.

He shook everyone's hands, accepted their sympathies, agreed when they talked about Reggie. What a guy! And nodded solemnly when they spoke of the way he died.

And when the congratulations came, congratulation for helping to solve the mystery of David Robertson's murder, Juke could only shrug. It had been a long night—helping Piccerillo, Zaretsky, and Old Maid Marion come to an understanding, a decidedly slanted view of what took place Monday afternoon at the Robertson home, what took place Friday evening.

Juke confirmed the obvious, that Sally shot Neil, and that her pistol and the gun used to kill David were one and the same. He told them that she had blamed Neil for poisoning Reggie's dog, blamed him for destroying their family, their lives. Then she took her own life. There was closure in these statements. More so than not.

He omitted two details, Megan Wechsler and Natalie Sussman, for reasons he knew in his heart were right. But these particulars wouldn't matter, just as the two unidentified sets of fingerprints found in the house could have belonged to anyone. The case was just open and shut enough for the Chief's liking, murder weapon and all. Time for Piccerillo and Zaretsky to move on. For the people of Harmony to move on. Time to heal. Neither the Chief, the detectives, nor Juke, could argue that fact.

When everyone but Anabelle had filed out of the viewing room, Juke stepped past the widow, and over to the coffin. There was something vaguely nostalgic about seeing Reggie this way. All those naps out on the deck. The only thing missing was the sound effects of him and the dog snoring.

Juke leaned in close, over the casket, and pressed his right hand over Reggie's.

"You were a good friend," he said, letting the leather pouch drop from the sleeve of his left arm, into the casket.

He discreetly pushed it deep with his fingertips, under Reggie's bulk. Then straightening, noticing nothing, he squeezed his neighbor's hand one last time, and stepped away.

They'd be together now. Reggie and Molasses chasing tennis balls and drinking Pabst in the holy land. Hope they find some shade, Juke thought. A nice spot for a picnic. For that cookout. And Maggie. She'd be pleased to see them again.

sunday

forty-six

He sat on the sunporch. It was a beautiful morning, mid-seventies, no humidity, as if Reggie was finally taking control of the thermostat up above. The time was after eleven, but still the Sunday *New York Times* was mostly untouched on the floor by Juke's feet. Instead he nursed a Pabst, the last can in the fridge, knowing that he'd never get used to the taste. He doubted that even from the grave Reggie would want him to.

He was thinking about yesterday. How as he left the Harmony Veterinary Hospital, Dr. Birnbaum called after him, "Make sure you bring her in for her shots."

"What was that?" Juke had asked, stopping in his tracks, turning to face the doctor, who jerked his thumb toward the bright yellow poster still thumbtacked to the bulletin board.

The details caught Juke's eye: "Free lab pups to good home. Meet their mom, Phoebe. Call 286-8194."

"Megan Wechsler called the other day," Birnbaum said. "Told me you called about the pups, but that she lost your phone number."

"So you gave it to her?" Juke said, the final piece of the puzzle slipping into place.

"Yeah," Birnbaum said. "When're you getting the dog?"

The doorbell rang.

He half expected Anabelle. She said she'd be going through Reggie's things, and if she found something she thought Juke might like, she'd bring it over. But the front door? Maybe after the other night, Juke thought, opening the door, then taking a half step back from the surprise of seeing the two of them.

"Mr. Miller," the familiar voice said. "I'd like you to meet my mom, Dr. Wechsler."

His attention was drawn to one side. Megan, a squirming black bundle of fur in her arms, stood alongside her mom. She was smiling.

"Eva," the woman said, extending her hand.

"Juke," he said, a little unnerved, but shaking it.

She was wearing jeans again, and a button-down cotton shirt, sleeves rolled up. Juke was wearing jeans and a button-down linen shirt, sleeves rolled up. He wondered if she noticed.

"I never thanked you for that drink," Eva said, then turning to her daughter. "The other night, Juke bought everyone at my table a drink."

"That was nice of him," Megan said.

"I owed Dr. Birnbaum a favor," Juke explained.

"You'll owe him plenty more," Eva said, staring at Juke, a small smile playing at the corners of her mouth, the same smile as when she sipped the wine, a little distraction in her tone.

"Excuse me?" he said.

"Megan told me you called. About how you missed your neighbor's dog." She shook her head. "I read the story in the paper today. You must be devastated."

"I'm glad it's over," he said, looking back and forth between mother and daughter, trying to comprehend. Had he missed something here? Had he—

"I'm hoping this isn't too soon," Eva said, misinterpreting his confusion. "I mean, after everything, but it is the perfect time. She just turned eight weeks old today."

"She?" Juke asked.

Megan stepped forward and handed Juke the bundle of fur. A wrinkled black pup, with a whip of a tail that was going a mile-a-minute. Juke reluctantly took hold of the dog, which licked at his face with a G-force tongue, causing Megan and Eva to laugh. Juke struggled to hold on to the excitable sack of loose hair and bones, himself finally breaking a smile.

"She's our favorite," Megan said.

"Cute as anything," Eva said.

"What's her name?" he asked, staring into the dog's deep brown eyes. Such mischief. "Hey, girl," he said, scratching behind her ear.

"Uh-uh," Eva said. "That's your job."

"I was saving her for a friend," Megan explained, staring at Juke, her eyes telling him everything he needed to know. "But he changed his mind. His parents wouldn't let him have a dog."

"I can't imagine life without a dog," Eva said, leaning forward, scratching at the pup's chin, her fingers brushing by Juke's. "I don't care what side of the bed you get up on in the morning, a dog will make your day." She looked up, catching Juke's stare, holding it for a heartbeat. "Their love is so unconditional. They're so happy to see you every time. They just," and she shrugged, her mouth beautiful and happy as she spoke the words, "make you laugh."

"Right," Juke said, watching her. The mother who could never know. Who could never see those photographs. And seeing them together, he now understood. Completely. Megan was not willing to risk this love, as unconditional as it might seem. How could he blame her?

But Juke also understood there was no way out. That he was trapped by the curious whims of the teenage girl. He adjusted the dog in his arms, to the right, to the left, flowing with the wriggle. Holding it finally cradled like a newborn.

"You'll get the hang of it," Eva said. "And if you have any questions, you have our number?"

"Of course he does, Mom," Megan said. "He called us, remember?"

"Right," Eva said, taking a step back. "It was nice meeting you," and there was the smile again, this time as she spoke his name, "Juke."

"My pleasure," he said, returning one of his own.

She backed off his stoop, and turned around.

Megan gave Juke a serious little wave and a crinkled little smile. She mouthed the words, "Thank you," then she too turned and followed step, walking side-by-side with her mother down the street. The two of them talking about something. Eva taking a quick look back, then both of them talking some more.

Juke stood in his doorway for a long while. Staring after the pair, the resolutions swirling through his head. A little personal closure. That wasn't Megan Wechsler in those pictures. The girl in those pictures didn't exist.

He shook his head in amazement at the healing power of youth, then wondered about the dog. Could Juke ever begin to return unconditional love? Could he be trusted to protect and, not serve, but provide? The puppy didn't have the answers he was looking for. She'd already fallen asleep in his arms.